ALEX GRAYSON

PRAISE FOR ALEX GRAYSON

"Secrets and lies, lives falling apart, hearts being broken and crazed killers all come together in a heady mix that just simply seethes lust, sexuality and, above all, love." **Old Dave's Romance Revue**

"Ms. Grayson is an incredible writer and the friendships and love stories that she has created between her cast of characters are not going to be forgotten after the last page is turned." ~ **Nance, Goodreads reviewer**

"Amazing writing, fantastic storyline and completely lovable characters. One again, Alex Grayson was able to pull me into the world of Jaded Hollow within the first couple chapters." **JC. Goodreads reviewer**

"This book was exceptional as usual with Alex. She gives you emotions of both funny and adventurous all in one book not to mention all the other emotions that pull at you." ~ **Nook Books and More Blog**

"This book will take you through the every emotion possible. I'm so glad I lost my M/M virginity to this story!" ~ **Desiree, Goodreads reviewer**

"Speechless! Such a moving story and written so beautifully, Unveil Me had me captured from the start. Alex Grayson has nailed it." ~ **Deborah, Goodreads reviewer**

This book is dedicated to all the people out there living with chronic diseases. Your bravery and tenacity inspire me. Here's to hoping some day we find cures for every one of these maladies, so no one ever has to suffer from them again.

Chapter One

Andrew

HAVE YOU EVER WANTED something so bad every muscle tenses and your body almost locks up with just the thought of having it? Your heart races, your palms sweat, your breathing escalates, and you feel a thousand tiny butterflies fluttering around in your stomach? You would do just about anything, say just about anything, *be* just about anything to get that one thing? You would take damn near anything out if it got in your way. And the thought of not getting it crushes your lungs so completely that it's hard to draw in breath, sending shivers throughout your body, leaving you physically ill. You would no longer care if your lungs drew in life-saving oxygen or your heart pumped blood throughout your veins.

That was the way I felt when Chris first showed me the picture of her brother, Jase. I was completely and utterly transfixed by the man in the picture. I knew right then and there, at that very second of time as I stared at the most beautiful man I had ever seen, I would do anything to make him mine. I have no idea what drew me to him; I knew nothing about him, hell, he could be a total dick, but it didn't matter. There was nothing anyone could do to stop me. It was inevitable and the solid truth.

I'm sure I probably bugged the shit out of Chris, and anyone else around, with the many times I asked her about him, or when he would be in Jaded Hollow. But I didn't give a fuck. I was impatient. The need to see him in person was suffocating. I literally felt like I couldn't breathe properly once she showed me that picture, and I knew I would get to meet the one man I would spend the rest of my life with.

I know it sounds crazy and irrational, but it was how I felt. Each time Chris told me the date was pushed back for whatever reason, I wanted to yank my hair out and throw a fit. Yes, a big grown man like myself with tats and piercings wanted to throw a fit like a fucking preschooler. And every time Chris revealed little snippets of the shit Jase had to put up with from his parents, I wanted to commit cold-blooded murder. Was it ridiculous? Absolutely. Did it make me seem crazy? Probably. Did I care? Fuck no.

For years I thought I'd found the man that I wanted forever. It didn't matter he was about as unobtainable as becoming the president of the United States would be for Adolf Hitler. I coveted him in secret, knowing nothing would come of it. I wanted Jaxon Walker like a starved man wanted a big juicy steak. It hurt every time I saw him with a different woman, but I knew it was never meant to be. I think what hurt the most was the reason behind Jaxon and his women. He didn't do it because he was looking for the right woman. He did it because of the pain he was going through *because* of a woman. I wanted to be there for him. I wanted him to choose me to comfort him, but I knew it would never happen. When Bailey came along, it didn't hurt so bad. I knew from the beginning she was different. She was what Jaxon needed all along. It still hurt, but I was happy for them both.

"Hey sweetie, would you like a refill?" Jaxon and Mia's grandmother, Maggie, asks, pulling me from my thoughts.

I look up at the woman the whole town has dubbed their Gram, and smile. "Yes ma'am. And can you add a slice of your apple crisp pie and bring me the check?"

She pats my cheek twice before refreshing my coffee and turning to get my slice of pie.

"Are you ever going to choose someone else's dessert, Andy?" she asks, handing me the slice of heaven and the white slip of paper with my total.

An ache starts in my chest at the use of the nickname. She's one of only two people I allow to use it. I've tried over the years to get her to stop, but it's no use. Gram does what she wants. Not wanting to hurt her feelings, I've stopped trying, even though I feel a twinge every time she uses it. I let everyone believe I hate the name because it sounds like a girly gay name, but that's not the true reason. Every time I'm called Andy it reminds me of a certain person who holds my heart. A person who very well may be unjustly wiped from the world. When *that* person calls me Andy, I can't help the big grin that comes across my face. Hearing Andy from their lips is one of the sweetest things ever.

I grab the container of sugar and pour some in my coffee as I tell her, "You know I'll never cheat on you with another dessert. Your desserts are the shit. Why would I want to try another?"

Every month customers submit desserts they want featured at Maggie's Diner. A few are selected and put on the menu. At the end of the month there's a vote to see whose was the best. The winner gets one free meal a day for the next month.

"Oh posh! You never give anyone's a chance. You may like some more than mine," Maggie says, unloading the drying rack.

"That may be so, but I don't plan on finding out. I've eaten your desserts since I was little and I've never come across one I didn't like. Sorry, Grams, but you're stuck with me always choosing yours." I give her a cheeky grin.

I dig in to the deliciousness before me and moan. Maggie just rolls her eyes and walks down to help another customer. I grin at her retreating back.

I hear the bell over the door jingle and turn to see who it is. Beautiful Bailey walks in first with her hair high on her head, a light pink diaper bag slung over her shoulder. The difference between the Bailey I first met and Bailey now is astounding. The old Bailey wouldn't be caught dead showing off the scar that runs from the corner of her right eye to her ear. This Bailey is self-assured and knows the scar shows her strength. It shows her bravery and perseverance. It shows that even though you may be beaten down to your lowest, you can still get back up and fight. I am so proud of her, and I'm one lucky bastard to be able to call her friend.

Right on her heels is Jaxon, carrying a wide-awake and giggling Amari on his arm. The kid is as cute and sweet as a button, but my gaze is captured, like always, by Jaxon. Jaxon would slaughter me if he knew the fantasies I've had of him. I feel my dick twitch in my jeans, remembering some of them.

I pull my eyes away from Jaxon and see Chris walking in next. Every time I see the woman I want to squeeze her neck. I feel this way because of all the help she's given Bailey over the years, when no one else was there for her. Chris is a very special person.

She has a huge grin on her face and I wonder why. I get my answer when the last person steps through the door. My eyes zero in on the one person it seems like I've waited my entire life to meet. The one man who has my blood pumping erratically every time I look at his now-worn picture. The man who has my breath catching and my body locking tight to keep me in my seat, because I don't want to scare him off by approaching and stealing him away.

Fuck!

Chris didn't tell me he was coming today. Today, of all days, is not a good day. I have to leave and there's no way I can get out of it.

Motherfucker!

Instead of finishing my pie and paying my bill like I need to, I sit there and take in all that is Jase in the flesh. How is it possible he looks even better in person? I thought he was perfect in the picture, but the man standing across the diner? This man is so damn perfect it almost hurts my eyes.

He's tall, not as tall as Jaxon or me, but still tall. Just like in the picture, he has his gorgeous dark-blonde hair in a low messy ponytail. I want to yank the band out and run my fingers through it, grab a handful and hold his head while I take his lips with mine. I bet his stubble would feel heavenly against my skin. The white t-shirt he's wearing molds to his chest, showing off the muscles beneath the material. His arms have multiple tattoos. Not sleeves, but there are definitely more than just a few. The faded jeans he has on hang low on narrow hips and I'm sure will showcase his ass perfectly. I can't see his eyes, something that's bugged the shit out of me from the moment I first laid eyes on his picture, because he has on a pair of dark shades.

I take a deep breath and feel my lungs expanding more than they have in a long time. The whole of Jase in the flesh is so much more than I thought. My fingers itch to touch him. My lips tingle to taste him. My nose twitches to take in his scent. My eyes gobble up every inch of him. My ears strain to hear his voice. And my fucking dick stiffens, trying to lead me to him.

All four of them stand there for a minute, looking around, trying to find a spot to sit. As it's still the morning rush, there aren't too many places. Bailey sees me first, sitting there drooling like an animal over prey. She nudges Chris on the shoulder and points to me. I see this out the corner of my eye, as there's no way can I take my eyes off Jase.

They make their way through the crowded diner toward me. I watch Jase's swagger, which makes my dick jump even more. He hasn't noticed me yet, so I have a few extra seconds to watch him.

I take a quick look at the others. Chris's smile gets bigger the closer they get. Bailey's lips tip up into a smile as well. Jaxon has a smirk on his. They all know of my obsession with Jase.

Finally, fucking *finally,* Jase sees me. He flips up his glasses to rest on top of his head, and I'm nearly knocked off my fucking stool at my first glimpse of his eyes. They are the clearest blue I've ever seen, and suck me in immediately. It takes damn near every bit of strength to pull mine away and look at Chris.

Chris stops right in front of me, almost bouncing on her heels in excitement. The girl is a complete loon, but I still love her. Bailey's on her right side, with Jaxon and Amari behind her. Jase steps next to Chris and a light smell of the ocean hits me. My eyes flicker to him before I forcefully bring them back to Chris.

"Hey, Chris, Bailey, and Jaxon." I look at each of them as I say their names, then back at Jase and rake my eyes all over him, not in the least bit hiding my interest, before saying, "Hey there, baby."

By the way his body jerks, I can tell he's taken aback by my comment, but he recovers quickly, tipping his chin up in greeting.

"Hi, Andrew," Bailey says in her sweet innocent voice.

Jaxon gives a chin lift, trying to catch Amari's hands that are grabbing at her mom's hair.

"Hey, Andrew!" Chris says in a chirpy voice. "What are you up to today?"

I narrow my eyes at her. What in the hell is she doing? She knows I've been waiting weeks to meet her brother. The little twat is making me suffer, and she's enjoying watching me do it. If she doesn't stop this shit, I'll introduce myself. I'm sure as shit not shy and can take care of it myself, but I'm trying to play it cool. He doesn't need to know that I already know who he is and have been waiting on tenterhooks for him to get here. That may freak him out just a bit.

With a tight voice, I tell her, "Not a lot. I'm leaving to go out of town in a few minutes. Got business to take care of."

Jase shifts beside Chris and another wave of ocean hits me. I grip the back of the stool and the counter tightly. I'm about to open my mouth when Chris finally puts me out of my misery.

"Aww… that's too bad," she says with fake sadness. "I wanted you to meet my brother, Jase, and ask if you wanted to have breakfast with us."

Through gritted teeth, I tell her, "Well, maybe if you had given me a heads-up I would have, honey, but since you didn't, I've already had breakfast."

7

Enough of this bullshit. I turn my head to Jase and hold out my hand, excitement running through me at the thought of finally touching him.

"Hey, Jase. I'm Andrew."

He eyes me for a second before he lifts his hand and places it in mine. The shock is instant and strong. Sizzles run up my arm as I grip his hand tightly. He has a firm grip and his hand is rough. I bet that shit would feel good gliding along my body.

I don't ever want to let go, but I know I need to. After holding on a few seconds longer than necessary, I reluctantly pull my hand back.

"Hey. What's up?" he says with a head jerk.

At his question, my head automatically turns down to my lap, which incidentally has something very *up* in it. My first instinct is to tell him my dick is up, but Chris jabs me in the stomach before the words have the chance to come out.

"Don't you dare, Andrew," Chris says, glaring at me.

Giving her a flirty grin, I fake innocence, when we both know damn good and well nothing I was just thinking was innocent. "What? I haven't done anything."

"You know *what*," she hisses at me.

Chuckling, I turn my attention to Jase, knowing it will be my new favorite thing to do: having my attention on Jase.

"How long are you going to be here in Jaded Hollow?" I ask, hoping his answer is going to be "forever."

"Not sure yet. Gonna check the place out first, and then I'll decide," he responds, his voice sending shivers down my back.

I seriously need to check myself. I'm on the edge of my seat wanting to jerk him to me, and I know I can't do that, which goes against everything that is me. I'm not used to holding my feelings or actions in. Everyone in town knows I'm the type of person who says what's on his mind. I'm a fun-loving guy who likes to make people laugh. Normally, except with Jaxon, I never hide when I want something. To not give in to the urge to make my feelings about Jase known to him is killing me, but I promised Chris I would keep it to a minimum. What's even worse is Jase's reaction to me, which is nothing. No spark in his eye, no tightening of his body, no abnormal breathing, just nothing.

I want him to react to me. I want him to notice me. I want him to see me as a potential lover.

"Let me know if you need someone to show you around."

Another chin lift and a, "Will do," are the only reply I get.

I'm frustrated, so I turn to face the rest of the small group. "What are you all up to today?"

It's Jaxon's deep voice that answers. "Just showing Jase a few places. We're headed over to Chris's next to settle him in. He'll be staying there until he decides if he wants to stay. Then headed down to the bar."

Chris lives in Bailey's old place, which is right above Jaxon's Pub. Bailey wasn't there long before she and Jaxon got together, and when Chris moved here to be closer to her friend, she decided to take it over. It's small and cramped, definitely not enough room for two people to live in. An idea forms in my head, and I turn back to Jase.

"Let me know if you decide to stay. I have an extra room at my place that's empty." The idea of him in my space gets my blood flowing and almost has my eyes rolling back in my head. I can't help the needy look I know is written all over my face.

"Thanks. I'll let you know."

UNVEIL ME

I glance down at my watch and see that I need to leave or I'm going to be late. I hate leaving when I just met him, but what I need to do is important. It doesn't just involve me, but others. Others that I can't and won't let down.

I get up from my stool. "I've got to go." To Chris and Bailey, I ask, "Will y'all be at the bar later?"

Please say yes, please say yes. Shit, I'm pathetic.

"Jaxon and I will be there. His mom's gonna watch Amari for me so I can hang out," Bailey says.

"We'll be there as well," Chris answers, wrapping her arm through Jase's and leaning on him. "I want Jase to see where I work part-time and get the feel of the place since it's a focal point of town."

I barely contain myself from jumping up and down like a five-year-old at Christmas. I'm on shift tonight, along with Mia. Even if I wasn't though, I'd still be there. I want to be wherever Jase is going to be. I want to get to know him and him me. I want him to see the real me, not the person standing in front of him, biting his tongue. To do that, he needs to be around me and my friends in a comfortable setting. Jaxon's is the perfect place for that.

I look around for Maggie to pay for my meal and see she's busy with a customer. I pull out my wallet and throw money on the counter, more than enough to pay for my breakfast and leave a tip. I turn back to Bailey and reach down to place a soft kiss against her lips. "I'll see you all later."

I then lean over her shoulder to do the same with Amari, tickling her side in the process, causing her to giggle and kick her little legs. When I pull back, I glance at Jaxon and see the pierced eyebrow is raised. He's waiting for my usual flirtatious move to try to get a kiss from him.

"Sorry buddy, not today," I tell him with a wink. He just rolls his eyes and shifts Amari around in his arms.

My lips tip up, and I turn to face Chris, who is still leaning on Jase. Leaning down, I kiss her lips as well. This may seem strange to some, but it's just who I am. I'm very open about my feelings, and these two ladies have come to mean a lot to me. When I pull back from Chris, I look her straight in the eye and say, "Thank you." She smiles and nods.

I stand to my full height and take in Jase one more time before I have to leave. His brows are puckered and it looks like he's concentrating on something important. His eyes shift from mine to Chris and then back.

"It was nice meeting you, Jase," I tell him with a sexy smirk. To the others I say, "I'll see you tonight at Jaxon's."

It takes everything in me to not look back at Jase as I walk away.

Jase is so much more than I expected. No, I still don't really know him, but from what Chris has said about him he seems like a good guy. I'm really looking forward to getting to know him. I just hope I can calm my raging body enough to do so before I turn him off me.

Chapter Two

Jase

FUCK! SHIT! SON OF A BITCH! Who in the hell is that guy and where can I get one?

The ridiculous thought pops into my head, and I want to do a face palm. I've got too much shit going on to be thinking like that. Shit that no one knows about. Shit that no one will know about if I can help it. That's the reason I'm in this little town anyway, to get away from the fucked-up mess back home. Between my parents and the other shit going down, I had to leave. I missed my sister like crazy, so this seemed like the place I was going to be for a while.

I turn my head and watch the sweet ass making its way through the door. I thank my fucking lucky stars I still had my glasses on when we first made our way over to him, because my eyes nearly bugged out of their sockets. The man is drop-dead gorgeous. Tall, dark tattooed skin, built, shaggy brown hair, and eyes so black you could get lost in them. My jeans get tight at the memory of him. When I saw the flash of desire in his eyes, I nearly dropped to my knees.

Chris tugs on my arm, grabbing my attention away from the door. "Come on. Let's grab a seat."

We make our way over to a freshly cleaned booth and take a seat; Chris and me on one side, Bailey, Amari, and Jaxon on the other.

I look across the booth at Bailey, who now has Amari on her lap. The last time I saw Bailey was a few years ago. The scar on her face makes my blood boil. We've never been very close. She and Chris have been friends since they were little, but with how Bailey's parents were, she was rarely allowed at our house. I never knew of the abuse she endured as a child. By the time we all were older and Bailey ended up in another shitty situation, I was off doing my own thing. Bailey made Chris promise not to tell anyone of the abuse she was enduring on a daily basis, and so Chris never came to me with her concerns. Had I known about it, I would have buried the bastard so far down his body would have never been found.

My eyes skip to Jaxon, and see complete adoration for the woman and child sitting next to him. He has his arm slung across the back of the booth, his hand playing with Bailey's hair. The look in his eyes as he watches them shows everyone he would do anything to protect and love them. Jaxon is a scary-looking motherfucker, and I feel sorry for anyone who messes with his family. I'm happy for Bailey. She deserves a bit of happiness in her life after what she's gone through, and the love shining in her eyes says she's found it.

Chris nudges my shoulder, and I look down at her. "It's amazing, isn't it?" she asks quietly, and looks at Bailey and Jaxon.

It really is amazing. Chris has updated me on everything that has happened, including what that sick fuck did to Bailey and Jaxon's sister, Anna, after he followed Bailey to Jaded Hollow. For her to overcome everything is incredible.

I smile down at Chris. "Yeah, it is."

Just then, a blonde waitress in a bright blue button-up shirt, purple skinny jeans, and heels walks up to our table, setting four empty coffee mugs and a pot of coffee down in front of us. Her name tag says Nitra.

"Hey guys. How's it going?" she asks, chewing obnoxiously on a piece of gum.

Everyone gives their nods and hellos, then Nitra faces Chris and me. "Who's the hottie?"

"This is my big brother, Jase," Chris introduces us.

She offers a manicured hand to me. "Well, hey there, handsome. Nice to finally meet you. We've heard so many good things."

"Thanks. Good to meet you too," I tell her.

"What can I get you all this morning?"

After we place our order, Nitra walks off.

"So, what did you think of Andrew?" Chris asks.

I turn suspicious eyes on her. "Why?"

"No reason. Just curious." She shrugs and tries to play the innocent, but I'm on to her. She's up to something.

"Chris, don't," I warn her. I don't know what she's playing at, but she needs to back off. My life is too unstable at the moment to be thinking about starting a relationship. Of course, Chris doesn't know that, and that's the way I want it to stay. She only knows about the issue with our parents, not the recent shit storm I put myself into. I just hope that I ran far enough it doesn't follow me. If it does, I'm not sure I'll make it out on the other side alive. And that's why a relationship is not in the cards for me right now. I can't afford to drag anyone else into this mess. My being here could already put Chris in danger, but I'm hoping he doesn't look for me this far away from home. He has no way of knowing where I am. But then again, the fucker doesn't give up when he wants something.

"I know what you're doing and you need to stop."

"Why don't you just wait and see for yourself? Andrew is a great guy. You may like him."

"I'm sure he is, but I can't. I'm not in a good place right now, okay?" My voice is firm, letting her know I'm serious.

"Jase, Mom and Dad—"

I cut her off before she can get started. "Just drop it, Chris. I said no. There are things you don't understand. Things I can't tell you. Until those issues are taken care of, I can't take on a new relationship. I appreciate what you're trying to do, and I love you for it, but you need to take a step back. It's not a good time."

Frown lines appear on her face as she takes in my words. I know my mistake immediately. I've said too much and now she'll hound me, wanting answers. She won't get them, and she'll make my life hell.

Jaxon speaks up from across the table, and I want to kiss him for changing the subject. Looking at Jaxon, at his irresistible eyes, I know it would be no hardship kissing him. He's not as hot as Andrew, but he's definitely a close second.

"Bailey said you were looking for work. What can you do?" he asks.

I turn from Chris, who is still looking thoughtful, and face Jaxon. "If possible I'd like to work with cars. I'm pretty good at it. Before I moved here, I was lead mechanic at one of the shops in town."

He nods. "Joe has a shop down on Big Bulge Road. He was just telling me the other day that he needed to bring someone else in. Work's getting too much for just him. We can stop by later so you can talk to him."

"Thanks. I'd appreciate it," I tell him, and pick up the coffeepot and pour some into my cup.

"It's been years since I've seen you, Jase. You look good. How have you been?" This is from Bailey. After stirring my coffee, I look up at her and smile.

"I've been good. Not much has changed since the last time you saw me." Of course, this isn't entirely the truth. Several things have changed, but those are things that I plan on keeping to myself. "You look good, too." I carefully approach the subject I'm sure is not easy on her, but I feel I need to say something. Even though I really had no way of knowing what was going on with Bailey, I still feel terrible. "Chris told me what happened when you were little, and what happened later, and then here. I'm so sorry for never doing anything. I had no idea that shit was going on."

She gives me a sad smile and reaches across the table to squeeze my hand. I look at Jaxon and see his jaw clenched, hatred and rage in his eyes.

"It's okay. You had no way of knowing. I was hardly ever allowed at your house, and when I was, it was only when I had no visible bruises. And I made Chris promise to not say anything because I was embarrassed and thought no one could help me." She pulls her hand back, snuggles up next to Jaxon, and kisses Amari on the top of her head.

"I still wish I knew. I would have done something if I had known."

I watch as tears glisten in Bailey's eyes, and I feel like shit. She doesn't let the tears fall, but I know this is a hard subject for her. I shouldn't have said anything. Jaxon drops his arm onto her shoulders and squeezes Bailey to him.

"I know you would have," she says softly. "I didn't want anyone to know, so I kept it hidden. Please don't feel bad."

I nod, but the guilt doesn't go away. It probably won't ever go away.

"It looks like you're doing good now, though," I tell her with a tender smile.

"I am," she responds, and tips her head back to look at Jaxon with a beautiful smile on her face. "So much better than I thought I would ever be."

Chris and I both watch as Bailey and Jaxon share a private moment. Bailey really does look happy. Chris told me that Bailey thought she wasn't able to have kids. I look at Amari, who is shoving a yellow ring in her mouth, and am truly happy for her. The shit she's been through would break just about anyone else. It's a damn near miracle she made it out on the other side sane. And for her to have a baby when she thought she couldn't, I think is God's way of rewarding Bailey for being strong and not giving up.

A couple minutes later, Nitra brings our food. We eat and make small talk. Chris tells me all the reasons she wants me to stay in Jaded Hollow. I tell her that I'm contemplating it. This seems to please her for right now. She also tells me about the new job she's starting soon at the school as a guidance counselor, happy that her degree is finally being put to use. Jaxon and I discuss me rebuilding an old car he's had in his garage for a while. Bailey plays with Amari, throwing in her input every so often.

Once we're done, we decide to head over to Chris's place to store my stuff. Chris and Bailey are going to Jaxon's mom's place to drop off Amari, while he and I head over to Joe's to talk to him about a job for me. We're to meet back up at Jaxon's Pub at three, where Chris wants to show me off. She actually said this, which caused me to roll my eyes. I have a fucking silly sister.

After paying our bill, which was when I met Jaxon's Gram, who is a sweet old lady I liked instantly because she gave me a piece of her delicious pie to take home, we head out the door. Jaxon and I say our good-byes to the girls and make our way to his truck. I have my own Jeep, but it makes more sense to just take Jaxon's ride since we're going to the same place.

We climb into his truck and take off. What I've seen of Jaded Hollow so far, and the people I've met, makes me believe it could be a place I'd like to settle in. I know being away from my parents is the best thing for me. When I told them that I was gay, my dad didn't take it too well. I knew he wouldn't. That's why I held off as long as I did, but he looked at me like I was a nasty contagious bug he wanted to squish beneath his shoe. It hurt, but it wasn't a surprise. I knew then that I needed to get away; it was just a matter of time. But when all the other shit went down, the time to leave became right then. I had no choice. Had I not left when I did, there was a big possibility I never would have. I would have ended up in a swamp, waiting to be gator bait.

I just hope me moving here didn't bring hell to Chris and the people of Jaded Hollow. Only time will tell.

Chapter Three

Andrew

"UNCLE ANDY! UNCLE ANDY!" A cute little black-haired girl comes barreling toward me as soon as I exit my car, long black pigtails flying behind her.

She's out of breath by the time she makes it to me. I squat down just in time to catch her in my arms and scoop her up. As I stand, she lays a big kiss on my cheek. My heart melts at the action, just like every other time she does it.

"Hey, skittles. How's my girl?" She pulls her head back, wraps her short legs around my stomach, and rests her hands on my shoulders. I take in her face, so familiar, and see pure happiness in her expression. However, her eyes look tired and there are dark rings around them. I can also see she's lost some weight, and up close her hair looks thinner than it once was. The slight bulge on her upper right chest sends a sharp pain shooting through me. My heart hurts looking at her haggard appearance, and I want to scream at the injustice of what this beautiful little girl is going through.

"I'm doing good, Uncle Andy!" she says animatedly, still trying to catch her breath. "I made a new friend at school. Her name's Mandy. Mom and Dad said I could spend the night with her tomorrow night for her birthday! We're going to tell ghost stories and have s'mores!

I smile at her excitement. "That's great, baby. Sounds like you're going to have a lot of fun."

"I am! This will be my first sleepover ever!" she says, before wrapping me in her six-year-old arms and giving me a tight hug. "I missed you, Uncle Andy," she whispers in my ear.

Fuck, but I love this little girl. She's the second and only other person I allow to use that nickname. No way in hell could I ever tell her not to. Hell, the girl has me wrapped so tight around her little finger that I would let her call me anything, and I'd still smile.

"I missed you too, precious," I tell her, and give her a tickle on the side, making her giggle and squirm in my arms.

"Where's your mom?" I ask her.

"I'm here," comes a breathless voice from behind me. I turn and see Becky coming our way. She has on a pair of worn-looking but still nice jeans, a green t-shirt with a few splotches on it, and a pair of black sneakers. Her light-brown shoulder-length hair is a mangled mess. Her eyes look tired, but she still sports a small smile as she walks up to us.

"Ally, what have I told you about running out of the house like that. Next time wait for me," she scolds her daughter. There's no heat in her voice, but she tries to look stern as she looks at Ally.

"But, Mom, it was Uncle Andy," Ally whines, and puffs out her lower lip in a pout. "It's been forever since I've seen him."

I try to hold it in, but I can't help the chuckle that slips past my lips. Becky's eyes turn to me and she tries to give me a don't-you-dare-laugh look, but fails when her lips twitch.

"Sweetie, you saw him last week. That's hardly forever."

"Well, it feels like a long, *long* time," Ally mutters, causing another chuckle from me.

"Go on in the house and finish packing for tomorrow. Your uncle and I are right behind you."

"Okay!" she says happily. I set her on her feet and off she goes again.

"You okay, Becs? You look a mess," I say, as we walk up the steps to the porch and into the house.

"Gee, thanks. I needed you to point that out," she utters dryly.

I shrug unashamedly. "It's true. You look like you're dead on your feet."

She sighs as we walk into the kitchen. I pull out a chair as she grabs glasses out of the cabinet and pours us both a glass of iced tea. Taking a seat at the table, she takes a swallow of the cold liquid before saying, "Yeah, everything's good. I'm just running around trying to get the house prepared for Brent's family. They're due to get here next Tuesday. The house will be full. I love his family, but I'm not looking forward to our space being invaded for several days."

I sympathize with her. I love to be around people, but I also like my own space. If I'm going to be surrounded by people, I would prefer it to be somewhere I can leave. Becky won't have that, because it's her house.

I pat her hand that's on the table. "It'll be okay. Toughen up, Becs. Besides, if they start to get on your nerves, just do what I would do. Set a tent up in the backyard, grab a twelve-pack, and get drunk off your ass."

She laughs at my suggestion and slaps my arm. "Yeah, I can just see that now. His family would flip out and think I'd gone crazy and try to commit me."

We sit for a few minutes in silence, the laughter leaving the room. I finally ask the question I'm dreading the answer to, but praying the news is good.

"How is she? Any changes?"

The look Becky sends my way has my heart plummeting down to my stomach. Not good news. The sadness I see in her eyes nearly has me losing my shit. I get up from my seat and pull her into my arms. She wraps her arms around my waist, buries her face into my chest, and I hear her muffled sobs. It takes iron will to keep my own eyes dry.

We comfort each other for a few minutes before Becky pulls back, wiping her eyes with the back of her hand. She takes a steadying breath before releasing me and resuming her seat. I take my seat as well and wait for her to tell me the bad news.

"The doctors say her white cells are still too high, not as high as they were, but still higher than what they hoped it would be at this point. The treatment's working, but not fast enough. They want to up the dosage, which will kill any remaining marrow in her bones. Since they've already tested you, they know you're a candidate to give bone marrow. They said to stand by and be available at a moment's notice."

I nod, ready to be where I'm needed. I would give my life for Ally. If giving my bone marrow can help her in any way, I'll do it in a heartbeat. Becky knows this. From the very beginning, when Ally was first diagnosed with leukemia, the doctors had mentioned the possibility of a bone marrow transplant. They tested Ally's closest relatives to find the match that was needed. Mine was the closest, and there was never any doubt I would do it.

"How has she been feeling?" I ask Becky.

"Tired, mostly. She's been sick to her stomach a few times. The doctors gave her some medicine to try to help. It's working some. She also complains of aches and pains. I'm sure you've noticed she's lost weight. The doctors say it's normal with the treatment." She looks down at her hands, clasped tightly together on the table, before looking up at me again with watery eyes and whispering, "She started losing her hair a couple nights ago."

Fuck! Her words hit me hard. I saw for myself that her hair was thinner than normal, but to see Becky break down again and confirm it tears me up. Why in the fuck would God deem it his plan to put such a sweet and innocent girl through something like this? I want to rip my hair out and howl in agony.

I scoot my chair back from the table and move it closer to Becky. I spread my legs wide enough to put them on either side of hers. Prying her hands away from each other, I take them into my own. I know there is nothing I can do to help make this easier on her, on either of us. The only thing I can do is be here for her when Brent can't. And I know Becky will be there for me as well.

"I'm so scared, Andrew." She continues to whisper. "What if the chemo doesn't work? What if—"

I don't let her finish, not wanting to even think of that possibility. It's not the end yet, and I refuse to think Ally won't make it through this. If I do, I'll break, and I'm not sure if I could ever be put back together again.

"Hey. Look at me." My voice is soft but firm, and it gets her attention. She brings her tortured gaze back to mine. "You can't think like that, okay? Ally is strong, and we have to be strong with her. She's going to get through this. We're all going to."

I lean forward and rest my lips on her forehead. I feel her tears dripping down onto our combined hands. I squeeze my own eyes shut, forcing the tears away.

We pull away a few minutes later. When I look into Becky's eyes, I see new determination in them. She's pulled her shit together, for now at least. A mother can only handle so much when it comes to the health of her child before she breaks down. This isn't the first one Becky's had, and I know it won't be the last. She never has them in front of Ally though, which is good.

"Has Mom been by?" I ask her, and scoot my chair back.

Becky gets up from the table, grabs a tissue from the counter, and blows her nose before replying. "Yeah, she was here yesterday. She's going with me to Ally's chemo appointment tomorrow."

"That's good. It's been hard on her as well. I know she wants to be here for you both as much as she can. How's Brent doing?"

"Better than me." Her laugh is strained. "He's been a godsend. I don't know what I would do without him. Without all of you. I just wish he was here more."

Brent's an engineer for a big company that makes textile machines. His position often requires him to leave town when there's an issue with one of his designs. I know it's difficult on him, being away so much. He loves his daughter just as much as we do.

The pitter-patter of little feet running across the floor interrupts our conversation. It's amazing that Ally has so much energy still left in her body after all the poison that's being pumped into it. Once again, she's out of breath when she skids to a stop in front of me.

"Ally, sweetie, you need to stop running so much. You're going to wear yourself out," Becky tells her.

"Okay, Momma," she says, breathing rapidly. She then turns to me. "Look at the picture I drew in art class, Uncle Andy!"

I take the white construction paper from her hand and flip it around. The scene on the paper breaks my heart. It's simple, but so much more. It's a picture of five people standing out in a field. There are trees in the background and flowers on the ground at the people's feet. Each person is holding the next person's hand. The last person in line, the smallest, has one hand up toward the sky, like she's trying to grab the sun, or reaching for heaven.

My eyes fly toward Becky and see she has her back to us, her shoulders shaking slightly. I bring my gaze back to Ally's, looking for any signs of sadness or resolve. She's only six years old, but she knows she's sick. Her parents decided to not hide it from her, which would be hard to do because of all the tests. They haven't told her there's a possibility she may not make it though. That would be too much for a child to handle.

Looking down at the picture again, I wonder if she senses something. Of course, this could just be a child and her imagination. Maybe the little girl, which I know is Ally, really is just reaching for the sun.

"Do you like it?" she asks in a soft voice.

I gather her in my arms and pull her onto my lap, turning the chair away from Becky to give her time to compose herself. Holding the picture in front of us, I tell her, "Of course I like it, skittles. It's beautiful. Now, tell me who these people are."

I already know who they are, but I like hearing her sweet voice and excitement. It's something I may not hear in the future. I wipe the thought away before it has a chance to take hold of me.

"That's Mom and Dad," she points to the first two people, "that's Grandma and you, and then there's me." She finishes by pointing to the last three people.

"You did a really good job, Ally. I'm proud of you." I lean down and kiss her temple.

"Alright, little lady, it's time for you to get washed up for lunch. I'm making your favorite," Becky says, spinning around and clapping her hands twice. She has a bright smile on her face for Ally's benefit, but it's plain to see to adult eyes that it's forced.

Ally jumps down from my lap and yells, "Yah! Tuna fish sandwiches! Is Uncle Andy staying for lunch?"

Becky looks to me for the answer, and in turn, I look at Ally. "Tuna fish sandwiches? Even huge spiders with gnarly teeth and hairy bodies couldn't keep me away." I mentally shudder at the thought. Spiders are one thing I do not do.

Ally giggles and skips off to do as her mother said. A few minutes later, she comes back down and we all sit and chitchat while we eat our tuna fish sandwiches, which also happens to be my favorite as well. After, Ally ropes me into playing Barbies with her in the living room while Becky does laundry.

See? Told you she had me wrapped around her finger.

After Ken and Barbie get married and live happily ever after, I help Ally clean the mess we made. I grab her hand and off we go to look for her mom. We find her in her and Brent's room, hanging up clothes.

"Hey, I have to hit the road. I'm on shift tonight at work." A mixture of emotions runs through me at the thought of leaving. I hate every time I drive away and leave Ally and Becky. But the thought of seeing Jase again has me reaching for my keys in my pocket.

"Okay. Will we see you next week?" Becky asks, walking out of the closet.

"Yeah, if not before then. Let me know if you need me." Becky catches my meaning and nods. As soon as the doctors say they need me, I'll be on the road.

Becky comes to me, and I gather her in my arms. At her ear, I whisper, "Everything is going to be okay, Becs. Stay positive. Love you."

She pulls her head back and places a kiss on my cheek. "Thank you, Andrew, for everything." There's more to her words than just thanking me for being here. I acknowledge her gratitude, knowing I would do it again in a heartbeat.

I squat down and then Ally is right there in my face. She grabs my cheeks and plants a big kiss on my lips. "Love you, Uncle Andy."

"Love you, too, skittles. You be good for your mom, okay? And have fun at your sleepover," I tell her, before wrapping my arms around her. I squeeze her tight, not wanting to let go.

She nods solemnly and says, "I will."

"I'll see you in a few days." I get up, and they both walk me out to my car.

After a couple more hugs, I get in my restored Dodge Challenger and wave another good-bye to them as I pull away. My heart feels heavy as I watch them in my rearview mirror, waving. But then it lifts slightly when I think about the man and the future I'm driving toward.

Chapter Four

Andrew

WHEN I PULL UP TO JAXON'S PUB, the parking lot is half-full. It's only five o'clock, so that's to be expected. More people will show up the later it gets. Pulling around to the back, I park my car next to Jaxon's motorcycle and climb out. I unlock the back door and make my way down the dark hall that leads to the front. As I pass by the kitchen, I knock the door open with my fist and yell a hello to Hoot, our cook. He hollers his own hello, and I keep walking.

As soon as I reach the mouth of the hallway, my eyes scan the room in search of Jase. At first I don't see him, and it irritates me. My emotions are raw after hearing the news about Ally. I need a distraction and Jase is the perfect one. I finally spot him when he steps out from behind a wall over by the pool tables. He has a pool stick in his hand, getting ready to take his shot, and laughs at something Mac's said. Chris and Bailey are both sitting on stools against the wall, watching them play.

A groan nearly rips from my throat when he bends over the pool table. His ass in those sexy jeans almost has me stalking over to him and rubbing myself against it.

"Get your ass behind the bar and help me, Andrew, and stop drooling over Chris's brother," Mia says, throwing a towel at me.

Forcing my eyes away from the irresistible sight across the room, I turn narrowed eyes on Mia. "You're just jealous it's not your ass I'm fantasizing about fucking."

"Yes, you're exactly right," Mia says dryly. "I'd much prefer you over the man over there who I've been in love with most of my life. Gosh, Andrew, you've found me out. However did you guess?"

I bend down to grab the towel she threw at me, and walk behind the bar. I tell her with dancing eyebrows, "Because everyone secretly wants a piece of me."

"Whatever," she mutters with an eye roll, and turns to walk away, flipping me her middle finger as she does so. I chuckle at her retreating back.

I grab a clean rag from under the counter and throw it over my shoulder. In an effort to keep my eyes off Jase, I decide to take inventory to see if we need anything from the basement. After seeing that everything is already stocked, I turn to the drying rack and start unloading it.

My eyes unconsciously make their way over to the pool tables. Jase has his arm lazily draped over Chris's shoulder, and his head bent, talking to her. She laughs at something he says and shoves him away. He winks before walking over to the pool table for his next shot. Once again, my dick jerks in my jeans as he bends over the table. After lining up his shot, he smoothly pulls the stick back and shoots it forward, sinking a ball in the corner pocket. The girls clap and cheer him on.

As if sensing my eyes on him, Jase turns and looks my way. I hold his gaze and let him see the heat I know is radiating from them. I may not want to scare him off by coming on too strong, but I also want him to know I do want him. He needs to figure that shit out now, because I won't give him long before I make it blatantly clear.

I would swear I see a flash of desire blaze in his crystal-clear blue eyes, but before I get a good look, it's gone and he looks away. I feel a rush of excitement at the thought of him thinking about me the way I'm thinking about him.

I turn away from him when someone comes up to the bar with an order. I spend the next thirty minutes going from one person to another. The place is starting to fill up and it takes my mind off the man across the room I want to do dirty things to.

Just as I turn to place some shots in front a couple of guys, I see Mac and Jase walking my way. My eyes stay glued to Jase.

"Hey, Andrew, can we get a couple beers?" Mac asks, taking a seat at the bar. Jase claims the stool next to him. Prying my eyes off Jase, I turn to Mac.

"Sure. Anything in particular?" I ask.

"Nope, just whatever," Mac says.

I look to Jase for his answer. "Sam Adams, if you have it."

"You got it," I tell them, and turn to get their beer.

After placing their drinks in front of then, I lean my elbows on the bar close to Jase.

"Please tell me you're kicking Mac's ass over there. Ever since he finally won against Jaxon a few weeks ago, he thinks he's unbeatable." I flick my eyes over to Mac and smirk.

"No, he's not. And fuck you, Andrew. No one's ever beat Jaxon before. I think that's a damn good reason to feel a bit cocky."

"Sheriff Weston," I say in mock surprise. "Shame on you. Mia was just saying that she's loved you most of her life, and now you're telling me you want me to fuck you?"

I hear Jase laugh and glance over at him. His stunning blue eyes sparkle, and *fuck*, he has a sexy-ass dimple in his left cheek.

"And what're you laughing at, baby? You want me to fuck you, too? All you've got to do is say the word, and I promise, I'm all yours," I tell him boldly. His lips tip up at the corners, eyes crinkling, like he thinks I'm joking.

Oh, honey, if you only knew how serious I am.

"Think I'll pass on that, as tempting as it is," he says, laughter still in his eyes.

Mac groans at Jase's side, but we both ignore him.

"What a fucking shame. I'm not worried though. I'll change your mind."

My body trembles as I think about reaching across the space between us, yanking him to me, and planting my lips against his. Would he let me or push me away? The way he's licking his lips while looking at mine makes me think he's not as indifferent to me as he lets on.

Oh yeah, baby. It's only a matter of time before you're mine.

Mia walks up to us and bumps me with her hip. "What are you guys over here talking about?"

I throw my arm across her shoulders. "Mac wants me to fuck him, but I told him I was at work and was busy later. I don't think he liked my answer too much. See, Mia? Told you everyone secretly wants me."

"Oh, for fuck's sake," Mac mutters, causing both me and Jase to laugh.

Mia looks over at Mac with mischief in her eyes, and asks, "Uh, Sheriff, is there something you need to tell me?"

Mac leans over the bar and crooks his finger at Mia. "Yeah, Pix. Why don't you come over here, and I'll tell you."

I watch as Mia's small frame leans over the bar toward Mac, knowing what's about to happen. Ever since these two made it official that they were back together, they haven't been able to keep their hands off each other. I can't say I blame them. The shit they went through at the hands of Shady and Tessa would make anyone cherish the moments they have with their loved ones.

Just as predicted, the moment Mia gets as far as her small body would allow over the bar, Mac reaches over, hooks his hands under her arms, and hauls her the rest of the way into his arms. She laughs loudly as she latches her arms around his shoulders and wraps her legs around his waist. Once there, they devour each other's mouths.

It's still strange seeing them like this. Before the truth finally came out and Mia found out Mac didn't cheat on her, her attitude toward him was volatile. Mac always had a sad, longing look on his face every time he looked at her. Now though, all you see on both faces is pure happiness and love.

I turn to see Jase watching me. I can't quite decipher the look in his eye, but it looks like curiosity. I wonder what he's thinking and feeling when he looks at me. Is he just as curious to know me, as I am to know him? Does he feel even a smidgeon of the desire I feel every time my eyes land on him?

We stand there and stare at each other until Mac and Mia pull away, breaking our connection. Jase looks away first and turns to face the two lovebirds beside him.

Mia releases her hold on Mac, and after another brief kiss, hops up onto the bar, swings her legs around, and jumps down beside me again. She has a cute flush to her face and it makes me smile, glad that one of my best friends is finally happy, like she should have been all along.

"Where did you head off to today, Andrew?" Mia asks casually.

I stiffen at her question, just as I do every time she asks me this. No one knows where I go when I leave town and visit Ally. They know about Becky and Brent, but have only met them a few times. However, they know nothing about Ally. I don't know why I haven't told them. Maybe because I've shared every other aspect of my life, and I feel I need to keep this part separate. It's certainly not that I'm ashamed of her. It's just the opposite, in fact. I'm very proud of the small family I'm part of. I just have this need to keep Ally to myself and not share her yet. Eventually I'll have to tell everyone, but I want to wait until after Ally is better and can handle the stampede that will enter her life. Because I know, once my friends in Jaded Hollow find out, they'll swarm her, and not let her up for air.

My fun mood starts to dissipate. It makes me sick to my stomach every time I think about what Ally, Becky, and Brent are going through. I hate that there's nothing I can do. I feel completely helpless and it pisses me off.

"It's none of your damn business. Stop fucking asking me that." I can't help the harshness in my reply, and I feel like shit when I see a flash of surprise, shock, and hurt enter Mia's face. It doesn't last long though. Almost as soon as the look appears, it is replaced with narrowed eyes. Mia is normally the type of person who'll bite you back if you catch an attitude with her. I never lose it with her, so I'm sure she's probably taken aback by my words. I've always been good about hiding this part of my life, but it's getting harder the last few months because of the leukemia. The news today that she's not getting better hit me hard.

I put my hands on the bar, close my eyes, bow my head, and take a deep breath.

This fucking sucks.

"Who pissed in your Cheerios today?" Mia asks. I grit my teeth at her smart-ass commit, not wanting to say anything else that'll antagonize her. Because that's one thing about Mia: she doesn't give up.

"Mia," I hear Mac say. "Just leave him alone."

"What the hell, Mac?" she hisses at him. "All I did was ask a simple fucking question and he thinks it's okay to cop an attitude? He knows me and should know better."

My stiff shoulders tighten even more. My grip on the countertop has my knuckles turning white. Mia has no idea how close I am to losing it. I'm on edge, and I'm clueless how to back away.

Taking a deep breath, I loosen my grip and tilt my head back up, and immediately clash eyes with Jase. The clear blue of his stare instantly calms the emotions raging inside me. His face shows concern, and something flutters in my chest. I like he's concerned about my abrupt change in demeanor, but I want to wipe that look from his face and replace it with something different, something carnal.

Not able to do anything about it now, and needing to apologize to Mia, I turn to face her. Her brows are puckered, and she's watching me with an expression that says she's unsure of what my next move will be.

"Sorry, Mia Pia. I've just got shit going on right now that I can't talk about. Please just leave it, okay?"

After watching me for a few seconds, she nods. "Okay, Andrew. Just remember, you've got friends here you can lean on."

"I know. Thank you," I tell her quietly. And I *do* know I have friends. Wonderful friends I know would do anything for me. I know I could count on them through this rough time, but I just can't reveal my secret yet. In time I will, but not yet.

Seeming okay with my answer, she smiles. Her attention is pulled away when someone down at the other end of the bar whistles, and she goes to take their order. Mac gets up from his stool and says he's heading to the bathroom, leaving Jase and me alone.

"How was your tour of the town?" I ask him, trying to take my mind off my dark thoughts and draw him into a conversation. He has a deep voice, and I haven't heard near enough of it. Every time he speaks it sends a shiver down my spine, and I want more.

He takes a swallow of his beer and sets it down. "It was fine. You have a nice little town here. I like how everyone seems so close-knit. Chris and I grew up in a small town as well, but everyone was so spread out you didn't get the vibe that everyone's family like you do here."

"Yeah, we're all close here and look out for each other. You fuck with one of us, you fuck with us all. You'll become a part of that if you decide to stay."

Fuck! Please let him stay. I'm not sure what I'll do if he chooses not to. I haven't completely ruled out kidnapping. Drastic? A big fucking yes. But I don't give a shit. No way am I letting him get away. Not now that he's here and I've met him.

"We'll see," he murmurs, twisting the beer bottle in front of him. I can tell by his tone and the way his eyebrows are drawn down he has something on his mind. And whatever it is isn't good. I wonder what it is.

In an attempt to wipe the look from his face and to get to know him better, I ask, "So, what did you do back home? I assume you'll be looking for work soon."

He lightly shakes his head, bringing himself back from wherever he was at. "Cars. Rebuilding and repairs. Some custom work. I'm damn good at it. Jaxon took me out to Joe's today. I start there tomorrow."

"Good. Joe is good people. He'll treat you right. And he needs help. He's the only mechanic around and he's getting too old to bring in more work. Some locals have to go to town for their repairs because he's not able to take on as much as he used to."

He nods in understanding. The old geezer is in his seventies and it's about time he realizes he can't keep up as much as he used to.

"So, why did you decide to come to Jaded Hollow?" I ask him. Of course, I know part of the story. Again, from Chris. His dickhead parents haven't made it easy on him. It pisses me off every time I think about the shit Chris has told me about them.

He avoids my eyes when he answers. "Our parents were giving me a lot of shit, so I thought it was time for me to get away and come visit Chris. It's been awhile since I've seen her."

There's more to the story than what he's saying. I can tell by the stiffness in his shoulders and the way his eyes turn hard. It takes a lot of self-control, but I decide not to delve further into it. I'll give him time to get used to me and see if he comes to me on his own.

We lapse into silence for a few minutes, Jase looking back down at his beer, me watching him. It's so damn hard to take my eyes off him, so I decide not to. My eyes roam all over the parts I can see over the bar. Several loose strands of his hair have fallen out of his hair tie, and they tempt me to reach over and rub them between my fingers. I force my hands to stay on the bar. The white of his t-shirt is a stark contrast to the dark tan he sports, and brings out the vibrant color of his stunning tattoos. The muscles bulging on his arms bring mental images of him bracing against a wall as I stand behind him, guiding myself into his tight ass. The sight almost has me jumping over the bar to get to him.

Jesus Christ! I've got to stop this shit. It's pure torture.

I'm forced to walk away from him for a few minutes when several customers come up with orders. Part of me is grateful for the distraction, but another part of me wants to kick every asshole out of here so Jase and I can be alone.

I walk back over when I see Chris and Bailey step up next to Jase, both giggling at God knows what. Chris drops down onto a stool and slides her beer bottle toward me, asking for another one. I grab one for her, pop the top, and hand it over. She raises her eyebrows in question and looks to Jase before looking back at me. I know what she's asking. She wants to know my take on him. I just grin. She'll know soon enough, everyone will, that I'm very interested. Of course, I already knew I would be, even before he got here.

"Nice shirt, Andrew," Chris says, laughing.

I look down at the black t-shirt I'm wearing. In big, bold, white letters it reads, "I bet my dick is bigger than yours. Wanna compare?" I look back at her and shrug. Everyone loves my shirts. They go with my personality. I'm not ashamed of who I am, so I won't hide it. Some people may find them extreme or vulgar, but those are the people I don't care to associate with anyway. So it all works out.

I notice that Jase is smirking as he looks at my shirt. He looks up at me, and I give him a flirty smile and a wink, letting him know without words that if he wants to compare I'm ready when he is. He holds my look, and I get the feeling he's not totally against the idea. My dick hardens and my blood heats up what feels like twenty degrees. I force my eyes away from his before I do something I'm not sure he's ready for.

I turn to Bailey, who has her eyes on something across the room. Before I get a chance to look and see what it is, she suddenly turns to me and asks, "Hey, Andrew, what are you doing Sunday after next?"

"Well, I'm not sure yet, Bailey girl. I take it you've already got plans for me, huh?"

"Maybe," she says, before turning to Chris. "When does your new job start at the school?"

"Umm... two weeks. The current guidance counselor extended her notice another week. Something to do with the sale of her house being delayed. Why? What's up?"

Instead of answering her, she then turns to Jase. "Do you know if you have weekends off?"

"Joe said it was up to me. He doesn't work the weekends, but said I could if I wanted to."

"Two weeks from Sunday, don't, please," she says, and turns back to the bar.

"What's going on, Bailey?" Chris asks, walking around Jase to stand by her.

"In a minute," Bailey says, causing Chris, Jase, and me to look at each other with questions in our eyes. This is strange behavior for Bailey. She's normally the quiet one, not openly making suggestions or giving opinions unless she feels it important enough. For her to be so cryptic is not like her.

She leans over the bar and hollers for Mia. After she makes her way over to us, Bailey asks her if she, Mac, and Trent, Mac's son, have any plans.

"Not that I'm aware of." Mia looks beyond Bailey and Chris to Mac and Jaxon, who are walking out from the hallway. Mia asks Mac if they have plans.

"No, I don't think so. Why?" he says, once he makes it to us.

We all bring our eyes to Bailey, well past curious as to what she has planned. Jaxon steps up beside her and she puts her arm around his waist.

"Can we close the bar down a few hours early two weeks from Sunday?" she asks him.

He looks down at her with the same expression he always reserves for her. Love and worship.

"I could, I guess. Why? What's going on?"

She gives us all a beaming smile and exclaims, "We're going to the fair!"

We're all silent for a minute, not expecting that to come out of her mouth. Not opposed to it, just not expecting it.

"Hell yeah, I'm game!" I'm the first to break the silence. I reach over and hold my palm up for Bailey to slap. She looks at it blankly for a second, then realized what I'm doing and slaps it. "I haven't been to the fair in years."

"Such a great idea, Bailey," Chris says, clapping her hands in delight. Bailey gives her a big grin.

"We're in," pipes in Mac. "T will love it."

"What about you, Jase? You good to go?" Chris asks.

"Sure, I'll go," he says with a shrug.

"Yah!" Bailey jumps up and down, barely able to contain her excitement. "This is going to be so much fun!"

We all smile as we watch her. Jaxon picks her up and plants a solid kiss on her lips before setting her back down.

I have to agree with her. This is going to be fun. It's not very often we're all able to get together. It's hard for

Jaxon because he has the bar to run, not to mention me, Mac, or Chris are normally here. Every once in a while, he'll close it down if plans are made for all of us. Obviously, he can't do that very often, or he'll piss off a lot of customers. They generally don't mind if it doesn't happen too often.

It's been a while. We're all due some downtime. This'll definitely be interesting. When we all get together, we always have a blast, because that's what friends do. With the added bonus of Jase being there, giving me another opportunity to be around him, I'm really looking forward to it. It can't get here fast enough.

I feel a twinge of guilt at the thought of Ally and Becky at home while I'm out having a good time. Ally may not have many more opportunities to enjoy life. And if anything happens to her, I know it'll be a long time before I will enjoy *anything*. I force the thought away. I refuse to believe God would be such a bastard and wipe the Earth of the beautiful little girl living a couple hours away. No fucking way would that happen.

Chapter Five

Jase

I WIPE THE SWEAT FROM MY face with my shirt as I enter the back door of Jaxon's Pub that leads to the small apartment upstairs. My breathing is labored and my heart is racing, but fuck, it feels good to run. It's a good way to keep my mind off shit back home. I think about that fucked-up mess entirely too much as it is. Any distractions are welcome. There's nothing I can do now anyway. Eventually I'm going to have to come up with an idea to get me out of the mess I'm in. No way do I want to live looking over my shoulder every day for the rest of my life. I don't regret what I did, I'd do it again in a heartbeat. The bastard deserved everything he got.

I push the thoughts away and my mind immediately turns to the other reason I run and need a distraction.

Andrew.

I grip the back of my shirt between my shoulder blades and rip it off in frustration. I walk to the fridge, grab a water bottle, and down the whole thing. Throwing the empty bottle in the trash, I lean back against the counter and tip my head back.

Fuck!

That man gets to me. And that's one thing I can't afford right now. I don't need the added stress of starting something with a guy. I've got too much going on to even contemplate that. But fuck if I don't want to. I've been here a week and every single fucking day he's been right in front of me in some form or fashion. And he's made it very clear he wants me. With the heated looks he sends me or the blatant flirting, there's no way I could mistake his interest for anything other than what it is.

He's constantly making insinuations and it's getting harder and harder to not take him up on his offers. He flirts with everything that's of legal age and has two legs, but it's different when he does it with me. The look he gives the others is flirty and you can tell it's in jest. The look he gives me is entirely different. I see the tension in his body, his eyes dilate, and he'll grip whatever's closest to him, like he has to physically hold himself back from getting to me.

There's even been a couple times my eyes have, of their own accord, drifted down, and I've noticed a bulge. Those are the times I want to say fuck it and back him up against the nearest wall and fuck his mouth with my tongue, among other things.

I grip the counter and grit my teeth, not sure how much longer I can hold off. I know if it happens—and I'm bound and determined to not let it—it'll be explosive beyond belief. No way would Andrew be the type to meekly sit there and let me do all the work. Fuck no, it'll be a battle to see who ends up on top. Literally and figuratively.

I hear Chris's bedroom door open, and a minute later she walks into the kitchen. She's still in her sleep clothes and she's walking with her head down. When she lifts it, I immediately know something's wrong, and my thoughts of Andrew fly away in a flash. Her eyes look sad and are red rimmed. I can tell she's been crying.

She notices me standing there and tries to wipe the look away. It doesn't work. The grief-stricken look still lingers.

"Hey, what's wrong?" I ask, as I walk toward her.

She dips her head and mumbles, "Nothing."

I put my hand under her chin and lift her head until I see her eyes again. I tell her gently, "Obviously, it's not nothing. You've been crying. Why?"

She looks at me with such defeat in her eyes, then bursts into tears and throws herself in my arms. I put my arms around her and bring her closer. I hate to see her so upset. I've noticed that since I've been here something's been on her mind. Every once in a while I'll see her stare off into space with a somber look on her face. I figured that if she wanted to talk about it she would come to me. Evidently it's more serious than I thought. And now I feel like shit because I haven't asked her about it before now.

She mumbles something into my chest that I can't make out. I pull back a little, but she doesn't let me get far.

"What is it, Chris?" I ask her again quietly.

"Everything is just so messed up," she murmurs tearfully, and it breaks my heart.

"What's messed up, sweetie?"

"Everything," she cries loudly. "Everything is messed up. I tr-try so hard to sh-show him how I feel, but h-he doesn't care. I hate this. I ha-hate feeling like this. I know he-he's hurting, but so am I. I want to help h-him, but I don't know how."

She becomes quiet, and I try to make sense of what she's talking about. I have no idea what the fuck's going on, but it clearly involves a guy. My fists ball up at her back. If some asshole has hurt her, I'll tear him apart.

"Shhh… Chris, I don't understand what you're talking about. Who are you trying to help? Who in the fuck hurt you?"

"You don't understand," she mumbles. "He doesn't do it on purpose." She looks up at me with tears falling down her face. I wipe at the trails on her cheeks.

"He hurts, too, Jase. Something happened a long time ago, and he's still hurting. I just wish he would stop pushing me away and let me in."

"Who, Chris?" I want to know who's hurt her. I don't care what the circumstances are, you don't hurt my little sister and think you can get away with it.

I can see her closing down. She's not going to tell me. Whoever it is, she's protecting him. I have no idea why, but I'll find out.

"No one," she mutters, and looks down. "Just forget about it. Forget I said anything. I'll just leave him alone from now on."

I want to punch the wall at her defeated look. I don't like seeing her this upset. I want to fix whatever her problems are, want to beat sense into whoever hurt her, but I can't if she won't let me.

She wipes her eyes with the back of her hand. Taking a deep breath, she looks up at me and there's determination written all over her face.

"Chris—" I begin, but she cuts me off and takes a step back.

"It's okay, Jase. Really. I'm fine now. Just please forget it," she pleads with me, and I hold whatever I was going to say. I'll keep quiet for now.

She tries to give me a smile, but fails miserably, "Do you want breakfast?"

I watch her for a minute, gauging her expression. "No, honey, I'm good. I'm going to jump in the shower, if you're okay?"

She nods and takes a deep breath before releasing it.

"Go. I'm fine here. You're all sweaty and you stink, sooo…," she says, with a slight smile.

I chuckle at her attempt at a joke. I can see her visibly trying to pull herself together. Chris has always been strong. I've always admired her for that. Our parents weren't the best in the world; not the worst by a long shot, but they still could have taken parenting classes.

As she passes me to walk to the fridge I grab her arm, and she looks up at me.

"You can talk to me, Chris. I know I haven't been around much, but I'm here now. Please, come to me if you need me. For anything." My voice is quiet, but no less meaningful.

She gives me a bigger smile than the one before, and the anger I felt a few minutes before dissipates some. Whatever was bothering her, she'll get over it. I can see the resolve, and I feel a sense of pride.

"Thank you, Jase. I've missed you so much. I'm really glad you're here.

"I am, too."

I lean down and kiss her forehead before releasing her arm. I turn to walk out the kitchen, but she stops me by calling my name. I turn to face her again.

"I may not be here when you get out of the shower. I'm meeting up with Bailey. We're going shopping in the next town over."

"Okay. You're on shift at the bar tonight, right?" At her nod, I continue. "I'll meet back up with you there. Have fun."

After another smile, I turn on my heel and make my way to the bathroom.

My nerves are completely shot, and I want nothing more than to have hot water beating down on my shoulders. I strip down, pull the tie from my hair, and step into shower, dipping my head under the spray. My wet hair falls forward and hangs around my head in a curtain. Taking a deep breath, I push back the images running through my head, not wanting to think of all the reasons I'm fucked. Now's not the time to dwell on them.

I stay in the shower for a good thirty minutes, soaking up the warmth of the water and releasing some of the stress.

Just as I step out, I hear a banging on the door. Grabbing the towel off the back of the door, I wrap it around my hips before making my way to the living room. When I open the door, I see Andrew on the other side. My initial thought is to yank him forward, but I hold still. My second thought is that it was a mistake opening the door. I know this from the look in his eyes when he sees me standing there in nothing but a towel.

"Holy mother of all that's hot," he breathes, and takes a step forward. "I've died and gone to fucking Andrew heaven."

I quirk a brow at his reaction, trying to hold back a laugh. He sure has a way with words that makes a guy feel damn good.

The possessive look in his eyes as he runs them up and down my near-naked body, and the way his breathing has become heavy, has me gritting my teeth. It looks like he's about to pounce. My dick hardens at the thought.

I'm at my wit's end when it comes to him. A man can only take so much from someone like him before he snaps. I'm almost at that point, but I can't let it happen. At any other time I would take him up on his offer in a heartbeat. Hell, I'd already have him up against a wall, beneath me, behind me, any way I could get him. Denying him feels so wrong on every level, but in order to keep my head, I have to. I need to keep my head in the game. The game of survival. Maybe once all the shit back home is taken care of...

Andrew takes another step toward me, stalking me, looking at the hand that's holding the towel around my hips. Every part of me wants to stand still until he reaches me, but I force my legs to move backward. I raise the hand not holding the towel in front of me in an attempt to stop him. If he gets too close, I seriously doubt I'll be able to hold off.

"Hey, hey," I say, and snap my fingers at him, trying to get his attention off my junk. His eyes meet mine. "This isn't happening." I gesture between the two of us.

"The fuck it's not," he growls, and comes closer. I nearly groan as a wave of his scent hits me. He's too close. I need him to stop. I'm on the edge, and it'll only take a slight push for me to go over.

"I'm telling you, Andrew, this shit can't happen right now."

"And I'm telling you, baby, that it is. There's no way you can stand in front of me, wrapped only in a fucking towel, and expect me not to get a taste. I'm not leaving here until I do."

I nearly become light-headed at his words. My blood heats and my dick goes from half-mast to hard as fucking titanium in a nanosecond. A shiver races down my spine, and I have to grip the towel tighter.

He's only a few feet from me when he stops.

"Lose the towel," he grits out, his voice going deeper and his eyes flaring.

My hand loosens on the towel, my resolve weakening.

Fuck, but I want him.

I know damn good and well that it'll be good between us. It'll be intense and sexy as fuck. There's something about him that draws me in, making me want to forget about everything else. I felt it the first time I saw him.

A jingle sounds in the room and the look in his eyes switches from something carnal to frustration. He yanks his phone from his back pocket and scowls down at it. Once he sees who the caller is, the scowl immediately turns to concern. I wonder at the abrupt change. Shaking my head, I breathe a sigh of relief at the interruption.

Andrew turns away from me while he answers the call.

"Hey. Everything okay?" he asks the caller quietly.

He's silent for a minute, then his body goes stiff. The hand at his side balls into a fist. All the air leaves the room as I watch Andrew drop his head, his shoulders going up and down as he takes in deep breaths. He looks defeated and it crushes something inside me. Whatever's being said on the phone is not good news. I don't like seeing Andrew like this. It's so unlike his normal magnetic attitude.

His voice is quiet when he tells the person on the phone, "I'm on my way. Give me about an hour and a half. Take a deep breath and stay calm, okay? Everything is going to be fine."

He listens to the caller for a second, then says, "I know, Becs. Just hold tight. I'll be there soon."

He disconnects the call and then tips his head back. His eyes are clenched shut. The phone is in a white-knuckled grip, and I don't see how it's still intact.

I take a step forward and place a hand on his shoulder. He jerks at the contact, but doesn't turn to face me. Whatever news he just got is obviously painful for him. I may not know Andrew that well, but one thing I have learned is not much gets to him. Seeing this beaten-down version of Andrew causes my chest to hurt.

"Andrew," I call his name hesitantly, not wanting to startle him. "Everything alright?"

He whips his body around and the pain I see clear as day in his eyes almost brings me to my knees. They look tortured.

"I've got to go," he says hoarsely.

I nod, not sure what to say. Whatever's bothering him isn't my business, even if I want it to be.

His eyes turn fierce again and his voice is stronger when he adds, "But this isn't over. We *will* finish it."

He doesn't give me the chance to refute his statement before he turns and practically runs for the door. The sound of the door slamming jars me and I twist my neck, trying to release the tension caused by Andrew's statement. And then the anguish written all over his face. Never have I seen eyes that looked so grief stricken.

I walk to the window just in time to see Andrew get into his car and take off, wheels peeling out on the pavement. I know it's only a matter of time before I give in to Andrew's pull.

Chapter Six

Andrew

I RUSH INTO THE EMERGENCY department and sprint toward the nurse behind the desk. When I'm refused the information of which room Ally is in, I have to force myself not to jump the desk and strangle the nurse. I realize she legally can't give out any information, but I'm beyond being reasonable. There's a little girl here who means the world to me, and I have no idea what's going on. I'm past the point of caring about regulations and legalities.

Just as I'm about to lay into the damn nurse and tell her to check the chart because my name is on there, I see Becky rushing my way. With a final glare at the bitch behind the counter, I turn just in time for Becky to barrel into my chest.

Her eyes are swollen and there's utter devastation written on her face. I clutch her shoulders and peer down at her.

"Tell me what happened," I demand in a soft voice, not wanting to make the situation harder on her.

Sniffing and then taking a deep breath, she rocks my world when she speaks.

"She passed out in the hallway. She had been looking pale earlier and she threw up a couple times. I was on my way to check on her when I found her. Oh, Andrew." Fresh tears start gliding down her cheeks. "At first I thought…" She stops herself and buries her head in my chest, shoulders shaking.

"Shh… I've got you." I rub her back and give her a couple minutes.

The lump in my throat is tight, and I have to force the tears away. My knees feel weak, but I force them to stay locked in place. The ache in my chest is debilitating. This is so unfair. I not only feel completely helpless, but I *am* helpless. There's not a damn thing I can do. But I have to be strong for her. For both Becky and Ally. They need me right now. As much as this crushes me, I can only imagine the pain Becky, and especially Ally, are going through.

I pull Becky back from my chest and ask her in a gravelly voice, "What have the doctors said?"

She wipes at her eyes, and I can see her trying to pull herself together.

"We're still waiting on a couple more test results to come through. She's in now getting an ECG done." She pauses and pulls in a lungful of air. The tears are coming back, and I know what she's going to say next won't be good. "They think it's her heart, Andrew," she whispers, barely loud enough for me to hear.

I jerk at her words and a wave of dizziness hits me. My lungs stop working, and I can't get enough air in.

"Wait. What about her heart? Is it bad?" I ask, desperate for her to tell me it's not.

"They won't know the details until after the rest of the tests. What are we going to do, Andrew? I can't lose her." Her voice cracks at the end. I put my arms around her and pull her against my chest.

"We got this. She's not going anywhere," I tell her, and hope it's not a lie. "Where's Brent?"

Taking a shaky breath, she leans her head back and looks at me. "He's on his way. He was about two hours away when I called him. He should be here soon."

I nod and take her hand "Come on. Let's go sit."

She lets me pull her over to the waiting area. There are several people in the chairs spread throughout the room. I lead her to the corner where there's no one. She takes a seat beside me, and I put my arm over her shoulders, pulling her close. She leans her head on my shoulder.

I can't imagine how hard it is on Brent. The man adores and worships the ground Becky and Ally walk on. To not be here when they need him must kill him. Unfortunately, his job requires him to travel, and it's the insurance that's paying for Ally's treatments. However, Becky did tell me a while back that if things get worse, Brent's boss said he'll station him here for a while so he can be with them. I think what's happened tonight will classify as bad enough for him to stay in town.

"When's Brent's family getting in?" I ask, trying to draw her into a conversation.

"Tomorrow afternoon. Ally's excited about seeing them. I have no idea if we'll even be home for her to enjoy them."

"Let's wait and see what the doctors say, okay?"

"Yeah," she says on a sniffle.

"How did she take her last treatment?"

"Not good. It made her more sick than usual. She ran a slight fever the rest of the day. Her hair is coming out in clumps now." She takes a minute to steady her breathing before continuing, "She finally agreed to shave it off. We had planned on doing it this afternoon."

When Becky, Brent, and I sat down with Ally to explain her illness, we told her of some of the side effects that could happen. Hair loss was one of them. We suggested we shave her head before it started falling out, I even offered to shave mine along with her, but she flat-out refused. We knew she's only six years old, but felt she needed to know what to look for, since it's her body being affected by this horrible sickness. We left the decision up to her to give her a sense of control.

"That's good. Watching it fall out is tough. At least this way, she'll say when it goes, not the other way around."

"Yeah. I just hate to see her like this. I feel so helpless and useless. I feel like I need to do more." She adjusts in her seat and sits up, causing my arm to drop from her shoulders. Reaching over, she grabs my hand. I can still see the tears in her eyes, but she's trying to push them away.

"What you're doing now is enough, Becs," I tell her. "Being her mom, loving her, and protecting her the best you can. Being strong when she can't. Holding her when she feels sick. All of those things are important. Those are things she needs."

"Thank you, Andrew. For everything you've done for us. For coming today. I don't know what I would have done if you hadn't."

I place both my hands on either side of her head and pull it forward until her forehead rests against mine.

"You know I wouldn't be anywhere else. I need to be here just as much as you." Her watery eyes look into mine and she nods. "That little girl in there is part of me as well. I love her and would do anything for her. You know this."

She nods again and gives me a half smile. There's not much to smile at right now, but she knows my words are truth. I would give my life for Ally, no questions asked.

Our moment is interrupted by the whoosh of metals doors being opened. Becky and I immediately stand. She grabs my hand and we rush over to Dr. Adams, Ally's oncologist.

"How is she?" Becky asks, a quiver in her voice.

"She's fine, Becky. Resting in a room at the moment," Dr. Adams says with sympathy in her eyes. "Follow me and we'll talk in private."

The grip Becky has on my hand tightens when she nods. I look over at her and see pain so sharp it also takes my breath away. I feel it, too. The look in Dr. Adams's eyes isn't promising. I feel a sharp pain in my chest, and I reach up to rub it.

We follow Dr. Adams into a private room that has a couch, a couple chairs, and a table. There's a phone and a box of tissues on the table. The walls are a plan white, with nothing hanging from them. No decorations are to be found. It's as if they know any decorations used in this room would be a wasted effort. None of it would be appreciated. I hate this room on sight. This is a room that's heard a lot of bad news. I'm sure the box of tissues is replaced often.

Becky and I sit on the couch, while the doctor takes a seat across from us. It takes her a minute before she starts talking.

"It was as I expected. Her heart isn't taking well to the doxorubicin, the medicine used in her chemotherapy.

It's put stress on her heart that it can't handle right now. It's beating too fast. That's what made her pass out."

I hear a strangled sob from beside me, and I use my shaky hand to pick up hers. My heart's beating a mile a minute.

"What do we do next? Obviously she still needs the chemo for the leukemia, but the medicine isn't good for her heart," Becky says.

"We'll give her something to bring her heart rate down. Although it'll put a strain on her heart, I want to up the dosage a bit more for the chemo. It's important to get her numbers where they should be. The medication for her heart should offset any problems. When we first started this, I had Ally tested to see if she showed any signs she couldn't handle it. All the results were good. It's rare that a person has this reaction. We'll try this new medicine and see how she does with it. We'll monitor her closely. I'm sending a blood pressure cuff home with you, Becky. I want you to check her blood pressure every six hours and write down the results. I'll give you a chart that shows what's acceptable and what's worrisome. I also want you to bring her in every three days for the next couple of weeks to get an ECG. If all goes well, then we'll continue with the higher dosage. If her heart continues to be strained, we'll reassess and see about using a different chemo medicine."

I sit there and listen to the doctor's words, not sure how to take them. She obviously won't survive if she doesn't have the chemo. My stomach drops at the thought, and I push it away. However, if she continues with the current chemo treatment, her heart could give out. Either way doesn't sound good. They're both life threatening.

Fuck!

"What are the chances of the chemo working with a higher dose?" I ask.

Dr. Adams looks at me and answers.

"Since we've started the higher dosage of doxorubicin, her white blood cell count has lowered, which is good. It means the chemo is working. I believe if we up the dosage a bit more it will lower her numbers quicker. However, it will also kill her bone marrow. That's where you'll come in, Andrew."

We both nod, accepting her explanation for what it is. Ally and Brent trust this doctor to do what is best for her.

Becky sits up straighter in her chair and pulls in a deep breath before saying, "Okay. Thank you. Can we see her?

"You can see her, but I want to keep her overnight for observation. With the rate her heart was going, I want to monitor it to make sure the danger is over. The medicine we gave her tonight has slowed her heart down. If all goes well and she's feeling better, then we'll release her in the morning." Dr. Adams gets up from her chair and holds out her hand for Becky and me to shake. "I want you and Brent both to stay positive. Her reacting to the chemo the way she did does not mean she's doomed, okay? Everyone is different and we all act differently to medicines. That doesn't mean we can't find something that will work for Ally."

Becky's watery gaze meets the doctor's and she nods. "Thank you, Dr. Adams. For everything."

Dr. Adams reaches over and squeezes Becky's shoulder and gives her a tender smile. "No thanks needed, Becky. We're doing everything we can for Ally. Take a deep breath and take one day at a time. You stay in here, and I'll send a nurse in to get you to bring you to Ally."

Before the doctor leaves, she asks me, "Are you following all the instructions we gave you when you signed up to give Ally bone marrow?"

"Of course," I tell her. No way would I not follow what the doctors told me I need to do. My number-one priority is doing what I can to help Ally.

"Good. Be on close stand-by for our call."

I nod before she turns on her heel and leaves us in the barren room. We sit in silence for several minutes, taking in what the doctor said.

A few minutes later a nurse enters the room to lead us to Ally. We walk down hallway and I feel like I'm going to my doom. Or rather, Ally's doom. I have no idea what I'll do if that little girl doesn't make it. She's such a pivotal part of my life that I refuse to picture it without her in it. The world will be a darker place if she doesn't exist.

I grit my teeth, clench my hands into fists, and pray with all that I am, with all that I'm worth, that God shows mercy and continues to shed Ally's light on us all.

When we make it to Ally's room, Becky rushes inside. I walk in behind her more slowly, afraid of what I will see. I stay by the door, wanting to give mother and daughter their time first.

The sunken-in look of Ally's eyes almost kills me. Her cute little face is pale, and I can see under the blanket that she's lost even more weight. Her dark hair, or what's left of it, is dull and lifeless. I'm glad she decided to shave it off. Watching it come off in clumps can't be easy. Maybe I'll surprise her and shave mine off as well so she won't feel so alone. The once vibrant, healthy, and carefree six-year-old girl is not who is in the bed across the room. I still love her just as much, but it tears me up inside to see her like this. To plainly see the pain she's going through. I want to bundle her up and try to outrun all the pain and heartache she's enduring.

"Hey, Uncle Andy," Ally says in a weak voice. She holds out her hand toward me, and the look in her eyes seems desperate. I can't take that look, and I quickly walk to her side and grab her hand.

"Hey, skittles. How are you feeling?" I ask, already knowing the answer.

"I'm okay. My head hurts a little, and I want to go home."

"I know you do. But the doctors want to watch you for a little while first, okay?"

She nods, and I can see it's taking a lot to stay awake. I look over at Becky on the other side of the bed and see her watching us. There's sadness present in her eyes, but there's also love shining in their depths. I look back down at Ally.

"Why don't you try to get some rest, and I'll try to talk your mom into letting me bring you some Skittles in the morning." Skittles are her favorite. She likes to separate all the colors and eat them until all the colors have the same amount. Then she'll eat one from each color, keeping the numbers even.

She puffs out her little bottom lip and it makes me want to smile, but I don't. It's hard to smile in a situation like this.

"Mama said Daddy will be here soon. I wanna see him," she says, giving a big yawn.

"Baby, you need to rest," Becky says. "When you wake up Daddy will be here, okay? And he'll be here for at least a few days. Remember, Grammy, Pops, Uncle Cal, Aunt Lena, and Kemmie are coming tomorrow. You need to be well rested so you can visit them."

"Okay, Mama." Her eyes are already drooping and it's not long before she settles into a peaceful sleep. Or at least I hope it's peaceful. I pray her dreams are made up of little girls playing in the park, eating ice cream, chasing after puppies, and feeding the ducks in the pond.

Becky pulls a chair over closer to the bed and sits down. She grabs Ally's hand and clasps it tightly in hers, intently watching Ally while she sleeps.

"She's going to be okay, you know," I tell her, and myself, if I'm honest. Maybe if I tell myself and Becky enough times, it will come true.

She doesn't remove her eyes from Ally, but she replies quietly and tearfully, "I know."

A few minutes later, the door opens and Brent comes sprinting in. He looks haggard. His blond hair is a mess, like he's swiped his fingers through it a hundred times. Stark pain is visible in his eyes. His normally clean-shaven face is covered in stubble. His clothes look wrinkled beyond repair.

His eyes briefly meet mine before they settle on Becky. As soon as Becky sees him, she jumps up from her seat and they meet in the middle of the room. Becky falls into his arms and starts crying softly. Brent rubs her back and whispers quietly in her ear. I can't hear what he's saying but she nods against his neck.

When they pull apart they both make their way over to Ally's sleeping form. I step to the side to give them privacy.

"Oh, Ally," Brent says hoarsely, grabbing her bony hand and kissing the back of it. He wipes at a few stray tears that leak down his face before turning to Becky.

"Tell me what happened," he says, his voice laced with pain.

For the next twenty minutes Becky tells him what happened at home and the reason we're all here. Then Becky and I both explain Dr. Adams's concerns and the changes in Ally's treatment.

He looks at me across the bed, and says, "Thank you for being here when I couldn't."

He knows how I feel about Ally, what she means to me, but I understand his need to show his gratitude. "I love them both. I wouldn't be anywhere else."

He nods and turns back to Becky. "I told Jim I'm done. He's got no choice but to station me here for a while. I can't keep leaving you here to do this by yourself. He said he understands. I won't be leaving again until she's through this."

Becky breathes a sigh of relief and collapses against Brent's chest. "Thank God."

We all stand surrounding Ally's bed in silence. We stay this way for a while, watching the rise and fall of her tiny chest. None of us say anything, each deep in thought. Ally doesn't shift once. She's so still. If it weren't for her breathing, I would be worried.

Several hours pass before I realize I need to leave. As much as I don't want to, I know I need to head back to Jaded Hollow. I have the earlier shift at Jaxon's. I make Becky and Brent promise that if there are any changes they'll call me.

"I'll come by once Brent's family is gone," I tell them.

I know I would still be welcome with his family there. I've met them a few times over the years and got along with them fine, but they need to have family time.

Becky nods. I give her a hug, Brent a handshake, and a gentle kiss to Ally's forehead, then head out to my car to make the trip back home with a heavy heart.

My thoughts turn to Jase once I'm on the road. When he opened the door earlier in nothing but a towel, I almost couldn't stop the urge to tackle him to the floor and devour his body. The man clothed is nothing but gorgeous, but the view of his bare chest, arms, legs, and stomach left me damn near speechless.

I couldn't hold it in any longer. I knew right then I had to have some part of him. I was no longer giving him time to get used to the idea. He was mine and it was about time he knew it. Just as I told him, I wasn't leaving without a taste.

But then Becky called and it all went to shit. As much as I wanted to continue my stalking of Jase, there was no way I couldn't come to Ally and Becky. They mean the world to me. Jase does as well, but Ally and Becky are different. They need me more than I need to have Jase. So, I left, but I left knowing I'm done waiting on Jase.

Jase has no idea what I'm capable of. He has no idea of my obsession with him. Has no idea of my need to be his and have him be mine. But he will. I'll make damn sure he knows. I'll also make damn sure he knows he has no choice in the matter.

Chapter Seven

Jase

I SIT ON A STOOL AT JAXON'S trying to enjoy a beer as I face the dance floor. I watch with narrowed eyes as Andrew, Chris, and Mia dance together. Both Andrew and Mia are supposed to be behind the bar working, but apparently a song came on that Andrew likes and, after looking my way, he grabbed their hands and dragged them to the dance floor. The place isn't that busy, so I don't think it's a big deal.

Mia is in the front, facing away from Andrew. One of her arms is thrown back and her hand wrapped around his neck. He has one hand around her waist, pulling her back and ass into his front, grinding away. Chris is behind him, one hand on his hip and one tossed over her head. Andrew's other hand is grabbing Chris's ass. All three are swaying seductively to the music.

I'd have never thought I would be jealous of my own sister, but sitting here, watching Andrew's hands on her, I want to stalk over there, rip them away, and demand he grind against me like he's currently grinding against them.

Shit! Just the thought of him rubbing his dick against me has my own getting hard. I adjust in my seat to relieve some of the pressure. My willpower is failing fast. No fucking clue how I'll be able to hold him off. Hell, I don't even know if I'll be able to hold myself off.

"If I didn't know Andrew would much rather suck my dick, or rather someone else's dick, than play with my girl, I'd be over there fucking his face up," Mac says ruefully from beside me.

I look over at him and see his eyes on me, clearly weighing my reaction, before turning back to the scene across the room. He has his beer bottle in a tightly clenched hand. Yeah, he feels me too, and doesn't like the scene either. We both know nothing would come of it, but it's still shitty to watch.

Looking back over to the trio, I watch as Andrew bends his head and nuzzles Mia's neck. My body tenses, as if it wants to get up and move across the room and tear them apart. I hold myself in place though. When she throws her head back against his shoulder, I hear a thump beside me. A second later Mac is making his way across the room and snatching Mia from Andrew. Mia laughs as Mac turns her to face him, starting his own grinding session with her, and slams his lips down on hers.

I see the humor in Andrew's eyes before he flips around to Chris and wraps her in his arms. I love my sister, I really do, but damned if I don't want to yank her away from him. I may still be in denial, but dammit, Andrew is mine.

They both look over at me, Andrew puckering his lips and sending me a kiss, Chris waving. I scowl at them both and hope they feel the heat radiating from my eyes. They just laugh and carry on their merry fucking dancing way.

I feel a presence beside me and see Nick taking Mac's seat. I don't know much about the guy, as I've only met him once, but it's plain to see he's always in a shitty mood. Even now I can feel the bad vibes coming off him. He also looks like hell. He has his hat low over his eyes, but it doesn't hide the haggard appearance he has going on. He looks worn down.

I've seen the way Chris gazes at him and the way he watches her. There's history there. I knew immediately this must be the guy that upset her the other day. The only reason I've held my tongue is because it's obvious the guy has been through some shit, and I know Chris would have my ass. I don't know what happened, but you can tell by the dead look in his eyes that it was harsh, and still is. I'll hold off until I deem it necessary for me to step in.

"Sup'," he says to me with a chin lift. Turning to face Jaxon, who just walked to our end of the bar, he orders a beer.

"Nick," I say back to him in the same emotionless tone he used.

After a greeting to Jaxon and getting his beer, Nick turns in his seat to face the dance floor and his body immediately stiffens.

"What in the hell are they doing?" he growls, his eyes going hard. "They're acting fucking ridiculous."

I shift in my seat, not liking Nick's attitude. No, I don't like the way they are all over each other either, but fuck if some guy is going to talk about my sister like that.

Before I get a chance to say anything, Jaxon's on the other side of the bar and is beside Nick with a hand on his shoulder. "Just leave it, man."

Nick shrugs the hand off and gets up from his seat. He sets his beer down and snarls, "Not fucking likely," before walking off toward Andrew and Chris.

When I get up from my seat to follow and make sure he stays in line, Jaxon says, "Give him a minute, Jase. There's shit between them that they need to settle."

"I'll wait, but if he fucks up then he's done," I tell him. I'm trying to stay out of my sister's shit, but I'll only allow so much.

Jaxon nods and we both turn our heads toward Nick's retreating back.

Chris stiffens when Nick makes it to them. Andrew steps to the side, but keeps a close eye on them, something I'm grateful for. Chris and Nick exchange a few heated words. You can see from their body language the words are angry.

When Nick grabs Chris's arm, I've seen enough. Without a look in Jaxon's direction, I move quickly across the floor. I'm about halfway there when Chris forcefully pulls her arm away, rears back, and slaps Nick's face. I feel a sense of pride when I hear her palm hit his cheek, but I'm also worried about Nick's reaction. My walk turns into a jog, but before I get there, Andrew steps in my path.

"Get the fuck out of my way," I grate at him, my eyes still glued on Nick and Chris. I see tears in her eyes, and I want to tear Nick limb from limb. Nick just stands there, glaring at Chris.

"Leave them be, Jase," Andrew says firmly, getting in my face. "He won't hurt her."

"Fuck that!" I growl. "There's other ways to hurt people than just physically. He's obviously hurt her." When I go to move around him, he steps in my way again.

I'm getting ready to push him out of my fucking way when he says in a more gentle voice, "Jase, baby, look at me." I pull my eyes to him and he continues, "They need to work through some shit, okay? They won't be able to do that if you step in. I know Nick. He wouldn't do anything that would permanently hurt Chris. Sometimes we have to go through pain to make it out on the other side happy. Give them time."

I look away from him and back at Chris. I still see tears in her eyes and it makes my chest hurt. Chris wears her feelings on her sleeve, while Nick is obviously in denial. Their feelings, whatever they may be, run deep. I know Andrew is right, but it's still hard to see my sister like this.

Nick grabs Chris's arm again and starts leading her toward the exit. I go to follow, because fuck, this is my sister here, but Andrew grabs my attention by saying, "Come on, baby, dance with me." My eyes land on him and he gives me a sexy smirk. "I know you want to. I saw you watching me while I was dancing with Mia and Chris. Were you jealous?"

A grunt is my answer. Damn straight I was jealous. I want to be the only person Andrew dances with. I won't tell him that, though. He's cocky enough as it is.

The door closes behind Chris and Nick. I want to follow, but instead let Andrew grab my hip and pull me in close. I'm giving Nick one last chance to get his shit straight, but if I ever again see him treat my sister like he did tonight, I'm stepping in, and fuck everyone else.

The rich smell I now associate with Andrew floods my senses. I breathe in deep and close my eyes briefly. When I open them, I see Andrew's lust-filled gaze. The fire there has my blood pumping and my dick growing. Seems like my dick is always making itself known when I'm around Andrew.

I keep my hands to my sides as Andrew pulls me closer to him, slowly swaying our hips to the soft beat of the music. I barely suppress a groan when our chests come into contact. I feel the ridge of his hard dick through two layers of jeans. I want to drop to my knees, unbutton and unzip his pants, and lick it like a fucking lollipop. My mouth waters at the thought.

Andrew's hand lowers from my waist and lands on my ass, squeezing, making the already sparse room in my jeans even smaller. I know he feels it, because he gives me a sexy smile.

"You want me too, don't you?" he asks huskily.

No sense in denying it any longer. "I may want you, Andrew, but that doesn't mean this is a good idea."

"Why the hell not? I think it's the best fucking idea ever."

"Because there's shit going on that you don't know about," I tell him. Before he can open his mouth to ask what shit I'm referring to, I stop him. "Don't ask. It's shit I'll take care of on my own."

He scowls at me for a moment before the sexy smirk is back in place. He leans down, and I stiffen. His warm breath on my neck and the bristle from his five o'clock shadow cause a shiver to race through my body. I'm no longer able to hold back my groan.

Andrew chuckles in my ear and says softly, "I'll just have to change your mind then, baby."

My body is on fire and my head tips to the side before I can stop it. I reach with both hands and grip his waist tightly. Andrew's lips graze my neck and my knees nearly buckle. Sheer force of will keeps them straight. I want to grab a handful of hair and yank his lips to mine. My lips tingle and it takes everything I have not to do just that. I bet his lips would taste like heaven.

"Fuck, Jase, you taste so damn good," he groans, licking his way up my neck, bringing goose bumps to my arms. "So many fucking things I want to do to you."

My hands flex on his waist, unconsciously molding our bodies closer, if that's even possible. Andrew's hips push against mine, and I can't help but push back.

"Andrew," I moan.

"I know, baby," he says against my neck. "You're lucky we're in the middle of the dance floor, or I'd take you right now. I'd sink my dick in your tight ass and fuck you so damn good."

Shit, I want that too.

We stay this way for a few minutes, slowly grinding on each other. Probably putting on a pretty good show for the people watching. Do I care? *Hell no.* It feels too damn good to care. I'd stay this way forever if I could. Actually no, I wouldn't. I'd want a bed close by and for everyone to disappear first.

When the song ends, Andrew pulls back, just far enough for me to see his eyes. They're dark, but I swear I see fire in them. We're both breathing heavily, and I think Andrew is going to lean in and kiss me. I silently pray he does, even though I shouldn't. I'm done. It's inevitable. Why fight something that's going to happen anyway? I'll just have to deal with the consequences later.

"Shit," Andrew mutters. "I've got to get back behind the bar before Jaxon slaughters me."

I'm tempted to tell him fuck it, Jaxon and Mia can handle things themselves, but I don't. I can't. I want to growl out my frustration. Now that I've decided to give in, I'm impatient. I want him *now.*

Instead, I take a step back from him and nod. "Go."

His eyes don't leave mine as he takes another step back, and then another. Before he can get out of hearing range, he says, "This isn't over. We're continuing this later."

I don't say anything, and after another moment, Andrew turns around and heads to the hallway, I'm assuming to the bathroom to get his dick under control before getting back to work. I stand there and watch his ass in his tight jeans and want to chase after him.

I've never had someone get me so worked up as Andrew does. All he has do is look at me with his black eyes and I'm ready and willing to forget all the other shit going on in my life. Even though I know it's a bad idea, there's no way I can continue to keep away from him. That ship has sailed and is a thousand miles away from shore.

With that thought in mind, I start walking toward the dark hallway Andrew is currently in. I've decided that Jaxon and Mia *can* handle things for a few more minutes. Just as Andrew said earlier, I'm not leaving without a taste. He's teased and taunted me one too many times and it's about damn time he follows through.

Just as I reach the mouth of the hallway, Andrew walks out of the bathroom. I briefly notice the white t-shirt he has on with the caption, "You must be this long to climb on this ride." There's a ruler underneath the lettering.

I beeline straight for him, determination in my steps. He doesn't notice me until I'm only a few feet away. He stops in his tracks with that damn sexy smile in place.

"You come back for—" he starts, but I stop him by slamming him against the wall. The next second my mouth is taking his in a brutal kiss.

And it tastes every fucking bit as good as I knew it would it.

There is no slow build-up of teases and touches and coaxing with my tongue. *Fuck that*. I go straight for the good stuff and shove my way into his mouth. Of course, none of that would have been needed anyway, because he gives as good as he gets.

69

I moan into his mouth and push my hard body against his, both our dicks still hard and straining toward each other. Andrew grips my hair and slants my head to the side, giving us both better access to the other's mouth.

I feel the vibrations of Andrew's moan against my chest and it just ramps up my need even more. I adjust my stance and shove one of my legs between his, gently rocking my thigh against his hardness. He growls against my lips and the sound brings tingles to my skin.

I pull back and start licking and kissing down his neck. Once I make it to his ear, I whisper raggedly, "No more fucking teasing. You want to fuck me, then fuck me, but know that you won't be the only one doing the fucking." I need him to know that I'm not just a bottom. I give and take. There's no way this will work if he doesn't realize that. No fucking way in hell I would be able to hold back from sinking my dick in his ass. I'm already so fucking hard I could hammer nails.

Andrew groans and grips my ass, kneading it. "You want my ass, baby?" I pull back and look into his eyes, not able to hide the fierce need, causing him to chuckle. In a low voice, he continues, "Oh, yeah, you want it bad, don't you? Well, you're in luck, 'cause it's all fucking yours."

I know my eyes flare with desire at his words, and I attack his mouth again. The thought of what's to come later has my blood pumping and my hands itching to rip his clothes off and take him now. My stomach flutters, and I feel light-headed. Sweat slides down my overheated body.

Andrew's hands run down my back until he reaches the hem of my shirt. When I feel his bare fingers slipping underneath the material, touching my back, I barely contain my shout of pleasure. I have no fucking clue how I'm going to last once we're alone and naked.

A throat clearing interrupts our hot and heavy make-out session, reminding us we're in a public place, Andrew's work, no less. It's a good thing too, because I have no doubt that another few minutes would have had one of us shoving the other into the bathroom to finish this.

My head drops back, while he turns his toward the mouth of the hallway. I take a few deep breaths to try to calm my breathing and racing heart, which causes me to breathe in Andrew's delicious scent. It does nothing to help my raging hard-on.

Fuck! He smells good!

"Really, hotness?" I hear the rumble of Andrew's voice. "You couldn't give us a few more minutes here?"

"No, I need you out front," is Jaxon's reply, no remorse in his voice. Instead I hear a hint of amusement.

"Fucking cock-block," Andrew mutters. My lips tip up at the frustration in his voice.

"I heard that, fucker. Now get your ass out here," Jaxon says, before I hear his retreating footsteps.

I hear a thump and bring my head back down to see Andrew leaning his against the wall with his eyes closed. He inhales deeply before lifting his head to look at me. His jaw is clenched, and I still see desire in the depths of his eyes.

"You're coming home with me tonight," he says in a tone that brooks no argument. As if he would get one from me after what transpired here in the hallway.

"You bet your ass I am," is my reply. No fucking way in hell would it be any other way.

He gives me his sexy grin again and dips his head for another quick kiss. Once his lips touch mine, there's nothing quick about it, though. He nips and licks and tortures me some more. However, I give back just as much, sucking his tongue into my mouth, getting more of what is fast becoming my favorite taste.

All too soon, we hear Jaxon barking, "Now, Andrew!"

With a growl, Andrew yanks his lips from mine and snarls back, "Hold your fucking panties, I'm coming!" In a quieter tone, he says, "Not really, but fuck, I want to be."

I laugh at him and he just glares back. We both take a minute to adjust ourselves before walking toward the end of the hallway. Once there, he turns to me and says, "Wait for me. You can follow me over in your Jeep." He leans over and places a kiss on my lips, then walks over to the bar and leaps over it.

Closing my eyes, I count to ten. Once I'm reasonably sure my body is somewhat back to normal, I walk over and take a seat at the bar. I glance up at the clock and want to growl at the offensive thing. Two more fucking hours to go.

Chapter Eight

Andrew

GIRLS HAVE IT SO DAMN EASY. When they get horny they get a little wet in their panties. I'm sure that gets pretty uncomfortable at times, but it's nowhere near the shit us guys go through. When we get horny, we have this big fucking pole hanging between our legs, looking for the nearest hole to sink into. That shit wants to stick straight out, but we have no choice but to tuck it between our bellies and the waistband of our pants. It constantly gets in the way, pinched, or rubbed raw. We also leak, just like girls. Except that shit doesn't stay in the seat of our underwear. Fuck no, depending on if the guy is big enough, as in my case, that shit gets smeared into our happy trail, making it sticky and stiff. That's definitely not something you want. And on the occasions we can't find a nice, warm, willing hole? We have to find a private place to jack the fucker to find release, have our balls feel like they're two-ton weights, or think of our grandmother's underwear.

Yep, girls get off so easy. I adjust my junk for the tenth time tonight and look over at Jase to see him sitting there talking to Ethan and Karyn. I've kept my eye on him for the past two hours—no way am I letting him escape unnoticed—so I know they've been talking for a while.

My shift is coming to a close, and I'm impatient to grab Jase and get the fuck out of here. Thinking back to what happened in the hallway has me damn near bouncing on my heels in anticipation. I feel like a teenage boy getting ready to receive his first blow job. The surprise I felt when Jase first pushed me against the wall and attacked my mouth lasted all of a split second before my instincts took over. When he pressed his hard body against mine, and I felt his cock against my stomach, it took every single bit of strength in me to not rip off his clothes and lick his body from head to toe. It's only been a little over a week since he's been in town, but it feels like I've been waiting on him for decades.

I finish up the last of the shit I have to do before I leave. There's not too many customers left and Mia is still working, with Jaxon in his office for backup. I let them both know I'm leaving, quickly wash my hands, and whistle loudly for Jase. He looks over at me, and I give him a chin lift, letting him know it's time to leave. I watch the desire return to his eyes, and it ramps up my blood pressure.

Neither one of us says a word as we walk out of Jaxon's and head to our cars. We both know what's coming. No words need to be said. I don't stray too close to him while we walk because I'm not entirely sure I'll be able to control myself if I do. The temptation of Jase is too much.

The drive home doesn't take long, as with just about every place here in Jaded Hollow. I pull into my driveway and see Jase's Jeep park behind my car. Without watching to see if he follows, already knowing that he is, I head up the steps to my two-story, unlock the door, and step inside. Jase is right behind me and closes the door.

When I hear the click of the lock, I turn and we both just stand there and stare at each other for a minute. Unable to hold back any longer, I slowly make my way to him, grabbing the back of my shirt and pulling it off on my way. His eyes flare wide as I expose my tattooed chest.

When I make it to him, I reach up and pull the hair tie from his hair. The dark-blond strands fall to his shoulders and an image pops into my head of me grabbing a handful as I fuck him from behind.

I place both my arms on the wall on either side of his head and lower my lips to his. The instant our lips touch we moan in unison. I don't think it's possible to ever get enough of his taste.

I grab his bottom lip with my teeth and suck it into my mouth. Jase moans again and places his hands on my abs. His rough and callused palms feel so fucking good against my skin. Goose bumps appear and I growl my pleasure.

"Shit. Don't fucking stop touching me."

"No way in hell," is his husky reply, before tracing his fingers up my stomach and chest to tweak my nipples. Ever since I got them pierced years ago, they've gotten even more sensitive. He flicks the metal and my already hard cock gets even stiffer.

My mouth leaves Jase's and I trace my tongue down his neck. I run the tip of it down the stubble the day has left behind. My hands leave the wall and make their way down to the hem of his shirt.

"Take this shit off," I tell him, and bring the material up his stomach.

He reaches back and quickly slips the material over his head, leaving a sight that has my mouth watering. I want to worship every bit of his body once I see his magnificent chest. There's muscle after muscle and it's lightly covered in light brown hair He has an eight-pack that I want to spend an hour exploring.

I dip my head and lay kisses from his collarbone, down to his pecs. I lick and flick my tongue against his flat nipples. He hisses in a breath through clenched teeth, and I move on to the next one.

Leaving his nipples behind, I trail my lips down his abs and head for the hair leading to his waistband. I get down on my knees in front of him and look up into his eyes. The color is no longer clear blue. Instead it's a storm-cloud gray.

"You want me to fuck you with my mouth, baby?" I ask him.

"Fuck yes, I do," he breathes, his voice hoarse and needy. "Put me in your mouth."

I give him a smile as I reach out and lay my hands on the waistband of his jeans. Without taking my eyes off him, I unbutton and unzip his pants. When I slip them down his hips, I bring my eyes to the sight in front of me. The hard cock that bounces out in relief captivates me. It's fucking huge and has a natural tan, the mushroom-shaped tip slightly pink.

There's a drop on precum on the tip, and unable to hold back any longer, I stick out my tongue and lick the drop away. I groan loudly at the taste of him. Jase's hips buck and he puts his hands in my hair.

"Ah, fuck, Andrew," he says with a deep moan.

Bringing my eyes back up to him, I lower my head and lick the underside of the head until I reach the slit. I

ALEX GRAYSON

open my mouth and bring the head inside. The moan that slips from the back of my throat is just as much for my benefit as it is his—I'm unable to hold it in. His dick is one of the best things that's ever entered my mouth.

Jase's grip on my hair tightens and his hips move forward. Wanting to please my man, I grip the base of his cock and suck him in my mouth until he touches the back of my throat. Jase's shout of pleasure sends a zing of satisfaction through me.

Pulling out, I slowly hollow my cheeks and then suck him back in. During the outward motion, I run my hand down his shaft. In and out. In and out. Jase's grunts and groans fuel my own need.

With my free hand, I grab his balls and give them a gentle tug. I feel Jase jerk in my mouth when I do. His body is tensing, and I know he's getting ready to blow.

Not wanting him to let go until I'm inside him, I release his cock and stand back up.

"What the fuck are you doing?" he growls at me.

I give him a half smile before saying, "Not yet, baby. I want to be inside you when you come."

"Then what the fuck are we waiting for? Where the hell is your room?"

"Horny much?" I ask with a raised brow, cocky grin in place.

"Fuck yeah, I am," I grinds out.

"What's wrong, honey? You don't want to build the anticipation? It's always better when you wait." I like taunting him, even knowing there's no way I can wait either. I love knowing he's impatient with need for me.

He takes a step towards me and snarls, "To hell with anticipation. You take me to your room or *I'll* be fucking *you* right *here*."

My whole body shivers at his words, and it's so damn tempting to let him follow through.

"Nah-uh. I've been waiting months to slide inside you. No way are you taking that from me."

He looks at me with a question in his eyes at my comment, and I realize what I just said. I still need to tell him that Chris told me all about him before he even got here.

"I've only been here a little over a week. How could you have waited months?"

"Later." I throw off his question and grab his hand. "Let's go." I take him to the hallway that leads to my room. He's got no choice but to follow me, his jeans sagging around his waist.

Once inside, I release his hand and turn to face him. I reach down and pop the button on my jeans and pull down the zipper. Jase's greedy eyes watch my movements. When I don't move to tug my jeans down, he looks up at me.

"Waiting on you, baby. We do this together, because once mine are down, there won't be time to remove yours." I speak the honest truth. Once I'm naked, there's not a damn thing that'll stop me from getting to him.

We watch each other as we tug down our pants in unison. Without taking my eyes off Jase, I reach down and yank off my shoes and socks and let my jeans fall the rest of the way to the floor. He does the same.

I stand back up, and just as I told him, I advance toward him quickly. I grab both sides of his face and slam my mouth down on his. Our bodies collide and mesh together, and his warm body against mine is a wonderful fucking feeling.

I turn us toward the bed and walk him backwards until his knees hit the mattress. There, I lift my lips from his and shove him down. He watches me from his reclined position as I climb on top of him and straddle his hips.

Our cocks come in contact, causing me to release a jagged breath.

I bend my head and attack his neck, nipping and sucking on the skin. Marking him.

Jase grabs my hips and grinds upward before sliding one hand around to grip my hardness. My dick jumps at the contact.

Fuck, that feels good! I never realized how much I need his hands on my. How much I crave it.

He slides his hand up and down my erection, and I feel myself getting closer to release. All it takes is one touch from him, and I already want to explode.

Knowing I won't last long if he continues, I pull back and sit up.

"On your stomach, Jase," I murmur.

Without protest, his eyes blazing, he flips around onto his belly.

The sight before me almost has me drooling like a fucking idiot. Scooting down a bit, I grab his hips and hoist him up onto his knees, and I swear I do drool.

He has the most magnificent ass I've ever seen. And it's all mine. It'll always be mine. Once I take him, there will be no going back. I don't know if he realizes it, but Jase Mathews is about to be claimed for life.

Reaching out, I lightly glide my hands along the tempting ass staring right at me. I hear Jase suck in a sharp breath. I lean over and place my lips on the base of his spine and run my stubble across his lower back. The scent that greets me is intoxicating, and I want to breathe it in forever.

I trail my tongue down to the firm ass cheeks in my face. I give them hot kisses and wet licks before I move toward the puckered hole that's begging me to take it. Lightly, I run my tongue over him.

"Oh shit. That feels so fucking good." Jase groans from deep in his throat.

I reach out and grab his dick. I give it a few good tugs and am rewarded by Jase rocking his ass back toward me.

"Oh yeah, baby, fuck my mouth," I say against him.

After a few more tongue kisses to his ass, I pull my hand away from his cock and place a finger against the tight bundle of nerves. Gently pressing forward, the tip of my finger slides in. I pull out and push back in with a little more pressure, until my finger is in up to the knuckle.

Jase's breathing becomes erratic and mine isn't much better. To have Jase like this is a dream come true.

I slide my finger in and out a few more times before I can't take it anymore. My cock and balls feel like they are going to explode if I don't get inside him soon.

I slowly pull my finger out, not wanting to hurt him. I reach over to the nightstand and pull open the drawer to grab a condom. I see Jase watching me with hooded eyes. I lean over and place a hard kiss on his lips, and then tell him, "I can't wait any longer. If I don't get inside you soon, I'm gonna go fucking insane."

"About goddamn time," he rasps out. I see the muscles on his arms bulging, and I know he's close to the edge himself.

He sure is an impatient bastard. But I like that about him. I thought I was going to have to work harder to get him to come around to the idea of being with me. Now that he's here, he's wants it just as bad, and it's obvious he wants it now.

Unwilling to make either of us wait any longer, I slide the condom on, hissing when my fingers glide over my cock.

I sit back up on my knees and pull his hips against mine, lining myself up against his ass. The tip of my dick nudges against his hole. He's already well lubricated from the saliva of my kisses, so the head of my dick slips inside easily.

The sensations surrounding the tip are almost too much to bear. I force myself to go slow and not pound into him like I want to. I grab on to his ass and open him up a bit more and slide another inch in. It's so goddamn tight and warm.

"Ahh... fuck, Jase." I throw my head back and moan.

"More," Jase grunts, trying to push back against me.

Gritting my teeth, I watch as my dick goes in another two inches.

"Shit, you're so tight, baby. This isn't gonna last long," I tell him. And it's the truth. I've never felt anything this good before.

"That's good, because I won't either. Now, give me all of it," he growls at me.

I give him what we both want, and slide the last several inches in. I throw my head back and inhale sharply. I have to still my movements for a minute or there's not a chance in hell I'll last. I feel my balls drawing up in anticipation of my climax. The feel of him surrounding my cock is overwhelming.

"Ah, fuck, don't stop now. Fuck me, Andrew. Fuck me hard." He pushes back again with his words. I see his hands clench the sheets tightly.

"I don't want to hurt you, Jase."

"You won't, just fucking move already."

I run my hands up his back and lean over to kiss his spine. By the time my hands reach his shoulders, my stomach is flat against his back. I grab on to his shoulders and lay my forehead between his shoulder blades. Pulling my hips back until just the tip of my cock is still inside, I ram my hips forward, impaling his warm body with my dick.

"Fuck, yes!" he cries out.

I pull back out and slam forward again. And again, and again. The headboard starts hitting the wall with loud thuds. I don't give a shit. We could bust the entire wall down, and I still wouldn't stop.

Each slam forward, I grunt and Jase groans. I'm getting close, and I don't want to go without him. I whisper in Jase's ear, "Stroke your cock for me, baby. I want you to come with me."

I feel movement and know that Jase is doing as I asked. I pick up my pace, my hips slapping against his ass. I feel myself get bigger, and the pressure on my cock is so damn intense. His muscles tighten around me, squeezing me for all I'm worth.

I lean up a bit and grab a handful of his hair. I yank his head to the side and attach my lips to his. We each take in the other's heavy breathing. Our tongues slip and slide in the other's mouth.

My world explodes, and I bite down on his bottom lip when I feel the first jet of cum leave my body and enter his. Tiny white lights dance beneath my eyes and it feels like I'm floating. Jase's ass grips my dick in a vise-like grip, milking every bit of cum I have in me.

Jase yanks his lips away from mine and shouts his own pleasure.

We both stay the way we are for a couple of minutes, our breathing heavy and our chests pumping. I lay my head back down on his back and give it a few open-mouth kisses, before I slowly pull my still semi hard cock gently out.

Pulling the condom off, I knot the end and drop it to the floor. Jase collapses beside me, still rapidly drawing in air. I lie down, roll his way, and reach out to place my hand on his chest. I feel the *thump-thump* of his heart against my palm. When Jase turns his head my way, one side of his lips tip up into a smile, causing something to swell in my chest. I love his smile. His long hair is damp from sweat and lies across my pillow in a tangled mess. His face is flushed from our fucking. This is the look I want to see every night from now on.

"Hey, baby. You good?" I ask quietly.

"Way past good," he responds.

"Thank you and you're welcome."

He lifts a brow in question.

Giving him a sexy smirk, I enlighten him. "Thank you for finally giving in and letting me fuck you. And you're welcome for fucking you so good."

He chuckles at my words, and I feel it in my palm. I slide closer to him and throw one of my legs over the top of his. He puts his hand on top of it and starts to rub my thigh.

We lie there just staring at each other, neither of us saying a word. I know he's got to feel the same thing I'm feeling. No way could anyone do what we just did and not feel the bone-deep need.

Loving looking at him, but exhausted beyond belief, my eyes close. Underneath my palm, I feel Jase's heartbeat slow, hear his breathing even out, and I know he's asleep. It takes me a few minutes to settle down, but it's not long before I drift off to sleep as well, knowing I finally have Jase just where I want him, and where he's going to stay.

THE NEXT MORNING I'M sitting on the side of the bed with my phone in my hand when I hear the shower turn on. Jase is in the bathroom, naked, with water running down his body. He asked me to join him, but I need to make a phone call first. I know that once I'm in there with him we'll be a while. I also want this call to be made in private. It's not that I don't want Jase, or anyone else for that matter, to know about Ally; I very much do. I'm just not ready yet to tell anyone. As of right now, my mom is the only one who knows what's going on. Ally's already got enough going on in her life, I don't want to add meeting a swarm of new people to the mix. I know that they'll love my second family and that Ally, will love my friends as well. I just don't want to overwhelm her. She needs rest, not too much excitement thrown her way.

It's been a couple days since Ally's been out of the hospital. When I spoke with Becky yesterday, she said Ally's heart rate declined a little, but still isn't back to normal. She's still extremely tired, but has some color back in her cheeks and a bit more energy.

I hold the phone to my ear and hear four rings before Becky answers.

"Hey, Jase," Becky greets me.

"Hey Becs, how are things there?"

I hear her sigh through the phone, but I can't tell if it's from relief or stress. "It's better. She still has a rapid heartbeat, but it hasn't risen to a dangerous level, thank God. She's sleeping a lot, but is more active when she's up. I'm sure I'm getting on the doctor's nerves with all my phone calls. We go back tomorrow for another ECG."

"Make sure you call me tomorrow and tell me what the doctors say, okay?"

"You know I will," she says softly. I do know that. She knows how worried I am about Ally.

"Are things going good with Brent's family?" I ask her.

"It's actually going better than I thought it would. They've been helping out a lot. I think Brent pulled them aside when they got here and explained what happened and asked them to tread carefully."

"That's good, Becs. You need all the help you can get. Going through this is stressful. Lean on them while they're there."

"I am. It's just hard. I've depended on Brent and you through most of this." She stops talking for a minute before she ask. "How have you been? We usually talk about what's happening with Ally. It's been forever since you've told me what's going on in your life."

"It's pretty much the same as it has been. Mac and Mia finally got back together." I've told Becky all about my friends. She was a little offended when I first refused to introduce Ally to them. It was hard to explain my reasoning, but she finally understood my need to keep these two worlds separate for the time being. She knows I'll eventually mesh the two.

"That's wonderful," she says excitedly. "From what you've told me about them, it seems like they were both in pain, but still in love with each other. I'm glad it worked out for them."

I tell her a less gruesome version of what happened between Mac and Mia. She doesn't need to know all the gory details.

After a couple minutes of idle chitchat, I tell her, "I've met someone."

"What?" she screeches loudly, and I'm forced to take the phone away from my ear.

"Damn, woman. Blow my ear out, why don't you," I grumble good-naturedly.

She laughs on the other end of the line. "Sorry, I'm just so excited! Who is he? What's his name? Does this mean you're over your fascination with Jaxon?"

Yes, I also told her all about Jaxon and my unrequited feelings toward him. She knows about the pain I've endured for years because my feelings were pointless.

"I've loved Jaxon for years, and I'll probably always love him. For a long time it hurt to see him with so many women, but then Bailey came along, and I knew right away that they both needed each other. It didn't hurt quite so bad. But Becs, what I feel for Jase is so much more. I knew about him before he knew me, and I was given the opportunity to know him better through his sister. We only met a week ago, but I've known for months that he's it for me. There's just something about him that draws me in and refuses to let me go. No one has ever made me feel like he does, not even Jaxon."

I stop talking and hear a sniffle in the background. Fucking tears. I should have known this would result in tears. Becky always wanted me to meet someone and be happy like she is with Brent.

"Are you crying, Becs? Jesus, stop that shit," I mutter.

"Oh, hush," she cries over the line. "These are happy tears. I'm just so glad you've finally met someone. You deserve to be happy. You're such a good guy, Andrew. Anyone would be lucky to have you."

"Yeah, well, I have to agree with you there. I'm one hot, fun guy. You'd have to be fucking blind, deaf, and stupid not to love me," I joke.

Becky laughs and the tears are forgotten, just as I planned. I don't care if they are happy tears or not, I hate knowing she's crying.

"Seriously, though. I'm the lucky one," I tell her quietly.

"I think maybe y'all both are lucky. I hope I get to meet him one day."

"You will. I promise." And she will. *Someday soon*, I tell myself. "Okay, I've got to go. My man is currently in the shower waiting on me to come service him in all ways possible."

"Ugh! Too much information, Andrew. Go. Have fun, but be safe. I'll call you tomorrow and let you know what the doctors said."

After telling her to give Ally kisses from me and to tell Brent and his family "hi," we hang up. I shoot up off the bed and yank down my jeans, impatient to get to Jase. Now that I've had him, it's going to be very difficult to keep my hands off him.

I walk to the bathroom door, and without knocking, turn the knob. My dick gets harder the closer I get to Jase.

I have a huge shower with clear glass doors. My eyes zero in on Jase's form through the steamed-up glass. He has his head bent and one arm extended, hand resting on the wall. His other hand is wrapped around his shaft, slowly stroking it. His lifts his head and turns it my way when he hears the door open. Even through the glass, I can see his pupils are dilated, swallowing up the clear blue. His breathing is heavy and his chest pumps even harder when he sees me there watching him. My own desire spikes at the sight of him pleasuring himself. I walk forward and yank the door open so hard I'm surprised it doesn't fly off the hinges.

"I see you've started without me," I say, need and want evident in my voice.

"Just warming up, waiting on you," is his husky reply.

He drops his hand and turns to face me. I advance quickly and back him against the wall, our bodies meshing together.

"Want me to finish for you?" I ask, licking along his jawline.

"You fucking better."

I quirk a brow at him and he gives me a sexy half smile. I drop to my knees and engulf his entire length in my mouth without warning.

Pure satisfaction slides through my body when he shouts, "Andrew!"

The sound of him calling my name almost has me shooting my load on the shower floor. It's music to my fucking ears. That's one thing I know with certainty I'll never get tired of hearing.

Chapter Nine

Jase

"WHAT'S YOUR FAVORITE COLOR?" Andrew asks me.

We're sitting outside Joe's garage at the picnic tables eating lunch. Andrew called about an hour ago and informed me he was on his way here with lunch from Maggie's. This is the second time this week he's brought me lunch at work. It's only been a few days since I finally gave in to Andrew, and I love every single minute of it. We haven't really gotten the opportunity to get to know each other much. Instead, we've been spending our time fucking. While those times are hot as hell, we both decided to play the generic get-to-know-you game.

So, here we are. Andrew eating his roast beef sandwich, me eating my Philly cheesesteak, while we play silly, girly games. I feel ridiculous, but at the same time, I'm enjoying learning about him.

"Gray," I answer. "You?"

"Green. What do you like on your pizza?"

"Chicken bacon ranch."

"Jase, man, that's fucked-up. Pizza is supposed to have red sauce, not white," Andrew says with a full-body shudder.

I chuckle at his overdramatic reaction to my pizza topping choice. "Not my kind of pizza. That red shit can stay the hell away from me. What's yours?"

"Plain old pepperoni, with extra pepperoni and light sauce."

After taking a bite and a swallow of my water, I tell him, "Okay, my turn. How old were you the first time you had sex?"

"Fourteen. It was with a fifteen-year-old boy from the next town over. We were friends of a sort. He was visiting his grandmother who lived here in Jaded Hollow. I was horny all the damn time, but it was always the boys that turned me on. One day, Michael caught me looking at his junk while we were skinny dipping in Jaxon's lake. He asked if I was into boys, I said yes, and then we were going at it like jackrabbits."

An irrational bout of jealousy hits me at Andrew's story. It's stupid to think, but I don't like the thought of him with anyone else. I want to pummel any fucker who's ever touched him. He's mine and should only ever have my scent on his skin.

"What about you?" Andrew asks, pulling me from my ridiculous thoughts.

I shake my head to clear it. "Thirteen. My first time was with a girl three years older than me. The thoughts and feelings running through my head scared the shit out of me. My family is the type that doesn't take being different very well. I knew my dad would have a fit if he knew I was attracted to guys. I rebelled against the feelings and fucked whatever girl that would have me, trying to force the thoughts away. Obviously, it didn't work." I smirk at him.

"And thank fuck for that," Andrew says.

That particular time in my life isn't something I'm proud of. When I told him I fucked any girl that would have me, I wasn't lying. And a lot of girls did. It didn't matter the age either, so long as she was my age or older. I was fifteen when I fucked a twenty-eight-year-old woman. She was a neighbor of ours. She was married but her husband was gone all the time. She would always watch me out the window when I was in the backyard mowing the lawn with my shirt off. Even back then I was fit and tanned.

My parents and Chris were gone one day while I was trimming the apple tree we had out back. The neighbor lady came over with a glass of ice water. We ended up in my bed screwing. Each time I had sex with a girl, I was never satisfied. I was able to finish, but I had to work hard at it.

Finally, at sixteen, I said fuck it and didn't try anymore. I officially moved my attempts to guys. After my first time with a guy, I knew that was it, there was no going back. And I haven't been back since.

"Have you ever been with a girl?" I ask Andrew.

"Yep. Once. Years ago." That's all he says, but I can tell by the softness of his eyes there's more to the story. I won't push him to tell me more if he doesn't want to, but it leaves me curious.

Our conversation is interrupted by the ringing of my phone. I pull it out of my pocket and look at the screen. I don't recognize the number but know it's from back home.

Thinking it may have something to do with my parents, I answer. "Hello?"

"Hello, Jase. Long time, no see," comes a voice I never wanted to hear again. "Where you hiding at these days?"

My body goes stiff, and I immediately get up from the bench. I take a few steps away from Andrew to stand beneath a tree. I really don't want him to hear this conversation. It's shit he doesn't need to know about yet. There've been a couple times he's asked me about my life back in Georgia, but I always deflect the questions.

"What the fuck do you want, Damien?" I hiss quietly into my phone.

I peek over my shoulder and see Andrew's eyes glued to me. He hasn't gotten up from his seat yet, but his body is tight, likes he's ready to pounce at the slightest provocation.

"Oh, you know just what I want. And I'm coming to get it. How are you enjoying your last days of freedom?" Damien laughs in my ear and it grates on my nerves.

"Fuck you, Damien. It's a wasted effort. You won't find me."

"Oh, see, that's where you're wrong, baby. When I want something, I get it. How's that pretty redheaded sister of yours?"

My blood runs cold at the mention of Chris. He has no reason to believe I'm with her. Unless he already knows. The whole time I was with him, I only mentioned her a couple of times. I purposely kept it that way, because I knew he was into some fucked-up shit. I didn't want him to think Chris and I were close, and therefore, a bargaining tool if it went bad between us.

Not sure which direction he's going, I feign ignorance, hoping he's not implying what I think he is. "I have no idea. I haven't seen her in almost two years."

"Come on now, Jase. You don't think I'm stupid, do you? I know you just saw her yesterday."

Son of a bitch!

"You stay the hell away from my sister, you motherfucker," I snarl into the phone. "She's got nothing to do with this."

I hear his chuckle on the other end and it grates on my nerves. I want to reach through the phone, wrap my hands around his throat, and squeeze the fucker until his head pops off. What the hell did I ever see in this guy?

"I think it's quite fair, don't you? An eye for an eye," he says, the laughter in his voice replaced by venom. "You took something of mine that I loved. Now it's my turn. Emilio isn't happy, either."

Fuck Emilio. Fuck Damien. Fuck every last one of them. I don't give a shit if they're happy or not. I just care about protecting my sister.

"I'm warning you, Damien, leave my sister alone. That bastard brother of yours deserved what he got and you know it," I tell him in a deadly calm voice. I'll do anything to keep Chris safe. The fucker better realize that before he does anything stupid.

"My baby brother had to get his kicks off somehow or another. His way was just a bit more messy than others. You took him from me when you had no right." The hard edge in his voice should worry me, but instead it just pisses me off even more. "What are you going to do, baby? I've got twenty guys at my back on this. How many you got in that podunk town you're living in nowadays? It's best you give yourself up now, or maybe me and that fuckable sister of yours will have a little fun before I snuff her out. I've never had a brother *and* sister before."

The hand holding my phone clenches. I barely hold in the scream trying to force its way out. I feel sick to my stomach that I let this sick fuck touch me. Frustration crawls through me. I've got no fucking choice but to leave. No way will I allow this asshole to come near Chris. For that to happen, I've got to give myself up. Rage surges throughout my body. I won't give up easily, I'll put up a damn good fight, but if Damien has the backing of Emilio like he claims, then the chance of me coming out of this alive is damn near nonexistent.

Before I get a chance to reply to Damien's threats, he continues, "We'll talk later, Jase. Give you time to come to terms with your fate. Who knows, maybe I'll keep you around for a while. We had some fun times together." And with that, the line goes dead.

Shit! Fuck! Son of a bitch!

My hand drops to my side and I hang my head. The thought of leaving Chris, Andrew, and everyone else in Jaded Hollow weighs heavily on my shoulders. Anger like I've never felt before courses through my blood and my whole body starts to shake.

"What the fuck was that?" a deep voice growls from behind me. I completely forgot Andrew was here.

My hand grips the phone tighter, and I squeeze my eyes shut. I really don't want to leave Andrew, but I know I don't have a choice. Keeping Chris safe is my number-one priority. The things Damien will do to her to get back at me even the strongest person would have a hard time handling.

I hear the crunch of leaves from behind me and brace myself for his touch. When it comes, my emotions finally let loose. I'm not only going to have to leave Chris, but Andrew as well. We haven't known each other long, but in the short time we have, he's come to mean a lot to me. There will be no more touches. No more jokes. No more heated glances. No more taking in his scent. No more running my fingers through his hair. No more feeling the warmth of him at my back.

"Andrew—" he starts, but I don't let him finish.

As soon as his fingers graze my back, I throw back my head and give an almighty roar. I ball the hand that still has my phone in it into a fist and slam it against the tree. The pain I know I'll feel later from the bark that's now embedded into my knuckles doesn't register. My phone breaks into pieces in my hand, and I'm sure bits of the plastic have sliced into my palm. I bring my hand back to punch the tree again, but I'm stopped by Andrew grabbing it and pushing me back a few steps.

He gets in my face. "Tell me what the hell's going on."

My chest heaves as I lift my head and look into his black eyes. It hurts to look, knowing I won't see them anymore. That I'll never see them flare with need again or crinkle at the sides with laughter.

I shove past him, needing to get my shit together and get the fuck out of Dodge. The longer I'm near him the harder it's going to be to leave. And the longer I'm here, the more chance Damien will show up. I need to make a clean break. Make plans on how I'm going to handle this. I won't go in unprepared.

I only get a couple of feet before I'm stopped again by Andrew. He pulls me up short by grabbing my bicep.

"Where in hell are you going? And who the fuck was on the phone?" he growls, taking a step closer.

"I don't have time to explain, Andrew. I've got to pack my shit and leave."

Of course, being Andrew, doesn't let me get away with that answer. Stubborn ass.

"I don't fucking think so. First, you're going to tell me what's going on that you think you have to leave, something that's not fucking happening. And second, we're going to figure shit out together."

"Fuck you, Andrew," I snarl in his face. "You don't know these people. If I don't leave, Chris gets hurt. Now let me go."

"I'd really like to right now, but I'm trying to help you figure out the mess you're in. I can promise you, though, that I'll fuck you later."

Normally his joking would bring a grin to my face. But now it just pisses me off. This shit is serious. I've seen the fucked-up shit Damien's done before. It's not pretty and downright gruesome at times. If he gets his hands on Chris, then it's over.

"Now's not the time to joke. If these guys get their hands on Chris, she's finished. There's no way she'll live through what they'll do to her. The longer I'm here, the closer they are to getting to her."

He steps closer to me, and I feel the heat from his body. His unique scent hits me, and I want to curl my fingers in his hair and yank his lips to mine. I have to hold myself together so I won't do just that.

"That's too damn bad, baby, because that's not happening. I didn't just find you after years of not realizing I was searching for you, to give you up. You're mine and you're going to stay that way, right here in Jaded Hollow. Whatever shit you're in, we can figure it out together. We'll protect Chris together."

"Fuck!" I throw back my head and scream. Why the fuck can't he just leave it and let me go? He doesn't understand the ramifications of me staying. He doesn't know the damage that could be done. If something happens to Chris, I'll never forgive myself. I'll never be the same. Chris and I may not have been real close before, but she's my sister and I love her. She's innocent in all this. She shouldn't have to pay for my mistakes.

I draw in a deep breath before letting it out. I don't know if it's a mistake or not, and pray that it isn't, but I nod at his words. I decide to tell him what happened. I have no idea how we can pull this off, but the thought of leaving him behind, of never seeing my sister again, leaves my gut clenching and my chest hurting.

Relief flashes in Andrew's eyes. I grab his hand and walk him over to the bench to take a seat. I bend over and rest my elbows on my knees, staring off into space. Andrew faces me and straddles the bench.

"I met Damien about a year ago. I was working at the local mechanic shop when he came in with his car that needed a new part. He let me know right off the bat he was interested in me. The feelings were mutual. We were together about a month before he introduced me to his friends. I knew right then that he was into some serious shit. Word out on the street was that Emilio, the head honcho of the group, was dealing drugs, selling girls, and running ammo. I wanted no part of it, but wasn't ready to give up Damien. I made it clear I didn't care what he did as long as he didn't involve me."

I glance down at my hands, clasped between my knees. I barely notice the torn and bloody knuckles. The images running through my head are ones I wish I could forget. That particular time in my life I'm not proud of. If I could go back and change the day I met Damien, I would in a heartbeat. But then again, had I not met Damien, his bastard of a brother would have finished the job I stopped.

I get back to telling Andrew what a fuck-up I am. I just hope he doesn't look at me with disgust once I'm finished.

"For the most part, I was clueless as to what was going on. Though, there were a few times Damien would come over with specks of blood on his clothes and his hands would be shredded. I ignored it, not wanting to know what happened. A few times he would reek of cheap perfume. I didn't care much if he was seeing women. I didn't even care if there were other men. We weren't exclusive and we both knew it. It was just good fucking between us."

When I look over to Andrew, his face is hard. There's a tic in his jaw and his hands are clenched tightly on his thighs.

"A couple of times he tried to talk me into joining the group, but I refused. He'd get pissed, but he knew it wasn't happening. However, I did attend parties he threw at his place, which included Emilio and some of his gang. I socialized with them briefly, but kept my distance. Damien was very close to his family. He had a sister, brother, and his mom. His brother, Drake, was in with the group. He was younger than both of us, early twenties, but was a cocky little motherfucker. He thought since he was part of it, nothing could touch him. Damien catered to him and let him get away with everything.

"One night, about a month ago, we were at one of his parties. I'd stepped outside to get some fresh air when I heard rustling around the back of the house. I walked around back and saw a light on inside the shed through a window. The music was loud inside the house, so I knew no one heard it. I thought maybe someone was trying to steal something, so I went to check it out. There was an unlocked padlock on the door with the key still in it."

I stop talking to draw a deep breath. I squeeze my eyes closed, trying to block the images from forming in my head, but they squirm their way in. Revulsion churns in my stomach, and I have to force away the vomit trying to make its way up.

When I start talking again, I do it with a hoarse voice. "What I saw when I opened the shed door is something I'll never forget. There, tied by her hands to the beam on the ceiling, was a naked girl. She couldn't have been more than thirteen years old."

"Shit," Andrew mutters beside me.

When he reaches out to touch me, I stand up quickly. "Don't," I tell him. "Don't touch me. Let me finish, or I won't. I need to get this out, first."

He nods in understanding, and I'm grateful. I've never told anyone this before. I don't like the thought of Andrew touching me while I spill out all this nastiness. Andrew's clean, while I feel dirty for being a part of this, even if it wasn't voluntary.

"Her tiny body was covered in blood. There were cuts and bite marks everywhere, bite marks so deep that blood oozed from them. Blood dripped from between her thighs, too. Her head was just hanging there, her tangled and dingy hair almost to her waist. She wasn't moving, so I thought she was dead. I leaned over just in time to throw up.

"When I stood back up, I took a step toward her to let her down, but before I could, I saw something out the corner of my eye. Fucking Drake was standing there with his pants undone, no shirt, blood all over his chest, and a bloody knife in his hand. He asked if I was there to join the party."

Andrew growls, but I ignore it. If I don't get this shit out now, I never will.

"I asked if his brother knew what he was doing. He said yes, that he helped him find the girls. He sounded proud when he said Damien didn't join in, but he'd sometimes sit and watch the show." I hiss when I say, "The man I had been fucking was stealing young girls so his twisted brother could rape and mutilate them. And he fucking watched!" I roar the last and punch the picnic table with my already damaged hand.

"Jase—" he starts, and starts to get up from the bench.

"NO!" I yell, and point a finger at him. "Sit the fuck down and let me finish! You wanted this, so shut up and let me continue."

I know I shouldn't be angry at him, but he forced me to tell him all this. I hate thinking about it, and when I do, I'm disgusted with myself all over again. How could I have been so clueless that Damien was involved in something so heinous?

Andrew doesn't say anything else, but I see the anger on his face. I don't know if it's directed at me for losing it, or if he's angry *for* me. I don't much care at this point. I just want it done, so I can come up with a way to get out of this shit.

"When he told me his brother was involved, I lost it. He must have really thought I was going to take part in it, because when I charged him, he just froze with shock. He didn't have time to defend himself before I got to him. I didn't think. All I saw was that kid hanging from the ceiling with her body almost unrecognizable.

"I guess I zoned out or something because by the time I was done, he wasn't breathing. I knew right away that I was in deep shit. No way would Damien let me live after I killed his brother. Even so, I didn't regret it. Still don't. I'd kill him a thousand times over for what he did to that girl, and probably multiple others. I grabbed a blanket off the makeshift bed in the corner and laid it out on the floor. When I went to grab the girl, she whimpered. Shocked the shit out of me, because I thought she was dead. I wrapped her in the blanket, ran to my Jeep, and left her at the emergency room before I blew out of town. I knew Damien would come after me, and when he did, it wouldn't be pretty. I was hoping I was far enough away that he wouldn't find me. Obviously, I was wrong. He knows I'm here and now he wants Chris in return."

Andrew's quiet for a minute, before he says, "He won't touch her. I promise you, Jase, he won't get his hands on her."

I look over at him and see he truly believes that. The black in his eyes make him appear deadly. I've never seen that look in his eyes before. His lips are set into a hard line and he's clenching and unclenching his fists. He looks as though he's ten shades beyond furious. But as much as I want to take his words for truth, there's no way he can guarantee Chris's safety.

"I can't take that chance, Andrew," I tell him. "The only way to keep her safe is to go to him. I won't go in unprepared, though. I don't plan on just giving myself over to him."

"That's not an option," Andrew growls, and gets up from the bench, walking my way. "You're not going anywhere near that fucker. You may as well forget that shit and help me come up with something else."

I blow out a frustrated breath. He just doesn't get it. This isn't something that can be easily taken care of. Damien, even without the help of Emilio, is a dirty motherfucker. He fights to win, by any means necessary. Fuck the repercussions and fuck anything that gets in his way.

"It isn't as simple as coming up with a plan," I angrily say back to him. "He has Emilio backing him up. That means he has all of Emilio's people. You really want to bring people like that to Jaded Hollow?"

He steps into my space and grabs me by the ponytail. I want to yank it from his grasp, but decide to hold still for the moment.

"We have people, too, Jase. We'll talk to Mac and see what he can do. We'll move Chris somewhere else for the time being so she's not alone." He steps closer and snarls in my face, "You're not fucking leaving. You're not fucking giving yourself up to that bastard. You're staying right here with me. You're mine and fuck if I'm going to let you go. Do whatever you need to do to get used to it."

When he's finished, his chest is pumping rapidly with his heavy breaths. I can tell there's nothing I can say to him that will make him change his mind. And in a way I'm glad. I don't want to leave here. I just hope we're not making a mistake Chris will pay the consequences for.

As soon as I nod, Andrew pulls me forward by the grip he still has on my hair and drops his head to plant a searing kiss on my lips. He doesn't wait for me to open to him, not that he would have to wait long anyway. He forces his tongue in my mouth to tangle with mine. I grip his hips and mold our bodies together. His hardness against my own has a groan coming from deep within my throat.

Never have I ever wanted someone as much as I want him, but it'll have to wait. We still need to talk to Mac. Tonight though, you better bet your ass I'll be taking his.

Andrew nips my bottom lip, and I want to howl in pleasure. Already, in the short time we've known each other, he knows just what to do to turn me on so damn much that I don't give a shit about my surroundings.

Andrew pulls his lips from mine and takes a step back. I have to force myself to not yank him back to me and demand he finish what he started. Still, an unfulfilled groan sneaks past my lips.

His lips quirk up into a smirk before tipping back down into a serious line.

"Chris will be safe, baby. Nothing will happen to her. She's like a sister to me, and I promise to do whatever it takes to keep her safe," he tells me softly, and I know he speaks the truth. Andrew is the type of man who would give his life for the ones he cares about. I've known from the beginning that he cares about Chris. I know she holds a special place in his heart for the help she gave Bailey when she needed it. I'm glad that she found that here in Jaded Hollow.

"I know," I reply, and see him smile.

"Come on," he says, taking my uninjured hand. "Let's clean your hand up. And don't do that shit anymore. Your hands are golden, and I need them to rub along my body. That hand is now out of commission, thanks to you mangling it up."

Although it's not the time for humor, I still laugh at him. The poor baby. He sends a cocky grin over his shoulder as he leads me into the bathroom in the garage. Thank fuck Joe isn't here today. I'd have hated for him to hear what I told Andrew outside.

"Oh, I'm sure I can use other parts of my body that you'd like just as much, if not more," I say with a wink.

"Damn straight you can, and if we didn't have shit to do, you'd be using them right now."

My body tightens up at his words and a shiver runs through me. What I wouldn't give to do just that. Waiting until tonight to have him might just be an impossible feat.

After cleaning and bandaging my hand, Andrew leans in for another dick-hardening kiss, before leaving me at the garage to finish up. He's headed into town to warn Mac we'll need to talk to him later.

Thinking of the reason for that talk sours my mood again. I'm disgusted that I was ever connect to that bastard, but I can't help but think maybe I was supposed to be, so I'd be there to help that girl. I have no idea if she made it. No clue of the condition she's in. I'm sure after going through what she did, for however long she was in that shed, she's probably not doing too well. Who in the hell would be after that? Still, I would like to know. Maybe once this is over, I can ask Mac to look into it.

Chapter Ten

Jase

A COUPLE OF DAYS LATER I'M sitting at Maggie's alone, eating breakfast. Andrew is out of town for the next few hours "visiting a friend." His words. When he told me this morning that he would be away for a few hours, I asked where he was going. Not because I'm a jealous lover and have to know where he is at all times, but because I am his lover and want to know more about what goes on in his life. That's part of getting to know each other, right? His answer was vague and stiff, like he didn't want me to know. That's fine. I don't have to know everything about him, but what bothered me was the way he acted after I asked him. He was quiet and withdrawn, not his usual carefree self. I'm nowhere near a sissy boy, but it still hurt that he didn't trust me enough to tell me. This isn't the first time he's left town and stayed away for hours. There've been a couple other times. And I get the feeling no one knows where he goes. I find it strange that normally he's so open, withholding nothing, but with this one thing, he's closed up tighter than Fort Knox.

We're going to his mom's tonight for dinner. He and his mom are close, and I'm looking forward to meeting her. Andrew told me his dad died when he was ten and his mom was so devastated she never remarried. She's still pining after his dad. He said he's tried talking her into going out to meet new people, but she would have none of it. She claims there was only one man for her, and he was taken from her too soon. It's a shame she feels that way. I agree we are all meant to find someone, but sometimes we're meant to find more than one. It doesn't mean you love the ones before any less.

I'm starting to wonder if Andrew is my "one."

I'm at the counter eating Maggie's delicious biscuits and gravy and listening to Jack and Jake bicker at each other behind me. They are two old men I met my first day at Joe's. They like to come hang out with him sometimes and it's funny to watch the two of them interact.

"I'm telling you, Jake, the girl was showing me her panties!" Jack says adamantly.

"Oh, shut it, Jack. Why in the world would someone want to show an old fart like you her drawers?" Jake asks Jack.

"'Cause she knows what's good for her. I may be old, but I still got it."

I can't help the laugh that slips out at Jack's words. The man can't be a day younger than eighty and is a skinny as a beanpole.

I try to cover up my laugh with a cough, but Jack doesn't fall for it.

"What you laughing at, boy?" When I turn in my seat to face him, he continues, "You don't think I can get a girl? Why, I bet I can snatch any girl out from underneath you." When I lift an eyebrow at his statement, he adds with a mutter, "If you had a girl underneath you instead of a boy, that is."

Jake laughs, and I grin over at him.

"Forget it, old man. Ain't no woman gonna want you. There's much younger fish in the sea."

"I still say she was showing me her panties," Jack mumbles.

Jake ignores his friend and asks me, "How you doing today, Jase? You headed to Joe's after breakfast?"

"Yep, but only for a few hours. Andrew and I are going to his mom's for dinner."

"'Bout damn time that boy's found someone else to moon over," Jack pipes in. "Poor boy had his eyes on Jaxon for years, even knowing he played for the other team."

His words are a punch to the gut. I never knew Andrew felt that way toward Jaxon. Yes, I've witnessed him flirting with him, but Andrew flirts with everyone. Does he still feel that way? Am I just a distraction for him? A simple fuck because he can't get it from who he really wants it from? And how long has he felt that way?

"Damn it, Jack, stop fucking opening your mouth before you think," Jake barks at his mouthy friend.

"What?" he asks. "It's not like the whole town doesn't know. Anybody could see the way that boy looked at Jaxon."

"Not everyone, you damn fool," he mutters, pointedly looking at me.

Jack catches his meaning and flushes. "Well, fuck me sideways."

"Don't worry about it. I know Andrew's had other interests besides me. Not like he was a virgin when I came to town."

"He most definitely wasn't, by the looks of all the men I've seen him with."

I grit my teeth and grip the counter top with white knuckles. The thought of Andrew with other men, makes me want to hit something. It's stupid to feel that way, because like I told Jake and Jack, I know he's been with other men, but I still don't have to like it.

Jake reaches over and knocks the back of Jack's head with a menu. "You're a damn idiot, you know that, Jack? I'm gonna lock you up in the house and throw away the key so you can't go out in public anymore. Let's go, you ass." He gets up from his seat and grabs Jack's arm, yanking him up as well. When he passes by me, he stops and says, "Just ignore him, he has hardly any brain cells left after all the drinking he did when he was younger."

"What the hell did I do this time?" Jake says, huffing and puffing. "I can't say nothin' right, can I?"

"No, you can't, that's why you need to be put in a nursing home so you're not in public."

With that, he pulls Jack behind him, pays for their food, and then drags him out the door.
With my good mood from earlier gone, I get up a few minutes later and pay for my own food.

A COUPLE OF HOURS LATER I'm at Andrew's house, waiting for him to get home. Since the first night Andrew and I fucked, I've been staying here. Andrew offered because I was sleeping on Chris's sleeper sofa and it isn't the most comfortable bed. I agreed because the thought of having Andrew anytime I wanted was too much of a temptation to pass up. We've been fucking each other senseless any chance we get.

After the incident with the phone call, Andrew and I met up with Mac, and I explained what went down back home. Mac said he would look into it. There wasn't much he could do until he found out more details.

I was leery on bringing Mac onboard because, well, he's a cop, and I killed a man. Mac's eyes blazed with hatred when I told him what I caught Drake doing to a little girl. I can tell he fought with himself over if he should bring me in or not, but in the end he said he would ignore that part of the story and work on running a check on Damien and Emilio to see if there are any warrants out for them. He's also checking into their pasts. The rest we'll deal with later.

The front door opening and closing pulls me from my thoughts. I'm standing in the closet when Andrew walks into the bedroom. His eyes heat when he sees me standing there in nothing but my jeans, button undone. Being eye-fucked causes my own desire to spike, and I take a step toward him.

"How was your visit?" I ask, still a little peeved by his attitude earlier.

Shadows pass over his face, and I see a flash of sadness before he looks down to his feet, avoiding my eyes. Andrew from this morning is still present.

"It was fine. You going to be ready to go in about an hour? I need a shower first."

When he tries to pass me to grab some fresh clothes, I grab his arm. He looks at my hand before lifting his eyes to mine.

"Not yet," I say, making it very clear what I want from him with a look.

"Not right now, Jase. We need to get to Mom's house," he says, surprising me.

Andrew always seems so ready and willing to fuck. For him to be uninterested is out of the norm. I don't like it. I also don't let it deter me. Ever since this morning, I've needed to show Andrew who he's with. To fuck any and all thoughts of Jaxon or previous lovers out of his mind. To show him I'm all the man he will ever need. He's fucking mine and when I get done, he'll know it.

Without releasing his arm, I take a step closer, leaving only an inch between our chests.

"I want you naked, on your hands and knees on the end of the bed. Ass in the air," I tell him gruffly, the mental picture I just conjured causing my dick to jump.

Andrew's eyebrows fly up and he hisses out a breath. I can tell my words have affected him just as much as me.

"That what you want, baby? To take me?" Andrew asks.

My grip on his arm tightens, and I close the remaining distance between us. I lean forward and run my tongue up his neck. Right before I get to his ear, I bite down. Andrew groans and it ramps up the ache in my cock.

"I'm gonna fuck you hard, Andrew," I whisper in his ear. "I'm gonna grip your hips and ram my cock in you over and over again, until you feel it in your throat. I'll be so damn deep in you that you'll feel it for days. Every time you take a step or sit down, you'll feel it, and be reminded of me taking your ass." I pull back from him and release his arm. "Clothes off now and get on the bed."

Not saying a word and keeping his eyes on me, he reaches back and yanks his shirt over his head. When his beautiful chest comes into view, I gobble him up with my eyes. His chest isn't completely covered in tattoos, but he does have quite a few. The one I'm most intrigued about is a small gathering of different-colored small circles. They almost look like Skittles candy, but I can't imagine why he would put them permanently on his body. There must be a reason though. The one in the middle of the group has the initials AD and the date 7-18-09. I noticed the tattoo the other day when I watched him sleep. I plan to ask him what it means, but not right now.

When I look back up at Andrew, he has his ever-present sexy smirk on his face. He turns on his heel, and I follow him to the bed. Once he climbs up onto it, with his ass in the air, all the air in my lungs whooshes out. The sight before me has me wanting to drop to my knees and worship his ass. I've never seen an ass that hot before. I could spend hours exploring it. But we don't have hours right now. We have to be quick. The fucking I'm about to give Andrew will be fast and hard.

I walk up behind him and run my hands up his back, looking at the black, leafless tree he has tattooed there. My jean-covered dick meets his ass, and I grind the denim against him, causing us both to moan. Even through my jeans, he feels good.

When he pushes his ass against me, I pull my hips back. Andrew looks over his shoulder at me with lust-filled eyes. I know mine reflect the same emotion.

Raising one of my hands, I slip a finger in my mouth, getting it good and wet. I then move the digit to Andrew's tight, puckered hole. Gently running my finger around the bundle of nerves there, I slip just the tip inside. Andrew drops his head and lets out a low groan. I push my finger in a little deeper and feel the muscles trying to suck my finger in further.

After a few in-and-out strokes, I pull my finger from him.

I reach for the condom and bottle of lube I placed on the bed earlier. I unzip my pants, pull out my throbbing dick, and slide the condom on. Uncapping the bottle, I look at Andrew, who has his eyes on me again, and drip some lube on his asshole. I grip the base of my dick and line the head up.

With iron will, I gently slip the tip inside.

Andrew grunts as I throw my head back with a loud moan. He feels so damn tight, damn near strangling my dick. I fucking love it.

Slowly, but steadily, I push forward until I have every inch of my cock inside. I clench my teeth and have to wait a minute to move again, or this will be over way too fast.

The grip I have on Andrew's hips gets tighter. I pull all the way out, leaving just the head inside.

"Who's fucking you, Andrew?" I ask him with a growl.

Turning his head to the side, he looks at me and replies with a ragged voice, "You are, Jase."

Andrew tries to push his hips back, forcing my dick back inside, but I stop his movement. I keep my hips still while I ask him the question that's fucked with my head all day.

"Do you still want Jaxon? Do you think about him fucking you?"

Andrew goes completely still below me. He grips the comforter beneath him.

"What the fuck, Jase?" he growls over his shoulder.

"Answer the damn question," I snarl at him, and ram my hips forward at the same time I pull his back to me. "Do you still want Jaxon?"

"Fuck!" he shouts at my sudden movement. The muscles in his arms strain as he holds himself up. "No, I don't want fucking Jaxon," he growls.

I pull out and forcefully drive back into him again. I reach forward and get a good grip on his hair and yank his face to the side. I look into his black eyes and ask him again.

"Who's fucking you, Andrew?"

He narrows his eyes at me and tries to pull his hair from my grip. I don't allow it, and instead yank it back more.

"I've already told you who's fucking me, Jase," he growls. "But if you don't stop dicking around and start moving, *I'll* be the one fucking *you*."

Shit, his attitude turns my dick to stone. I angle my lips over his and kiss the ever-lovin' shit out of him.

I pull back just enough to separate our lips and say, "Don't you forget it. *I'm* the one fucking you. I'm the *only* one who will ever fuck you again. Got it?"

"Goddammit, Jase!" he says through bared teeth. "Yes, I fucking got it!"

Satisfied with his answer, I release his hair, grab his hips, and plow my dick in as far and hard as I can, immediately pulling back out and pounding back in again. The force of my thrusts causes the bed to shift. The need to dominate and show Andrew I'm the only man who will ever have him this way is uncontrollable.

I reach around to wrap a hand around his cock. Squeezing hard, I give it a few strokes as I continue to fuck him for all I'm worth.

I feel my balls tighten and draw up. I'm getting close, and I want Andrew right there with me. Below me, he grunts with each of my strokes, both of my dick and my hand. Knowing that he is enjoying this as much as I am spurs me on. I want him to want more. I want him to always want to come to me for his sexual needs.

I grind my hips into his ass, trying to get even deeper inside him. Leaning forward, I wrap one arm around his stomach. My stomach is pressed to his back and most of my weight is now on him. I pull my hips back and slam back inside.

The pace of my strokes on his dick quickens. Andrew reaches back and grabs my ass, trying to bring me in further. There's no way, though. I'm as far in as I possibly can be.

"Fuck, Andrew, you ready, baby? I can't hold it any longer," I groan against his back.

Andrew's answer is to tighten his muscles around my dick and shove his ass back against my hips. My lips find his back between his shoulder blades and I bite down with a growl. I mark him with my teeth as my hips and hand pick up speed.

Fuck, I've never felt anything so good in my life. The feel of Andrew tightening around me has my stomach clenching and me tipping over the edge with a loud shout. Just as I hit my peak, I hear Andrew's own shout and feel his warm release on my hand.

My frantic thrusts slow slightly as I carry us both through our climax. I drive forward a few more times before I slow my hips and rest my head against his back. We both lie there trying to catch our breath.

After a moment, I gently pull out of Andrew, dispose of the condom, and fall to my back beside him. The bed jumps a little and I look over at Andrew, who is on his side with his head propped up on his hand. His breathing has slowed and he lies there watching me.

"What the hell was that about?" he asks quietly, his brows arched in question.

I turn my head away and look up at the ceiling. Throwing my hands up behind my head, I answer honestly, "Jack mentioned today that you've had a thing for Jaxon for a while. I let it get to me and didn't like it."

Andrew doesn't say anything for so long that I look back over at him. He has a grin on his face, which piques my temper. I'm glad he thinks this is something to smile about. I personally hate it. I've never felt jealousy before and it's not a pleasant feeling.

"Jase, honey, you've got nothing to worry about. I haven't looked at another man, including Jaxon, for months, since the first time I saw you," he says, smile still in place. The look in his eyes says he's sincere.

This isn't the first time Andrew's mentioned seeing me months ago. There's no way that's possible, because I've only been here a couple of weeks. I ask him to clarify.

"A couple months before you got here, Chris showed me a photo of you. She told us you were planning a trip here and wanted to introduce us. She didn't tell you because she was worried it may scare you off. From the beginning, when I first saw you in that photo, I knew right away I had to have you. I felt an instant connection, even from a simple picture. So yes, I did have feelings for Jaxon, even though I knew he didn't share them, but from the moment I knew about you, I've never, not once, thought about Jaxon that way again. All I can think about is you. I'm sure Chris wanted to snap my neck a few times because I bugged her for information about you and hounded her about when you were coming to town."

By the time he's done talking, he's scooted over to my side of the bed and is running his fingers through my chest hair. It feels good and my body starts to respond again.

I'm not exactly sure how to feel about what he just told me. On one hand, I feel deceived because Andrew knew about me before I got here and didn't tell me. But on the other, it's hot as fuck that he's wanted me from the beginning, before he even met me.

I look at the time on my watch and decide to let the subject go for now.

I turn to my side and lean over to give Andrew a kiss before murmuring against his lips, "I don't like the idea of you thinking about another man. It pisses me off and makes me want to hurt someone. But I know you had a life before me. I have to accept that, and I will."

"Believe me, baby, you've got nothing to worry about," he says. "There's no other man out there I want besides you. Jaxon will always mean something to me, but you're the one I will always want. You're stuck with me, whether you like it or not. Now, get your ass up and dressed so we can go." He finishes with a slap to my ass.

He chuckles against my lips at my growl, before pulling back and getting off the bed. I watch as he saunters into the bathroom for a shower, his tight ass making me wish we had more time.

I get up from the bed to grab the jeans I had on earlier and finish getting ready. Ten minutes later, Andrew comes out of the steamy bathroom, puts his own clothes on, and then we leave to go have dinner at his mom's place.

ANDREW, HIS MOM, SANDRA, and I are all sitting around the table finishing up dinner. When we first got here, Sandra welcomed me with open arms. Literally. When we walked up the steps to the porch she was already waiting for us. As soon as Andrew introduced us, she grabbed me, tugged me forward, and wrapped her arms around my waist. She left me no choice but to do the same.

I wouldn't say I was worried that she wouldn't like me, but a little part of me, the part that's still hurt over my parents' reaction to me revealing I'm gay, was a little leery. She immediately put me at ease, and I knew I was going to like her. I enjoy watching Andrew and her interact. They are so easy with each other and you can plainly see the love they share.

I never really had that with my parents. Chris didn't either. They weren't bad parents, but they weren't there for us like they should have been. We always had the material things we needed, we just didn't have any emotional support.

"So, Jase, do you plan to stick around Jaded Hollow long?" Sandra asks me from across the table.

I shift in my seat, unsure how to answer. Andrew and I have talked more about what's going down with Damien. He's adamant I stay here and let him and Mac help, but I'm still not sure if that's the best thing to do. If it were up to me, I'd never leave; however, if I feel it's best I leave, I will. I won't play around with Chris's safety. And I have no doubt Damien will do what he threatened.

"I'd like to, ma'am, but we'll have to see how it goes," I tell her, and then feel Andrew squeeze my thigh underneath the table. I glance over at him and see irritation in his eyes.

"Well, I hope you do. Andrew needs someone to keep him in line and curb is tongue. I'm hoping you can do that for me." She says this with a twinkle in her eye, and looks over at her son.

"Sorry, Mom. There's no chance of that happening. No one can take out the awesomeness that is me," Andrew says, winking.

"See what I mean?" she asks me with a smile.

"Well, I do have to admit, Andrew is pretty awesome, and as much as he can be a bit boisterous at times, I wouldn't change him. Andrew's special and one of a kind."

"Ha!" Andrew says with a big grin on his face, and points his finger at Sandra. "Told you so! Even Jase sees that I'm special and there's no one else like me. He has great taste."

"Oh, dear Lord, help us all," she mutters to the ceiling, but I see mirth in her eyes. She dips her head back down and looks at me, her expression turned serious. "I'm glad you feel that way," she says quietly. "My boy *is* one of a kind and not just anyone can make him happy—the kind of happy he truly deserves. I think he may have found that person in you." She has tears in her eyes when she gets done talking.

My chest tightens at her words. I hope I'll always live up to her standards and never let her down.

"Thank you," I tell her, and let the truth in my words be heard through my tone.

After smiling at me, she gets up from the table and grabs her plate. "Andrew, grab Jase's plate and come help me load the dishwasher."

I get up from my chair to help, but she shoos me back down.

"No, no, you stay here. Or better yet, go make yourself at home in the living room. Guests don't help with dinner dishes. We'll be back in a few minutes."

I watch as Andrew and his mom leave the dining room. I look around the room and see a few pictures hanging on the walls. Hearing the tinkling of the dishes, I get up from my chair and make my way over to one of the pictures. Andrew, Sandra, and a beautiful light-brown-haired woman I've never seen before are sitting on a porch swing. Andrew is seated between the two women with his arms draped over both of their shoulders. All three are smiling big at the person holding the camera. Judging by the younger look of Andrew, I would say that the picture was taken several years ago. The unknown woman is heavily pregnant. I wonder who she is.

Just as I'm about to walk out of the dining room, I hear Andrew's mom's voice drift through the door. Now even more curious about Andrew, I continue my perusal of the photos, not even trying to tune her out.

"How is Ally doing?" comes Sandra's concerned voice.

"Not too good," Andrew replies to his mom's question, his own voice laced with worry. "The last couple of days have been hard. The treatments are really starting to get to her because of the higher dosage."

I turn toward the door they are behind. I have no idea who they are referring to. I've never heard Andrew mention someone by the name Ally before, but she clearly means something to them both. Is she the woman in the photo? Is she the one Andrew visits when he leaves town?

"My poor girl," Sandra continues. Even through the door I can tell her reply is tearful. "Something's got to give. Every time I see her she seems weaker. She's strong, but a body can only take so much."

I move on to another photo as I listen to them talk. This one is of young kid of about eight or nine, Sandra, and an older man. The young kid has to be Andrew, judging by the looks. The man, who is the spitting image of Andrew now, I assume is his dad. All three of them are out on a boat in a lake. Andrew is standing between the man's legs. Both are laughing. Sandra has one of her hands on the other side of Andrew's head, pulling it toward her and kissing his temple.

"I know, Mom. Becky said the doctors are doing everything they can for her. Unfortunately, it's a waiting game. With her recent heart problems, they have to be more careful."

"I'm just so scared for her," Sandra says sadly.

It turns quiet after Sandra's heartbreaking reply. I may not know who they are talking about, but I still feel for the unknown Ally. Obviously, she's sick and not doing well. She's important to Andrew, and therefore, she's important to me. It saddens me to think that someone that means so much to Andrew and his mom is suffering.

I make my way out of the dining room and into the living room. Taking a seat on the couch, I grab the remote and switch on the TV. A football game is on. I watch the game without really paying attention to it as I wait for Andrew and his mom to reappear.

It bothers me that Andrew hasn't confided in me about this Ally person. She's undoubtedly a big part of his life. I care for Andrew, and I know he feels the same way. And because I care, I want to be a part of every aspect of his life. I want to be there for him while he goes through whatever he's currently going though. I just hope eventually he trusts me enough and reveals whatever it is he's trying so hard to keep from all his friends.

Chapter Eleven

Andrew

"YEAH, BABY, GET 'EM!" I yell at Jase, and watch him ram his car into Mia's, who in turn hits Bailey's, both of whom decided to attack me.

"I got your back," he hollers back at me, puts his car in reverse, and proceeds to push both girls out of the way so I can get out of the corner I'm stuck in.

Once I'm free, I turn my car in their direction to help out my man. Pushing the gas pedal down as far as it will go, I creep along at a whopping eight miles per hour. Just before I make contact with Bailey's car, I'm hit from the side by Chris. I'm thrown off course and smack into a wall.

"Hey, what is this? Gang up on Andrew day? What'd I do to y'all?" I ask Chris.

She just shrugs and says with a laugh, "Nope, just seemed like something I should do."

I narrow my eyes at her as she slowly drives away. I back my car up and align it with hers. I'm on one end of the bumper car platform and she's on the other. She's paying me no mind, already forgotten that she just bumped me off course. I look over at Jase, and see he has help from Jaxon, both chasing Bailey and Mia.

Gripping the steering wheel with both hands, I jam my foot down on the gas pedal. Chris is just ahead, laughing as she chases after two kids on the ride with us. I dodge left and narrowly miss Mac. Then to the right to avoid hitting Trent, Mac's son. I straighten my steering wheel and am only feet away from paying Chris back.

She glances up and sees me coming for her, but there's nowhere she can go. She's surrounded by unused bumper cars and the person who has blocked her against them. Her eyes go wide, which causes a huge toothy grin to pop up on my face.

Right before my car plows into hers, it starts to slow down. My car comes to a complete stop, just barely tapping hers.

"No!" I groan loudly, hitting the steering wheel with the palm of my hand. I'm pouting and I know it, but I was so damn close! "That's not fair! I wanna go again!"

"Aww… suck it up, Buttercup," Chris laughs, getting out of her car. "Maybe you'll get me next time."

I unfold my tall frame from the car and make my way over to the exit. Jase and the others are already there waiting on me.

"So, where to next?" Mia asks.

"Ferris Wheel!" Bailey yells.

We head in that direction and get in the short line.

"Wanna make out if we get stuck at the top?" I ask Jase quietly, but obviously not quietly enough.

"Ugh! Please! I really don't need to see my brother making out with another man," Chris says, slapping my arm.

"Then don't watch," Jase says to his sister, laughing.

"There are kids around. You can't do that shit," pipes in Jaxon, his eyes pointing in Trent's direction, who is standing at the front of the line with Scott, his friend.

"We'll be at the top. No one can see us." I shrug.

"You're a horny bastard, you know that, Andy?" Mia says. She has her arm wrapped around Mac's waist with her hand in his pocket.

Her use of the nickname Ally calls me by sends a sharp pain to my chest. Ally, Becky, and Brent should be out enjoying themselves as well, but with Ally being so sick and tiring so easily, it's not possible. She needs as much rest as she can get.

Guilt enters my system at the thought of Ally never going to the fair again. Of never getting the chance to be a kid again. I shouldn't be here like this. Why should I be out having a good time when a little girl is stuck at home, sick and barely surviving?

I wipe the thoughts away and plaster a fake smile on my face, keeping up the act with my usual comeback.

"Damn straight I am," I tell her, unashamedly. "Have you seen my man?" I face Jase and give him a quick kiss on the lips. There's no way I could ever get enough of him. He's intoxicating and I'm completely addicted. "Besides, I'm not the person currently feeling my man's ass." I hold my hand up, warding off her retort. "And, you call me Andy again, and I'll dump you over in that dunking booth over there."

"Bring it, big man."

"I will. Just as soon as I finish feeling Jase up on the Ferris Wheel," I tell Mia, and chuckle when Chris makes gagging sounds as we make our way to our seat.

After a few heated kisses and some mind-blowing groping, we get off the ride and decide to grab something to eat and drink. As we pass by the dunking booth, I look over at Mia and see her watching me. I smile at her.

"Don't you fucking dare," she says, pointing a finger at me.

Ignoring her warning, I grab her, put my shoulder in her belly, and throw her over my shoulder. She immediately starts pounding on my back with her tiny fists, which doesn't faze me at all. I hear everyone behind us laughing.

"Put me down, you jackass," she says with a slap to my ass.

I stop and ask, "Are you going to call me Andy again?"

"Probably."

"Wrong answer." I start walking again toward the pool of water.

"Mac!" she yells, squirming and wiggling on my shoulder. I slap her behind to get her to stop.

"Sorry, Pix, you're on your own with this one. You know he doesn't like to be call Andy." You can hear the amusement in his voice.

"Traitor!" she yells back.

I'm almost to the abandoned dunking pool when I feel a sharp sting on my ass. The little minx just bit me!

"Ow!" I quickly put Mia on her feet and rub my butt. "Did you just bite my butt?"

Looking smug, she folds her arms across her chest and juts out a hip. "Yes."

"My ass is off-limits. I know it's tempting and all, but only Jase can bite it."

"You put it in my face, it gets bit," she says with a smirk.

I take a step toward her, ready to get her back for her little stunt, when Jaxon walks up to us and puts his hand between our chests. "Children, children, that's enough now."

I feel Jase walk up behind me and I turn to face him. "She bit my ass, Jase. Kiss it and make it better later?"

Giving me a sexy smile, which shows off his dimple, he winks and says, "You know I will."

With just that look, my dick starts to harden. *Fuck!* I can't wait to get him home. I let my eyes tell him what I'm thinking. His own flare back at me. If we were anywhere else, I'd haul his ass somewhere and fuck his brains out.

"Alright, enough with the mind-fucking," Chris says, shuddering for effect. "I'm hungry. Let's go eat."

We all make our way over to one of the concession stands, order expensive and unhealthy food, and sit under one of the pavilions.

"How's Joe doing?" Mac asks Jase, after taking a bite of his greasy burger.

"He's doing better. The damn fool said he would be back to work middle of next week. I told him I've got things covered, but he's being stubborn," Jase replies.

Unfortunately, Joe's granddaughter had to rush him to the hospital last week because his left arm started going numb and he kept getting dizzy. He refused to go at first, insisting he was fine, until Heather threatened to call an ambulance and have him hauled off that way. Turned out he'd had a minor stroke. Luckily, it did no lasting damage.

The stubborn old man is refusing to take it easy. It's no surprise, really. He's old enough that he should have retired two decades ago. We all figure he'll probably die in that shop.

"Hey, Dad, can Scott and I get on the Zipper?" Trent asks Mac, carrying his trash over to the trash bin.

Mac looks over to the ride Trent is asking about and back to his kid. "Yeah, but when you get off, come straight back here, okay?"

Trent and Scott take off running toward the ride that'll flip this way and that. My stomach does a little flip as I watch it sling the carts around upside down. I use to be able to handle those things, but not so much anymore.

"Has anyone heard or seen from Nick lately?" Bailey asks everyone. "I invited him to come along with us last week. He said he'd let me know, but I haven't seen him since then."

"He was in the bar a few nights ago. Drunk off his ass," Mia says.

"He seems to be doing that more and more lately," Chris says sadly from beside Jase. Jase reaches over and puts his arm around her shoulders, bringing her closer. It's plain to see the hurt in Chris's eyes at Nick's continued downward spiral.

"I'm worried about him." Bailey says what we're all thinking.

We all thought Nick would eventually snap out of his mourning after a while. We get that he's hurt over losing Anna, particularly the way Anna died. Hell, we all felt the loss, especially Jaxon, Bailey, and Mia. But he seems to be getting worse. Nothing we do seems to be working.

Jaxon pulls Bailey to his side and kisses her forehead. "We'll give him a bit longer. If he continues the way he is, we'll figure out what to do."

Bailey nods, tears glistening in her eyes.

My body tenses when I hear Chris ask Jase, "Have you heard any more from that guy Damien?"

Everyone looks to Jase for his answer, me included. They all know of the situation and understand why he did what he did. They also understand why he ran and the potential danger.

"No, which worries me. Damien isn't the type to keep quiet. I can't help but think he's up to something."

My hands ball into fists at the thought of something happening to Jase. If that fucker thinks he can come into my town and take away or hurt something that belongs to me, he better fucking come prepared. Chris and everyone at this table are included in that category. No one fucks with my family or friends. I have every intention of stopping the bastard, damn the consequences.

"Still no leads on where he is?" Jaxon asks Mac.

"No, he's disappeared. When they pulled Emilio in for questioning, he claims he has no idea where he is either."

"If he's in cahoots with Damien, he's lying. He'd be running the show and would in no way let Damien just go off grid. Emilio's top notch and doesn't let anyone run over him."

"So, either Emilio's lying about Damien's whereabouts or Damien's lying about Emilio wanting revenge as well," Chris finishes for Jase.

"Maybe I should call Emilio myself and ask him," Jase suggests. "I have no idea what I'm dealing with here."

"What *we're* dealing with," I tell Jase, reminding him he's not alone in this.

Our gazes lock for a minute. I don't hide the anger I know is blazing in mine. The anger at the situation and the rage I feel at the thought of Jase contacting Emilio. I know it's probably the smart thing to do. We need to know if this Emilio is after Jase and Chris as well, but I still hate the thought of him associating with those pieces of shit.

"Let me talk to the guys down in Georgia, see if they've got anything else on Damien or Emilio, before you do that," Mac says, gathering his and Mia's trash. "Either Emilio is keeping a low profile for the time being, or he's not in on this mess. I'll let you know in the next day or two."

Jase gives him a nod and turns his attention to Chris.

"How are you holding up at Jaxon and Bailey's?"

When it came to light that Damien, and possibly Emilio, was after Chris, we all decided it was best if she stayed with Jaxon. His place is the most secure.

"It's great. I get to spend time with my best friend and I get to see and play with little Amari any time I want. But I still miss having my own space."

Jase's voice lowers when he replies to Chris, "I'm sorry this is happening. I wish I hadn't come here, putting you in danger. Or at least I wish I had come sooner, before all this started."

Jase's words piss me off. Not only because of the reason he wishes he didn't come to Jaded Hollow, but because he regrets it. This is where Jase needs to be. Around friends who care about him and are willing to help. There's no better place than here. I'm about to tell him so when Chris's words stop me.

"Don't you dare say that, Jase," Chris says heatedly. "I've missed you and am so glad you came here. I hate what's happened to you, what you've been through, but here is where you should be. Here is where you have friends who will help. You won't be alone." Chris looks over at me when she says this, and I understand her unspoken message. She shifts her eyes back to Jase before continuing. "As far as my safety, I know you won't let anything happen to me. I've also got these guys who'll help protect me." She gestures to Mac, Jaxon, and me.

"She's right, Jase," Jaxon says, and Bailey nods. "You shouldn't have to deal with this by yourself. You need help taking care of it. You're Chris's sister, so you're family. We protect our families."

And this is why I'll never leave this town. This community is filled with people just like Jaxon. The people here are close-knit and will do anything to protect their own. Jase is now part of the town.

I lay my hand on top of Jase's thigh under the table. When he looks over at me, I tell him, "Baby, you won't find a better place to be. We've got your back, no matter what. Those fuckers will find out soon enough that you don't fuck with the people in Jaded Hollow. If I hear you say you regret coming here again, I'll spank your ass, and it won't be one that you'll like."

His brows jump at my comment, but I see mirth in his eyes. "You really think you're big enough for that?" he asks.

He has no damn clue what I'm capable of when I set my mind to something. I wasn't lying to him. He says that regret bullshit again, I'll tie his tight ass to the bed and give him the ass slapping of a lifetime.

"Don't try me," I warn him. "You may not like the outcome. When I want something, I get it. You should know this already."

His lips tip up into a smile, showing off that damn dimple again. My mood goes from serious to carnal in a split second. That dimple is dangerous. Every time I see it I want to lick it.

Jase breaks our connection and turns to the rest of the table.

"Thank you all. When I spoke with Chris on the phone about coming here, she told me what a great place it was, but I never imagined I would find the friends I have."

Trent and Scott come running up to our table, breaking the gravity of the situation. They chatter to Mac and Mia about the ride. Bailey and Chris break away from our table and head over to grab cotton candy from a vendor. Jase, Mac, Jaxon, and I talk about the upcoming basketball game for the local high school.

I feel a vibration in my pants and reach into my pocket for my phone. Looking at the screen, foreboding envelops me at seeing Becky's name on the screen. I get up from the table and tell the others I'll be back. I take a few steps away and answer, heart pounding in my chest. I get that feeling every time Becky calls me lately.

"Becs, is everything okay?"

I hear a sniffle on the other end of the line before Becky whispers, "Andrew, we need you."

My gut clenches at the tone of her voice. She sounds lost and broken. I know the feeling. From the moment I was told Ally had leukemia, I've felt a hole in my heart. A hole that keeps getting bigger the weaker she gets. I know that if the worst were to happen that hole would stay there forever. Nothing would ever be strong enough to fill it. I send up a silent prayer, asking God to keep Ally safe and whole.

"What happened?" I ask, afraid of the answer.

"She's in acute renal failure. We don't know anything else right now. They're running tests."

Becky lets out a pained cry and my gut clenches at the sound. I hear a shuffle on the line, and a second later Brent's on the phone.

"Andrew, we need you here as soon as you can. They want to go ahead and take bone marrow from you and store it for when she's better." His voice breaks at the end and he stops to clear his throat. "She's not doing too good. Everything is piling up at the same time. Once they have her kidneys working properly they want to do the transplant."

"I'm on my way, Brent. Let the doctors know I'm ready, and I'll be there as soon as I can."

"Alright, we'll see you in a bit."

After we hang up, I turn to face the others, prepared to give whatever excuse I can come up with for needing to leave. The words die on my lips, and I know my time is up. If I know anything about these people, it's that they won't let me get away with lying anymore. They've obviously heard my conversation, judging by their worried expressions, and know something's happened.

Even though I know I need to explain, I don't have time at the moment. I need to leave and get to the hospital.

With my hands shaking and my heart pumping double time with fear for Ally, I tell the group, "Something's come up. I've got to go."

They all stand at the solemnity in my voice, but it's Jase who's by my side in a flash.

"What happened? What's wrong?" he asks.

I look in his eyes and see the concern there. I want to reach out and touch him, but I don't.

"I don't have time to explain right now," I tell him, and then look to the others. There's worry in their eyes as well. "I'll tell you all later. I've got to go now. I'm sorry."

I lean forward and give Jase a quick kiss. When I pull back and turn to leave, he stops me.

"Wait. I'm coming with you," he says.

I don't have time to argue with him, so I just nod. If I'm honest with myself, I'm glad he is going with me. I've kept this part of my life a secret for so long that it'll be nice to share it with someone. I don't want to do it alone anymore. Telling Jase and the others will lift a huge weight off my shoulders.

After a quick good-bye to the others, I practically run to my car. Jase doesn't say anything as he easily keeps up with me. I know he's worried though. I see him casting me troubled glances out the corner of my eye.

The drive to the hospital is made in silence. I think Jase knows I need the quiet right now, and I'm grateful for that. I need to think. I need to process what's about to happen. I'm not scared of giving marrow. I'm scared of the reason I *need* to give the marrow. What if it's too late? What if Ally's body rejects it? The thought of either of those things happening causes my heart to nearly stop, and I feel more emotions than I've felt in my life. I can't live in a world without Ally in it.

We make it to the hospital in record time. I don't take the time to park, instead asking Jase to park it for me after stopping at the entrance.

I rush into the main entrance and head straight for the nurse behind the desk.

"I'm here for Ally Dawson," I tell her, before I even reach the counter. "I'm donating marrow. Her doctor's name is Adams."

She presses a few keys on her computer, then looks up at me and asks, "Name?"

"Andrew Donovan."

"Okay, Mr. Donovan. I'll page Dr. Adams and let her know you're here. Someone will come get you in a few minutes." She hands me a clipboard with papers and a pen. "In the meantime, I need you to fill out these papers."

I grab the clipboard and head over to the small waiting area to take a seat. I stare at the papers in front of me, not really seeing them. This is really happening. I have no idea what condition Ally is in. Becky told me it was bad, but how bad? Not knowing is killing me inside.

I jot down the answers to the questions on the paper, take them back to the nurse, and stiffly start pacing the floor. I'm about to lose my shit and demand someone go get Dr. Adams when Jase walks through the door. A sense of calm rushes through me and my shoulders sag as he heads my way.

"Everything alright?" he asks when he reaches my side and grabs my hand.

Before I get a chance to answer him with a growled "I don't fucking know," Jaxon, Bailey, Mia, Mac, Trent, and Chris come rushing over.

"How did you know I was here?" I ask the people I regret keeping this secret from. I know I'll need them later.

"We followed you," Jaxon answers.

I must have been so deep in thought on our way here that I didn't notice them behind me.

I nod and run my fingers through my hair. I'm jittery and the longer I stand here not knowing what is going on, the closer my control gets to the edge.

"What's going on here, Andrew," Mia says, coming to stand beside me and placing her hand on my arm.

I give a slight jerk at the touch, my nerves getting the best of me. I feel so helpless just waiting here. Why haven't they come and got me yet? This waiting bullshit is driving me insane.

I pull in a lungful of air and look to Jase. He gives my hand a squeeze. Unbeknownst to him, he's giving me the courage I need to tell everyone the truth. A truth I worry will have everyone disappointed in me. I know they will forgive me. That's just the type of people they are. They love me just as much as I love each of them, but I still don't want to see displeasure in their eyes.

I never planned on keeping Ally from them for so long, but it's just the way it happened. Becky's parents made it impossible for me to tell them from the start, then Bailey came along and everyone needed to focus on her. After that, it was just easier to keep the secret. I also wanted to hold on to Ally myself just a little bit longer. But I don't need to anymore. I know I'm going to need their support in this.

"Hey," Jase says, taking a step closer. "Just as you told me earlier, whatever it is, we'll get through it together. Everything will be okay. Trust me, trust us."

This man will never know how much he means to me. There will never be enough words to express my feelings for him or how grateful I am he's here.

Gathering the courage that Jase's words and actions just gave me, I tell everyone my secret.

"Ally, a six-year-old little girl, is currently fighting for her life. She has leukemia, but the treatments weren't working as fast as her doctors need it to, so they've upped her chemo dosage, which has killed her bone marrow. My phone call earlier was from her mom, Becky. Her kidneys are failing. I've signed up and am a match to donate marrow if Ally should need it. They want to go ahead and take my marrow now for when she's better and her body can take the transplant."

My eyes stay on Jase as I talk. He's the one keeping me grounded right now. I feel a weight lift from my shoulders as I'm talking, but it also makes the situation even more real. For the most part I've always been able to keep this life away from my life with Ally, Becky, and Brent, and in a sense I've been able to hold off the emotions while in Jaded Hollow. But with my friends knowing the truth, those two lives converge. There's no way I can't fight the emotions and fear anymore.

My eyes flick to Bailey and Chris, who both have tears in their eyes. Jaxon pulls Bailey to his chest. Jase reaches over with his other arm and places it over Chris's shoulders.

"As you know, I met Becky and Brent twelve years ago in Bakersville when I was visiting my cousin Richard. I saved her from being robbed."

I was seventeen at the time. I remember the fear on Becky's face when I made it behind the building, and the relief when she saw me. I knocked the guy away and was checking to make sure she was okay when he took off. I wanted to chase him, but didn't want to leave her alone.

"You all have meet them a few times, but what you don't know is we've gotten really close over the years. Seven years ago, Ally came along, and I fell in love with her. She's the most precious thing to ever grace the earth."

I stop talking for a minute, remembering the first time I saw Ally wrapped up tight in a pink blanket in the hospital. The tiny fragile baby girl I held in my big hands took hold of my heart tight in her fists. And the older she gets the tighter that fist gets. There's nothing I wouldn't do for her. I would give my life in a second if I knew it would help her. If there was any way I could change places with her, I would.

I look up at the others and see compassion written on their faces. These people deserve to know Ally, but more importantly, Ally deserves to know them. Becky and Brent both need all the support they can get, and this bunch is the most supportive you can get.

I'm pulled from my thoughts when I hear someone call my name frantically. I look up just in time to catch my mom in my arms. She wraps her arms tightly around my neck and squeezes. I feel her tears soak my shirt.

"How is she? Have you seen her yet? Why aren't you back there getting ready?" she asks, pulling back from me.

I put both of my hands on either side of her head and focus on her tearstained face.

"I haven't seen her yet, so I don't know how she is. All I know is she's in renal failure. I'm waiting on them to call me back."

"My poor baby girl," she says, and more tears slide down her face.

I gather her in my arms again and rock her gently. Looking over her shoulder, I see everyone's eyes on both of us. Jase has moved to the side with Chris. He hasn't said anything this entire time, and I wish I knew what he was thinking. Mia is standing with Mac's arm around her shoulders. Trent stands beside his dad. Jaxon has Bailey in front of him, his hands on her hips. Each pair of eyes are watching my mom and me with open curiosity. I know it looks strange to them for my mom to be so upset over someone else's child.

The door that leads to the back whooshes open and a nurse appears. "Andrew Donovan," she calls.

I look from the nurse to Jase. I don't have time to explain, but I also need him and the others to understand the importance of Ally and her role in my life. I know this is big, but I hope he gives me the chance to explain later.

Taking one last look at Jase, I tell him with eyes that say I'm sorry for hiding this from him.

Right before I turn to follow the nurse, I tell him and the others, "One more thing you all should know. I'm Ally's biological father."

Chapter Twelve

Jase

"I'M ALLY'S BIOLOGICAL FATHER." Those words play over and over in my head.

I'm sitting on one of the hard gray plastic chairs in the waiting room and stare at the door Andrew walked through ten minutes ago. When he dropped that bombshell down everyone was left with their mouths hanging open and their minds reeling, me included. After a few moments of stunned silence, the room exploded with murmurs and shocked whispers of what this revelation meant. It was obvious Sandra knew about Ally and the situation. She avoided questions as best she could, until I stepped up and told everyone to back off.

"Leave her the hell alone," I growl to the crowd. "It's not her place to explain anything. Andrew will tell us what's going on when he can."

After my small outburst, the group dispersed with guilty faces into small separate groups, talking quietly amongst themselves. I understand everyone's need to know what the hell is going on, but it's clear she's upset and doesn't need to be interrogated. Hell, I'm just as shocked as everyone else and dying to know how Andrew became a father, but I also know Andrew is the only one who can tell us.

Sandra left to grab coffees for everyone. I offered to go with her but she insisted she needed time alone. I can't say I blame her.

I run my fingers through my hair and grab chunks of it as I bend over and place my elbows on my knees. The look on Andrew's face right before he walked away tells me he regrets me finding out this way, all of us finding out this way. I'm not upset he kept this from me. I'm just surprised and curious, and I have to admit, a bit intimidated. He obviously cares for this Ally girl deeply. The sadness and desperation in his eyes while he talked about her illness showed he's hurting. I hated the look and wanted to wipe it from his face. My need to be there for Andrew is strong. I wish there was something I could do to help, but all I can do is be there for him and comfort him if the outcome isn't good.

I have no idea how serious Ally's condition is. I just hope for her and Andrew's sake whatever treatment she's getting works. No little girl should have to go through what she has. My heart hurts for her, Andrew, Sandra, and her family.

"Hey, how are you holding up?" Chris asks, taking the seat beside me.

I release my hair and glance up at her. "I'm alright. Just shocked and worried. Andrew's back there giving bone marrow to a daughter I knew nothing about. A daughter who could be dying. I feel like I need to be back there with him. I can't imagine the pain he's going through right now."

Andrew's a strong person, but it doesn't matter how tough you are when it comes to the possibility of losing a child.

Shit. It's weird to think he has a child.

"He'll get through this," Chris says quietly, grabbing my hand. "He's got you, me, and everyone else to help him. He won't be alone, no matter what happens."

She's right. As much of a shock as it was to find out Andrew has a daughter, there's no way I would abandon him. Andrew is quickly becoming a vital part of my life. Imagining a life without him in it has my stomach cramping and a cold sweat breaking out. He has so forcefully woven his way into my heart that if I were to lose him it would destroy me. He doesn't know it, but my heart belongs to him. Wherever he is, my heart is right there beside him, keeping him company.

Chris and I sit in silence, both deep in thought. I wonder if and how this will change my and Andrew's relationship. It's clear he's part of Ally's life. This is where he goes when he leaves town. Will he want me to be part of her life as well? Or will he continue to keep the two lives separate? I have to admit, I want to meet her. I want to meet all of his second family. And that's what they are. The way he talked about them, especially Ally, shows he loves them and considers them his family.

My tumultuous thoughts are interrupted when Sandra comes back with coffee. She hands everyone a cup from the tray she's carrying and takes a seat on the other side of me. The others sit close by as well.

"Does anyone know how long this process takes?" Mac asks.

It's Sandra who answers. Of course she would know because they've prepared for it.

"The process itself takes about an hour," she says in a small voice. "There's also prep and recovery time. It'll probably be a few hours before we hear anything. He'll probably stay overnight since it's already so late in the day."

"What about Ally? When she gets the marrow, how long before we know if it works for her?" I ask.

When I turn to face her, there's such anguish in her eyes. "It could take a few weeks before we know if her body took to it or rejects it. Her body will be weakened because of the extensive chemo and the transplant, not to mention the renal failure, so she'll be susceptible to infection. It'll be a waiting game."

I gather her in my arms when a tear trails down her face. The pain she's going through must be horrible. First, she has to watch her grandchild suffer this terrible illness. Then she has to witness the grief of her son while he suffers with her.

I look over her shoulder at the others. Bailey and Chris both have tears in their eyes. Their men have them in their arms, comforting them. Mia is standing with Mac. The expression on her face is unreadable. She's been quiet and in the background this whole time. I know she and Andrew have a close relationship, and I wonder what she's thinking right now.

Several hours pass with us all sitting and waiting. There's not much talking going on. My nerves are getting the better of me. I want to jump out of my skin, wondering how things are going. I know very little about donating bone marrow, but I do know it's not a dangerous procedure. I'm not really worried about the procedure itself, I'm more concerned with Andrew's state of mind. I have no idea how he's kept this to himself for so long. How he's coped with this by himself. Yes, he's had his mom and I'm sure that's helped, but when you've got friends as close as Andrew does, it has to be hard to keep a secret like this from them.

A sound off to my left startles me, and I glance up just as a nurse comes through the door. We all stand up quickly as she makes her way toward us.

"Mrs. Donovan?" the nurse calls.

"Yes, that's me," Sandra says.

"Andrew's in recovery. As expected, the procedure went fine. He's still a little groggy from the anesthesia, but should be up and running soon."

I hear Sandra take a deep breath from beside me before she asks, "What about Ally? How is she?"

The sympathy I see in the nurse's eyes says a lot and it causes a sharp pain in my stomach.

"I'll have to check to see if you're on her privacy statement, but I can tell you she's okay. Dr. Adams is in with her and her parents now."

My hands clench at my sides. I understand the policy on privacy, but fuck if it doesn't piss me off just the same. Sandra's been worried sick out here for that little girl and she still can't find out how she's doing.

"Can we see Andrew?"

"Yes, if you'll follow me, I'll take you to him."

Sandra nods and takes a step to follow the nurse. I want to demand to go in with her, but it's not up to me. Everyone behind me has known Andrew longer and deserves to see him first.

She's only taken a few steps when she turns back to face me. "Are you coming?"

I look back at the others and watch as they nod. "You two go ahead. We'll give you both a few minutes before we come up," Jaxon says.

Turning back to Sandra, I ask, "Are you sure?"

"Yes. He'll want to see you."

Relief floods through me at her words, and I follow her and the nurse. The walk down the hallway takes forever. The smell of antiseptic and cleaner stings my nose. The white walls on either side of the hallway close in on me, and I have to shake my head to clear it. Nurses and doctors pass by us, talking quietly. The world continues on as usual, but it seems like mine just flipped on its axis.

When we make it to the door, I let Sandra enter first. She immediately rushes to his side because his dumb ass is trying to climb out of the bed.

"Andrew Donovan, get your butt back in that bed!" Sandra scolds him.

Andrew whips around at his mom's sharp tone. He sways a bit before righting himself. If the situation wasn't so serious I would have laughed at his expression. He looks like a child who just got caught sneaking a look at Christmas presents.

"Do you know how Ally is?" he asks in a scratchy voice. "I can't get anyone to tell me a damn thing. I was just getting up to find someone…"

He stops when he sees me standing in the doorway and we just stare at each other. He looks ridiculous in his white-and-green checked hospital gown. But even so, he's still sexy as fuck. I want to go to him, but don't. I'm unsure of where we stand at the moment. Revealing that you have a child to your lover has the potential to alter a relationship.

"The only thing they've told me is she's okay. The nurse said Dr. Adams is in with her, Becky, and Brent, speaking with them," Sandra says, breaking the spell between us. Andrew looks away from me and toward Sandra.

"Fuck," Andrew hisses, and lies back down on the bed, frustration and fear evident in his tone.

I take a step toward him. My need to go to him is too strong to ignore. I hate knowing Andrew is in pain, whether emotionally or physically.

"If you don't get your ass over here, Jase, I'm coming after you, and you'll be the one dealing with my mom bitching at me," Andrew says, pinning me with his eyes.

That's all the prompting I need. The next second I'm standing beside the bed and he has his hand on my neck, pulling my lips toward him. We meet in an easy kiss, nothing carnal or rushed about it.

After we pull apart, I rest my forehead against his.

"You okay?" I ask.

"Yeah. I'm sorry I kept Ally from you," he says softly.

I shake my head. "No, don't apologize. We'll talk more about it later."

He nods, and I pull my head back. Sandra's standing on the other side of the bed watching us with a small smile. I can see the strain still around Andrew's eyes. The worry is obviously still there, but his expression seems lighter.

A few minutes later, the door whooshes open and in walks a female doctor who looks to be in her forties. As soon as Andrew sees her he sits up in bed, wincing slightly without complaint.

"Hey, take it easy," I tell Andrew, and push him back down.

"He's right. You'll probably be a little tender the next couple of days," the doctor says, walking up to Andrew's bed.

He ignores her concerns and instead asks, "How is she, Dr. Adams? How's Ally?"

"Relax, Andrew, Ally's fine," she says kindly. "She's resting right now. Becky and Brent sent me down here to explain things because they knew you would be worried. Luckily, we caught the renal failure fairly quickly through random blood tests. Since it was at the beginning stages, she should only need one dialysis treatment. Once her kidneys are functioning properly and her body can handle it, we'll do the BMT."

Andrew relaxes against the pillow and closes his eyes, Sandra mutters a "thank God," and I let out a sigh of relief. I may not know the little girl who means so much to these two, but I'm glad she's okay. No child should be put through this.

"When are you starting the dialysis?" Sandra asks Dr. Adams.

"Normally we would take the time to create a blood vessel in her arm to connect a vessel to an artery, but since we're on a tight time schedule we'll be giving her a neckline. We'll start dialysis in a couple of hours. The filtering phase will last for about four hours."

"How soon will we know if it worked?" Andrew asks.

"We'll know within twenty-four hours if the treatment filtered the pollutants out of her system sufficiently."

Listening to Andrew, Sandra, and the doctor talk cements the fact this is very serious. It's also obvious they've prepared for any outcome and problem along the way. Through their questions it's plain to see they've done research and know what questions to ask.

"And her heart? Can her heart handle all this?" Andrew asks.

"We've managed to get her heart rate down, so it shouldn't be a problem. I'm more worried about getting her through dialysis so she can have the BMT. Her blood work shows the leukemia is dormant." She stops to let them take that in. Both Andrew and Sandra let out a sigh of relief. "Once dialysis and the BMT are complete, and if her body takes to the new marrow, she should be on the mend."

The atmosphere in the room lightens slightly. The news that the cancer is dormant is good. That's one less fight to deal with at the moment. Now the battle is to overcome the rest.

"Thank you for letting us know, Dr. Adams. When can we see her?"

"Let's give it until tomorrow morning, once she's had the dialysis treatment. She needs to get as much rest as she can in order to be strong enough for the transplant. We'll be sedating her to avoid any trauma due to the line we'll be putting in her neck."

After a few more words, Dr. Adams leaves with the promise to let them know if there is any change with Ally. Sandra fusses with fixing Andrew's pillow, and I can't help but smile as he grumbles at her. His eyes turn to me and narrow.

"What are you smiling about?" he mutters. "She's acting like I just had major surgery or some shit. It's ridiculous."

"You watch your language, Andrew. And let me be. I'm your mother. If I want to fuss over my baby while he's in a hospital bed, then I'll damn well do it, no matter how serious the reasoning is." I laugh at her word choice, because she just got on to him for cussing. "Besides, if I don't do this, then I'll think about…"

She stops midsentence and lets out a sob. I feel like an asshole for laughing. This is definitely not a time to laugh.

Andrew sits up and pulls his mom into his arms. As she cries against his shirt, I walk around and rub her back. Watching the emotions these two are going through is hard. I want to comfort them and make everything better.

Only a couple minutes pass before the door opens again and a rush of people file inside the small room. I step to the side as Bailey and Chris hurry over. Andrew releases Sandra and she discreetly wipes her eyes. Jaxon, Mia, Mac, and Trent stay back a few steps. I'm surprised Mia isn't in the middle of the cry fest Bailey and Chris are having. Her expression is still closed off, and I wonder if she's upset with Andrew for keeping Ally from her.

"Mia," Andrew calls, when he realizes she's still across the room.

She stays put for a couple of moments before slowly walking over to him. Bailey and Chris move away so she can get close. As I get a better look at Mia's face, I see tears glistening in her eyes and her lips trembling. When Andrew tries to grab her hand, she takes a step back.

"Why?" she whispers raggedly, barely loud enough for us to hear. "Why would you keep this from us? From me?"

"Oh, Mia, I'm so sorry," Andrew says, brows pulled down into a frown. "When Becky and Brent first came to me about donating sperm, they asked me to not say anything for a while. Becky's parents were firmly against anything other than a natural child from both married parents. The plan was to ease them into it. For years, I watched them suffer multiple negative pregnancy tests. The devastation each test brought them was destroying them, and I hated seeing them like that. Brent found out later that he's infertile."

Andrew again tries to reach out for Mia, but she just shakes her head.

"Why has it taken this long though? You said she's six, which means it's been about seven years. I get they wanted to wait, but for seven years?"

A tear streaks down Mia's face, and I feel Mac stiffen beside me, wanting to go comfort his woman. Mia's not the type to shed tears. She always seems so strong and stubborn. To see her upset like this must be tearing both him and Andrew up inside. The pain I see on Andrew's face as he watches the tear trail down her cheek has my own emotions boiling to the surface. I understand her feeling of betrayal, but what Andrew's been through hasn't been a walk in the park either, I'm sure. I can't imagine the internal struggle he's faced on a daily basis.

"Come here, Mia, please," Andrew says, his voice tight.

After a few seconds, Mia reaches out and grasps Andrew's hand and steps toward him. He brings her hand to his mouth and kisses the back. More tears fall silently down her face.

"In the beginning, they were only supposed to wait a few months after Ally was born to tell them. But things became strained between Becky and her mom. I don't know all the details, but they've always had a close relationship and it was hard on her and the rest of the family when their relationship went downhill. They spoke with me first to make sure it was okay that they waited longer to tell them. I told them to do what they felt was best. I didn't want to be the cause of an even bigger rift between her and her family. That would only hurt Ally.

"Once everything was settled between Becky and her family, I was the one that wasn't ready. I don't know why, but I wanted to keep Ally to myself a bit longer. I had gotten into a routine, and I wasn't for it to change. Before I knew it, years had passed by. I know that makes me selfish, and I'm sorry."

Andrew stops for a minute and looks at Bailey and Jaxon, his eyes softening. "Once I was ready to tell everyone, it got put on hold again. Everybody's attention was needed on Bailey. And after what happened to Anna, everyone was grieving. It wasn't the right time."

When Bailey starts to apologize, Andrew holds up his hand. "No, honey, I'm not blaming you. You were priority at the time. We needed to focus on you. I had already waited years, a few more months wouldn't hurt. Don't you dare take any blame for this."

Bailey comes to the bed and kisses Andrew on his cheek. She pulls back, wipes the tear that's fallen, and nods.

Looking back at Mia, Andrew continues, "Everything settled down after Amari was born, but that's when everything went down with you and Mac. Again, it wasn't the right time." He looks from one person to the other, ending with his eyes back on Mia. "I'm so sorry I never told any of you. But there was never a good time."

"Does she know you're her father?" Mia asks, and I hold my breath, waiting on his answer. Does Ally call him Dad?

"No, she knows me as Uncle Andrew."

Bringing Andrew's hand up to her face, Mia places it on her cheek. "We've missed so much of her life," she says tearfully.

"I know," replies Andrew.

They both stare at each other for a few moments. Everyone's quiet in the room, giving them their private time. It's hard to watch these two people who obviously love each other be at odds. Andrew's told me a little about his and Mia's relationship. They've been best friends since grade school. I feel a pang of jealousy at the closeness they share, but push it away. It's ridiculous to feel that way.

All of a sudden a beautiful smile comes across Mia's face, causing her blue eyes to shine brightly.

"You have a daughter, Andrew!" she says excitedly. "I can't believe it! I know we're not able to right now, but when can we meet her? Can you tell us about her?"

Andrew laughs at her excitement and the dire atmosphere fades. Everyone relaxes. Although the seriousness of the situation is still there, it's clear Andrew loves talking about Ally to his friends.

His eyes keep straying to mine and every time they do, I smile at him. We haven't gotten a chance to talk alone, so I tell him through my smile I'm okay with this. It'll be strange seeing him with her, but I'm looking forward to it. And I'm especially looking forward to meeting this precious girl who's irrevocably captured my lover's heart.

Chapter Thirteen

Andrew

I'M SITTING ON THE EDGE of the bed, back in my own clothes instead of the hospital gown from hell. I grip the back of my neck and bounce my leg in irritation and impatience. I'm waiting on the nurse to come back with my release papers and information on whether or not I can see Ally. She left here with a muttered "I'll be back soon." That was—I look down at my watch—thirty-two fucking minutes ago.

Jase is across the room sitting on the windowsill, watching me like a zookeeper watches a rabid animal. I get up from the bed and start pacing the room, feeling a little twinge on my hip, but I ignore it. Being stuck in this room waiting makes me feel like a caged animal. Don't these fuckers know how important it is I see Ally?

"Andrew, baby, you need to relax and calm down," Jase says soothingly. I'm sure he's worried I'll bite his head off if he talks to me with anything other than a cautious tone. I know I'm on the edge right now and need to take his advice, but my head keeps screaming at me to get to Ally.

"The damn nurse should be back by now. What the hell is taking so long?" I growl.

It's a rhetorical question. Andrew doesn't know why the nurse is taking her sweet-ass time, but I'm hoping he'll at least attempt to answer. If he's talking it helps keep my mind settled. I love the sound of his deep voice.

"I don't know, but I'm sure she'll be back soon. And I'm sure Ally is fine as well. You heard the doctor last night. She'll let you know if something changes."

I close my eyes, take a deep breath, and let his voice soothe my boiling nerves. He's right. I know if something changed with Ally, someone would let me know, but it's still hard to just sit here.

When I open my eyes again, I look over at Jase. He's still sitting there watching me. Of course, now my body picks the most inconvenient time to become needy. Seeing him sitting there with his sleeves pushed up to his elbows, showing off his tattooed muscles, and his hair in a sexy messy ponytail has my body hardening. My body may have picked a bad time to react, but damn if I won't take a taste. After all, the last taste I had was last night, and that's just too damn long.

My strides quickly eat up the distance between us. The closer I get, the darker Jase's eyes become, and the harder I become.

He hasn't moved an inch. He's sitting there on the edge of the windowsill with his hands on either side of his hips. When I make it to him, I rest my hands against the window on both sides of his head and lean in. He still doesn't move or talk.

Greedy for a taste, I lean down and run my tongue along the seam of his lips, waiting for him to open up. He doesn't disappoint, and I immediately slip inside. He tastes so fucking good.

I slant my head and deepen the kiss, tangling my tongue with his. My body vibrates with pleasure and it takes everything in me to not flip him around and sink my dick in his tight hole. If we were anywhere else and if the situation was anything but what it is, I would.

Jase groans and grips my hips, bringing me closer to him, which spurs me on more. I grab a handful of hair and yank his head to the side. He has scruff on his cheeks and neck from not shaving today and it feels fucking amazing against my lips.

"Jesus, I've missed your taste," I murmur against his ear, before taking a bite.

Reaching around, Jase grabs my ass and starts to knead. My ass cheeks tighten in response.

"It's only been since last night. That's not enough time to miss it." Jase moans.

I pull back from him and tilt his head so we're looking at each other. He really has no idea what he does to me. It's about time I enlighten him.

"Jase, as soon as your lips leave mine, I miss your taste. As soon as your touch leaves me, I miss the sensation. If we're not in the same room together, I miss your presence. I crave you all the time, baby. There's not a second that goes by that I don't want you, that I don't want your scent on me, your touch on me, or your eyes on me. There's never a time that I *don't* miss you."

I watch Jase, gauging his reaction to my confession. Every word I just told him is true. He has become such a pivotal part of me that, if I were to ever lose him, I'd lose parts of myself as well. He's burrowed himself so deep in my heart that he'd pull big pieces out with him if he left. And nothing or no one would be able to fill those gaps left behind.

As I stand there and watch Jase, his lips all of a sudden form a huge smile, showcasing his dimple. I'm just about to lean down and run my tongue along it when he says teasingly, "So, you like me, huh?"

I laugh at his ridiculous question and grip his hair tighter. "I'd say I more than like you," I tell him, and do what I wanted to do a minute ago and lick his dimple.

I pull back a minute later and rest my forehead against him. "Thank you for understanding about Ally. I know it's fucked that I didn't tell you or the others, but I just couldn't find the right time."

"I get it, Andrew. I know why you couldn't and it's okay. But you don't have to go through that shit alone anymore. Let us be there for you. I don't have any experience with this, but I know it had to be tough holding it all in when you were around us. No more of that."

His words hit home, because he's right, it has been tough not going to my friends when things started going downhill with Ally. Not being able to depend on them for support was one of the hardest things I've ever done. I may be a man and men are supposed to be able to handle hard situations, but I don't care how strong you are, no one can handle something like this by themselves. I had my mom, Becky, and Brent, but most times they weren't physically there.

"Mr. Donovan, are you ready?" the nurse says, as she comes back into the room.

I pull back from Jase and turn to face her. As she's standing there holding a clipboard, an orderly comes in behind her with a wheelchair.

I don't fucking think so.

"You can take that back, I don't need it," I say, gesturing to the wheelchair.

"I'm sorry, sir, but it's policy. I can't let—"

"I'm sorry too, but I'm not getting in that fucking thing. I can walk just fine on my own."

The good mood I had a moment ago because of Jase is quickly being replaced with irritation. First she took her sweet-ass time and now she expects me to be wheeled around in that thing? *Not fucking likely.* I narrow my eyes at the nurse and watch as she swallows.

"Please, sir—"

"It's okay, Janet, let him be. He'll be fine," Dr. Adams says as she steps into the room.

With a thank you and a smile, Dr. Adams takes the clipboard from the nurse and dismisses her. Walking over to me, she hands me the clipboard. I sign my release forms and hand it back.

"How is she? Do you know if the dialysis worked?" I know I probably sound frantic, but I don't give a shit. This keeping me in the dark is driving me fucking bonkers. I spoke with Becky late last night, but haven't this morning.

"She's doing much better," Dr. Adams reassures me, and I sag in relief. "And the dialysis did work. Her liver function has improved. We're giving her one more day just to be sure and to let her body recover some before starting the marrow transplant."

"Thank God," I mutter, and briefly close my eyes.

I feel Jase step up to me and rest his hand on my back. His touch gives me comfort.

I open my eyes and ask the doctor, "Can I see her now?"

She smiles and says, "Yes, I'll take you to her."

"I have family and friends here. I don't want to put too much pressure on Ally, but they're anxious to see her as well. When can she receive outside visitors?"

"As long as you keep it calm, she should be fine to see them now. Just don't overdo it."

I nod and Jase and I walk out hand in hand behind Dr. Adams. I need to call my mom and let her know she can come see Ally. I know she's been worried sick as well. I made her go home last night with the promise I would call her this morning with an update. After I speak with Becky and Brent and make sure it's okay, I'll call everyone back home and let them know they can come meet Ally for the first time. I'm a little nervous at the thought of them meeting her. Anyone would be nervous when they introduce their friends to a child they've kept a secret for years. However, the thought of knitting the two together has me excited and impatient.

We come to a stop at one of the doors, and Dr. Adams pushes it open for us to enter. I take a deep breath and pull Jase in behind me.

The first thing I see is Brent hunched over in a chair in the corner, asleep. When he hears movement, he jerks awake, looking first at Jase, then at me. I don't really pay him any mind because my eyes have moved to the bed. Becky is lying on the edge of the small mattress, her hair hanging off the side. I can't see her face or Ally because her back is blocking our view.

With my heart in my throat and fear at what I'll see, I slowly walk around the bed and get my first glimpse of Ally.

My breath whooshes out at the frail body I see lying in bed. It's only been a couple of days since I saw her, but she seems even smaller now. Ally's always been big for her age, courtesy of my genes, but now she looks underweight and so fragile, like the smallest of movements will break her. Her arms are thin and her face gaunt. The beanie she's wearing doesn't hide the fact that her hair is gone. She has dark shadows under her beautiful eyes. There's a bandage on the lower portion of her neck with a tube sticking out and she has several catheters in her hands and arms.

It breaks my fucking heart to see her like this. I want to fix everything that's wrong, but I can't. Being helpless is one of the worst feelings in the world.

Ally is reclining against a couple of pillows, playing a handheld video game. When she sees me, a gorgeous smile crosses her face and it nearly brings me to my knees.

"Uncle Andy," she says happily, her eyes lighting up. Her voice doesn't sound as strong and cheerful as normal.

Becky jerks awake. "What's wrong?" she asks, looking disoriented. It only takes her a second to realize everything is okay and see me standing by the bed. Her eyes flick to Jase standing behind me before returning to mine.

"Sorry, Mom," Ally says with a frown.

"It's okay, baby," Becky leans downs and kisses the top of Ally's head. "Hey, you two."

Grabbing Jase's hand, I step closer to the bed. "Hey, skittles. How're you doing?"

She puckers her lips into a pout and says, "I'm okay. I feel better today."

"That's great, precious," I sit on the edge of the bed, careful not to jostle her any. "I came to see how you're doing and introduce you to someone."

She looks behind me at Jase and then back to me, brows pulled down. "Is it him? Is that Jase?"

I turn to Jase and see surprise on his face. I may not have told my friends about Ally, Becky, and Brent, but they know all about my friends. It was only a couple of days ago that I told Ally about Jase. She was excited about meeting him.

I pull him closer. Once he's standing beside me, I tell Ally, "Yeah, this is my good friend, Jase. Jase, this beautiful girl is Ally."

Ally watches him for a moment, before smiling and saying shyly, "Hello."

I fall a little more for Jase as he lowers himself to his knees beside the bed, so he and Ally are face-to-face.

He gently grabs her hand and brings the back of it to his lips, placing a light kiss there. "Hey, sweetie. It's an honor to meet you."

She giggles her little girl laugh at his noble gesture.

I look over at Becky. She has her hand at her mouth, but I can see the corners tipping up into a smile. She has tears in her eyes.

"Do you like Skittles, Jase?" Ally asks, and I have to stifle a laugh. I know exactly where this is going.

"I do," he responds, eyes crinkling at the corners.

"Do you think you can talk Uncle Andy into getting me some?"

Releasing Ally's hand, Jase brings the tip of one finger up to his lips and gives it a tap.

"Hmm… I don't know if I can do that," he says, causing a frown to appear on Ally's face. "But you can have this bag if you want."

Surprising us all, Jase brings out a sharable-size bag of Skittles from the pocket of his cargo pants.

The frown on Ally's face is quickly replaced by a breathtaking smile, and I want nothing more than to kiss Jase senseless for causing it.

Before handing the Skittles over, Jase says, "You have to ask your mom if you can have them first."

Ally nods vigorously and turns to her mom. "Can I, Mom?" she asks hopefully.

Gazing at her daughter with affection, she pats her cheek and says, "Let's wait and ask the doctor before you eat any, okay?"

"Okay." She turns back to Jase. "Thank you!"

"You're very welcome, sweetie," Jase says, and stands up.

Brent walks over, and I introduce him and Becky to Jase. All four of us sit and talk for a while about nothing in particular, trying to avoid the elephant in the room. Ally needs as much normal as she can get. She entertains us with silly little stories, making us all laugh and eat up her attention.

After a while, Ally's eyes start to droop. Leaning down, I place a kiss on Ally's forehead. "Get some rest, Skittles. We'll be back later today, okay?"

"Love you, Uncle Andy," she mumbles, already half-asleep.

"Love you too, Ally," I tell her, my voice thick.

I let Becky and Brent know that Jase and I will be staying in a hotel close by, in case they need anything or something happens. I've already cleared the time off with Jaxon. He understood my need to be close to Ally. Not to mention, I'm under doctor's orders to not work for the next three days.

Becky and Brent walk us to the door. I turn to them before walking out.

"I've told the rest of my friends. I know they're anxious to meet Ally and you two. If she's up for it later, would it be okay for me to bring them by?"

Becky comes up to me and engulfs me in her arms, squeezing the life out of me.

She has tears sliding down her face when she pulls back. After quickly wiping them away, she says, "Yes, please bring them. We want to meet all of your friends. We've heard so much about them it feels like I already know them. And I know Ally will love meeting your friends as well."

Stepping up beside his wife, Brent reaches out to shake my hand. "Your friends are our friends, Andrew. You've done so much for us and there's no way we could ever thank you."

I nod, knowing I would do it all over again.

After Jase gets a tearful hug from Becky and a handshake from Brent, we leave the hospital. I have to force myself to walk forward and not turn around and go back, but I know there's nothing else we can do right now. We all have to hope and pray everything turns out okay.

Chapter Fourteen

Andrew

JASE AND I ARE IN THE Waffle House down the road from the hospital having lunch while we wait on our crew to get here. I called them a couple of hours ago to see if they wanted to meet Ally. Just as I expected, they were excited about the idea. They should be here soon.

A sense a relief washes through me at the thought of no longer keeping Ally a secret. I hated lying to my friends. The guilt ate at me every day. But now I have to deal with the feelings of not having Ally with me all the time. When I first agreed to donate sperm to Becky and Brent, I was happy to help them. I still am happy that I helped them. I wouldn't change that for anything. But once she came along, I immediately fell in love with her and wanted her for my own. I know she'll never truly be mine to raise, but I can't help but wish she was. She's not really my daughter, but I still refer to her as such.

I was able to keep the feelings at bay when everyone back in Jaded Hollow didn't know about her, because it was easy to distract myself. In order to keep up appearances, I *had* to distract myself. Now that everyone knows, those feelings have free run. It helps some knowing I can see her anytime I want. Becky and Brent know my feelings, as I've never kept them secret. They understand and give me free rein to see Ally as much as I want. They know I would never try to take Ally away or jeopardize her happiness. She's where she should be.

Mom came by earlier after visiting the hospital. She stayed in the same hotel Jase and I did, but decided to head home. She works at the only pediatric clinic in Jaded Hollow and couldn't afford to take time off work. She did say she'll be back every day after work, and if she was needed for anything else to let her know.

"I have a question," Jase says, interrupting my thoughts.

He's leaning back in his seat with an arm casually thrown over the back. His hair is in a low ponytail with a few strands loose. I watched this morning as he pulled it back without care. I like that he doesn't care if every hair isn't in place.

"What's up?" I ask, and pick up my lukewarm coffee.

He doesn't speak right away, but instead looks at me with his brows pulled down, like he's contemplating whether or not he should ask. This makes me curious. What could have him so undecided?

"How did you donate your sperm to Becky and Brent?" he asks, throwing me for a loop. This is one question I didn't expect him to ask. I knew it would come up eventually, but not yet.

"The one girl I had sex with?" He nods at my reminder. "That was her."

Jase's eyes flash with surprise. "And Brent was okay with you having sex with his wife? Why not do the whole artificial thing they do nowadays?"

"This was before Brent's promotion. He was just an assembly line worker and the pay was terrible. They couldn't afford artificial insemination. It was their only choice at the time. They struggled with the decision, thinking Brent would never be at ease with his wife sleeping with another man, but also refusing to give in. They had been let down so many times before and when they found out Brent was sterile, they were devastated. It took them years to get up the courage to ask me. They said I was the only one they felt comfortable enough asking, because of my sexual preference. They knew I would never develop feelings for her, or her me."

That was one conversation that I never thought I would have. To say it was uncomfortable is an understatement. Not so much on my part but on theirs. I've always been open about my sexuality. Talking about sex comes naturally to me. It's a part of human nature. What's to be embarrassed about?

At first I was worried Brent wouldn't be able to cope with the thought of Becky having sex with me, but he was adamant he would be fine.

"What did…" Jase's voice is hoarse and he stops to clear it before continuing, "How did it happen?"

I don't know if Jase is uncomfortable with this part of the conversation or slightly turned on. He doesn't seem like the embarrassed type, so I'm thinking it's the latter. My dick twitches, which surprises me because of the current situation. Jase does that. When I'm with him my mind is occupied with other things, making the bad disappear.

"Does that turn you on, baby, thinking about me and a woman?" I ask in a low voice.

"Anything to do with you and sex turns me on."

I quirk my lips up when his eyes heat. His ass is mine tonight when we get to the hotel. He better prepare himself for the fucking of a lifetime. We've had sex every night since the first time I took him. It may sound ridiculous, but I think I'm going through Jase withdrawal.

Getting back to the question at hand, I tell him, "It was all very sterile feeling mostly. Becky and I both knew what we were there for. It was nothing more or nothing less than that."

"And Brent? Where was he? In the living room while y'all got it on in the bedroom?"

"Actually, yes, he was. We all debated whether he should be in the room with us, but decided against it. It would have made it weirder having him there. We weren't in there long, both wanting to get it over with. I left afterward and didn't hear from them for a few weeks. Later Becky told me that Brent withdrew a bit from her, but they eventually worked through it. I understood his need for time and space. I couldn't have been easy knowing his wife slept with another man."

Jase doesn't say anything for a few seconds, processing my words.

"And she got pregnant the first time?"

"Yes. Come to find out, Becky is very fertile, which was good because I don't think she or Brent would have been able to go through that again. It took a few months, and it was extremely awkward in the beginning, but they were so grateful it worked they welcomed me to be a part of the pregnancy and Ally's life."

Jase turns quiet again before saying softly, "She's beautiful, Andrew."

I smile at him, glad he feels that way. Ally and Jase are the two most important people in my life. I would love for them to get to know each other.

"Thank you," I say, and straighten in my seat. "Now, I have a question for you. The Skittles. How did you know about them?"

He laughs and says, "Your tattoo kind of gives it away. You also call her Skittles. Not to mention all the Skittles packages you have in your glove box. I've never seen you eat them yourself, so I knew they were for someone else. Ally was the only logical person."

I'm pleased he recognized the Skittles for what they are. I got the tattoo a year ago in honor of Ally. She was tickled pink when I showed her. Becky, of course, teared up. It was two years ago that I started calling Ally by that nickname. Again, she loved it.

My phone starts vibrating, and I pick it up off the table. It's a text from Chris, letting us know they are five minutes away from the hospital.

"Come on. That was Chris. They'll be at the hospital soon." I take a last swallow of my now cold coffee and get up. I pay the bill while Jase brings the car around to the front.

Twenty minutes later, we're all walking up to Ally's room. Grabbing the handle, I pull the door open to find Ally in bed watching *Sponge Bob*. Becky is in the chair beside the bed, reading, and Brent's sitting on a chair on his laptop. I texted Becky an hour ago to let her know we'd be there soon.

Something seems off with the group though. I don't know if it's because they're getting ready to meet the daughter I've kept hidden, or something else is going on. Chris is jumpy and keeps frowning at her brother, Jaxon's features and body movements are stiff, and he's keeping a tighter hold on Bailey than usual, and Bailey, the poor girl, looks worried about something. Mac's quiet and seemingly distracted, while Mia has a scowl on her face. She's hasn't said a word as we make our way to Ally's room.

Jase notices too. We look at each other, wondering what has the others so disoriented.

When I stop at Ally's door, I turn to them and ask, "Alright, what's going on?"

Nobody says anything for a moment, just looks around at each other. Finally, Mac says, "Nothing you need to worry about right now. We'll talk later."

"Has something happened?" Jase asks, mirroring my own thoughts and concerns.

He takes a step toward Chris, who quickly looks up at Mac. After a second, she turns back to Jase, smiles, and says, "Everything's fine. Let's go meet Ally and we'll let you know later."

He takes a moment to contemplate pressing the issue, but eventually Jase nods.

I let the issue go myself for now, but later they'll tell me what the fuck is going on.

When we walk in the door, Becky and Brent get up from their seats to meet us.

"Becky and Brent, I'd like you to meet my friends, Mia, Mac, Jaxon, Bailey, and Chris." I point to each as I say their names.

They all say hello, but I notice Mia standing off to the side, keeping away from the gathering. I know she's still hurting from my deception and I hope she holds no ill feelings toward Becky and Brent. Her eyes keep wandering to the bed. I notice them going soft. Out of all my friends, I knew Mia would hurt the most. She and I have always been close.

After making sure it's okay with Becky and Brent, I grab Mia's hand. "Come meet Ally."

Her hand squeezes mine tight, and I feel a slight tremble as I lead her over to the bed. Ally's lying there looking at Mia, unsure. She can tell something's off.

"Hey, Skittles, I've got someone here who wants to meet you. Actually, I've got a bunch of people here."

She nods, but keeps her eyes on Mia, who is watching her in return. Emotions clog my throat when I see Mia swallow. Her eyes don't stray from Ally's, but I know she's taking in her haggard appearance.

After a few short seconds, Mia speaks hoarsely. "Hi, Ally, I'm Mia."

"Hello, Mia," Ally says in a small voice. "Uncle Andy told me about you. He said you were his best friend."

I hear a gasp from Mia when Ally calls me Uncle Andy. When I look at her, shock is clearly written on her face, before it's quickly replaced with understanding, and then sadness. Tears glisten in her eyes.

"Are you okay?" Ally asks, pulling our attention back to her. "Are you gonna cry?"

Mia lets out a strangled laugh before composing herself. Taking Ally's hand in hers, she tells her, "No, baby, I'm not going to cry. I'm just so happy to finally meet you."

"Okay, good. I know Mama, Daddy, and Gramma cry a lot because I'm sick. I don't want people to cry anymore. It makes me sad, too."

Fuck! This is hard.

My heart breaks at her words, and I know Mia's does as well. I can see her force the tears away. Becky steps up on the other side of the bed. I know she's holding back tears, too. I feel a hand at my back and know it's Jase.

"Honey, we're just all worried about you," Becky says, laying her hand on Ally's cheek. "We love you and want you to get better."

"I know Momma, but God's watching me. The angel told me I'll be okay."

We all stand there in stunned silence, not sure what to say. The others gather closer around the bed.

Finally, Brent steps up, takes his wife's hand, and asks Ally croakily, "What angel?"

Ally smiles so big her cheeks puff up and you see her teeth. "The one in my dream. I was playing in the sandbox at the playground and she came and played with me. She told me God was keeping me safe and to not worry. He was going to make me better again."

Several gasps are heard throughout the room, all of us secretly wondering if we should dare hope this was some sort of premonition. I pray silently for all I'm worth that this isn't just a child's cry for help. That someway, somehow, God's looking down on Ally and has mercy for her. I haven't been to church since I was a kid, but I've always held faith that there is a God.

Becky bends and places a soft kiss on Ally's cheek. Pulling back, she says quietly, but loud enough for us to hear, "You are going to get better. I know you will."

I introduce Bailey and Jaxon next. Ally, being a child and not afraid to voice her thoughts, immediately notices Bailey's scar and says, "It looks like God was looking after you, too. Did an angel visit you?"

Bailey gives her a watery smile and replies, "No, I wasn't lucky enough to have an angel visit me, but I do believe God was watching down on me."

Ally looks from Bailey to Jaxon, who has his arm around her waist, and then back to Bailey, before saying softly, "I think maybe God did send you an angel."

Bailey looks up at Jaxon, smiles, and then brings her eyes back to Ally. "I think you're right.

Ally beams her brilliant smile and turns to Jaxon. "You and Bailey have a baby, right?" Jaxon nods. "Can I meet her? I love babies."

"The next time we visit we'll make sure to bring her," Jaxon answers.

Ally's grin gets bigger. She turns toward Chris. "You're Chris, aren't you?"

Chris steps up to the bed beside me. "Yes, ma'am. I'm so happy to meet you, Ally."

"You're Jase's sister. Why do you have a boy's name?" Ally asks.

Chuckles are heard around the room. The stuff that comes out of kids' mouths is funny as shit.

Still smiling, Chris replies, "It's just a nickname. My name is Christabelle. That's a lot to say, so my family decided to cut my name short to Chris."

Ally scrunches up her nose and says, "I like Christabelle better than Chris. Can I call you that?"

"Sweetie, you can call me anything you'd like."

The last in the room to be introduced is Mac. He steps forward and extents his hand. Ally puts her little one in it.

"Hey, Miss Ally. I'm Mac."

"Hello, Sheriff Mac," Ally says with a serious tone. "Can you come closer?"

Mac bends down and puts his ear close to Ally's lips. She whispers something to him that has him standing back up laughing.

Chuckling, Mac says, "I don't know, you let me know if he's still doing it when you go back to school and I'll see what I can do."

We glance from one to the other, curious at what she told him.

Mac enlightens us all.

"Seems Miss Ally here has a boy at school that likes to pull her hair. She wants me to arrest him and throw him in jail."

We all laugh, glad the mood in the room is turning lighter. Kids do that. They make dire situations seem not-so-serious.

That is, until Ally asks, "Where's Nick? I want to meet him too."

We're all quiet for a moment, sadness etching our faces again. Becky and Brent know what happened with Anna and the effect it had, and still has, on him. It's been a couple of weeks since any of us has seen or heard from him. We're all starting to worry.

"Nick is out of town for work right now. Maybe you can meet him next time we visit." I tell her.

"Oh." Her face drops.

We stay in Ally's room for a bit and talk about anything and everything. Ally has always been very animated and talkative. Being sick and in the hospital has drained a little life from her, but her personality hasn't changed. In any setting, she can come up with the funniest things to say, keeping us all on our toes and laughing.

She already has everyone wrapped around her little finger, just as I knew she would. A sense of pride settles in me. I may not be her dad, but she's still half me, and I am so damn proud that I had a part in creating such a wonderful girl.

A couple hours later, everyone says goodbye to Ally, Becky, and Brent. I tell them Jase and I are heading to the hotel and we'll be back later after dinner.

When we walk out into the parking I stop everyone. It's time they tell Jase and me what happened. I understand them not wanting to tell us before we went into Ally's room, but we're done here and it needs to get out into the open.

"Alright, what the hell happened that had everyone acting strange earlier?" I ask.

Before answering, Mac and Jaxon share a look. I grind my teeth to keep from growling at them. Whatever it is, it's obviously important or they wouldn't be so hesitant to say anything. A thought crosses my mind, and I wonder if this has anything to do with Damien or Emilio.

Just as I'm about to open my mouth to demand answers, Jaxon turns to Jase and starts talking.

"When we got home last night, Chris had a surprise waiting for her. Her bedroom was trashed and there was a message on her mirror. It said, 'Tick tock. Are you ready?'"

"What the fuck?" Jase explodes. "Why in the hell didn't anyone call me?"

"Because," Chris says, walking up to Jase and laying her hand on his arm to calm him, "I made him promise not to. We called in Mac, but I begged them to wait to tell you. You and Andrew had other things to worry about."

Jase scowls down at Chris before yanking her in to his chest. She smashes her body to his and wraps her arm around him. I hear him murmur against her hair, "Next time, you call me. No matter what. You don't keep shit like this from me. I deserve to know. Promise me."

She nods against his chest. "Promise. I'm sorry."

I ball my hands into fist, ready and needing to hit something. This Damien asshole is fucking with the wrong people. You don't come into my town and threaten my family or friends. He wants to play that game, then he needs to grow some balls and show himself. He's going to learn really fucking quick how much he's underestimated the situation.

I walk over to Chris and run my shaky hand up and down her back, not hiding from Jase the venom I know is spewing from my eyes.

With a tight voice, I tell Chris, "I appreciate you not wanting to say anything because of the current situation, but don't ever keep anything like that from Jase or me again. This fucker is dangerous and we need to know everything that's going on if we want to catch the asshole."

She pulls back from Jase's chest and looks at me. "I'm sorry," she says, wiping a stray tear from her cheek. "I just didn't want to add any more stress. You were already dealing with so much."

I nod stiffly. "I get that, but your safety is important, too." I turn to look at Jaxon. "Next time, don't fucking keep this shit from us. Jase has a right to know."

Jaxon's eyes turn hard at my tone, but he nods. I know he was in a tough position. On one hand, he feels like he owes a debt to Chris for helping Bailey when she had nowhere else to turn. But his loyalties also lie with me due to a childhood friendship.

In his deep rumbling voice, he says, "You know I'd never let anything harm her. She was safe at the house with me there. You think I would have let my family stay if I felt otherwise? The fucker was in my house, where my family sleeps. I told her I would give her one night, but after that, she had to tell you or I would."

I accept his words for what they are. I know Jaxon would protect Chris with his life, just like he would his family. Chris is more than just a friend to him, she's a sister. I have no doubt he felt it safe enough for them to stay. If Jaxon is one thing, it's protective of the people he cares about. And he's damn capable of protecting them.

"Did you find anything?" I ask Mac.

He shakes his head. "No. No prints. He busted out the window in the utility room and came in that way. As far as I could tell, he only went to Chris's room. No other rooms were disturbed."

ALEX GRAYSON

"And no one's seen anyone in town that shouldn't be there?" Jase asks.

"I had a couple of people say they saw an unknown man around town, but thought it was just someone passing through. The description fits Damien. Unfortunately, he was on foot so they didn't get a look at what he was driving."

"Fuck!" I snarl, and grip my hair, frustrated that we aren't getting anywhere.

"When we get back to the hotel, I'm calling Emilio. We need to know if he's involved with this. If he is, at least we'll know what kind of man power he'll have backing him up."

It's on the tip of my tongue to tell Jase he's not calling Emilio. I don't want him to talk to, see, or associate in any way with that bastard, but I know we need to find out what we're dealing with.

"I think that's a good idea. I'll come along. Jaxon, you mind taking Mia to your house until I get back? The threat isn't to her, but I'd feel better knowing she's with you."

"Don't even need to ask," is Jaxon's instant reply.

Mac bends and gives Mia a brief kiss on the lips. "Stay safe. Love you," he murmurs.

"Love you, too."

She walks to me and wraps her arms around my waist. She's so tiny that her head comes to mid-chest on me.

"She's one of the most precious things I've ever seen, Andrew. I'm so proud of you," she says after pulling back.

I smile down at her and joke, "Did you expect anything less? After all, she's got my blood running through her, so she's bound to be perfect."

Rolling her eyes and laughing, she takes a step back and hugs Jase as well.

"You stay with Jaxon, okay? Or with Mac once he gets back. Don't go anywhere without either of them until I get there. Understand?" Jase tells Chris, his expression stern.

He looks at Jaxon to make sure he's fine with that. Jaxon, of course, nods in understanding. "You have my word she'll be safe."

"Thank you." Turning back to Chris, he says, "I'll be home in a couple of days. You need me or if anything else happens, call me or Andrew." The look he gives her says she better do as he says.

After the rest of us say good-bye, Jase and I get in my car, with Mac following us in his, and head to the hotel. Although it wouldn't make a difference, because no matter the outcome, these fuckers are going to pay, I hope Jase's phone call to this Emilio guy proves Damien is working of his own accord. I know Jase can take care of himself, but damn if I'm going to let him.

Damien is going down, and I'm the man who's going to take him there.

Chapter Fifteen

Jase

I'M ON THE COUCH IN OUR hotel room with my elbows resting on my knees. My head is bent, my loose hair falling around my face. I have my phone gripped in my hand. I really don't want to make this phone call. It's not that I'm scared, it's just that when I left Georgia, I had no intention of ever going back or associating with anyone I left behind, except maybe my parents, if they ever came around and accepted that I am the way I am. I knew Damien would never let it slide that I killed his brother; Damien is very protective of his family. But I had hoped he wouldn't find me. It was a foolish hope.

I look over at Andrew, who is leaning against the dresser with his arms crossed over his chest, showing off muscle and tattoos. He's angry, and I can't say I blame him, but he understands the importance of finding out what we're dealing with. Even if Emilio says Damien is working of his own accord, we still need to be careful and vigilant. Emilio isn't normally the type to lie, unless he has something to gain. I don't really see him gaining anything from taking me out, but I still wouldn't put it past him.

Mac is sitting across from me in another chair. He runs his hands through his hair, something I noticed he does when he's agitated. I know the feeling. This shit is getting old, and I'm ready for it to be done with.

A small part of me wishes Damien would just go ahead and come for me. I wouldn't give in easily, and at least Chris would be out of danger. If Damien is alone, I'm not really worried—we're evenly matched—but if he has the help of Emilio and his men, then I'm pretty much screwed.

I release the tight grip I have on my phone. Another shattered one is the last thing I need. I scroll through the contacts I had to retrieve from the hard drive of my old phone, and find Emilio's number. It rings four times before he picks up.

"Well, hello, Jase, it's been too long," Emilio says smoothly, his Spanish accent barely distinguishable.

I'm not surprised he knew it was me. Emilio is the type of gang leader who keeps tabs on all his men, including the people they associate with. I'm sure I logged my number the first week Damien and I started seeing each other.

"Emilio," I mutter into the receiver.

"I must admit, I'm a bit surprised you called me after the way you left town. Bad business there."

I find that hard to believe. Emilio isn't easily taken off guard. He expects the unexpected and looks at shit from all angles. Nothing surprises him.

Not willing to play his games, I get straight to the point. "I'm not calling to play games with you, Emilio. I know you're smarter than that, and you know I'm smarter than that. I'm sure you've been waiting on my call. What I want to know is, are you behind Damien and his vengeance to take me down?"

There's silence for a few seconds, before I hear Emilio laughing on the other end of the line. I grit my teeth, and choke back my retort. It's best to not piss him off too much. I need information only he can give me. We *need* to find out where he stands.

"Boy, you've got big balls calling me and demanding shit. Fortunately for you, I've always liked you. Damien has gone off the fucking deep end. I never agreed with what that bratty little brother of his was doing, but I kept my mouth shut because it didn't affect me. Now though, I have no idea what that bastard will do next, and that's something that *can* affect me. You know I don't like being left in the dark."

I breathe a sigh of relief. I have no doubt Emilio would lie, but through his tone and words, I don't believe he is. The last several months of my and Damien's relationship, I noticed Damien acting strangely. He seemed to be more secretive. There were several times he came home angry with Emilio. He never showed his anger to Emilio; he wasn't stupid and knew that shit would land him in a world of pain. But he'd stomp around the house, and I'd hear him cursing him under his breath. I never asked what the problem was; I didn't want to be involved.

"Did you know he's looking for me?" I ask.

Emilio releases a breath and it whooshes across the line. "I do. He came to me wanting my help. When I told him no, he stormed out, and I haven't seen him since. Good riddance to the little shit. I was about to cut him loose anyway. Too much drama. I don't need attention drawn to me and he was becoming reckless."

"Fuck!" I hiss over the receiver. "No one on the street has seen him? Do you know what man power he has?"

"No, Jase, I don't. All I know is he came to me wanting to use some of my men. He's lost his mind if he thought I was going to allow him to use me or what's mine for his own gain. My men are loyal to me and many others out on the street don't much care for Damien, so whatever he has can't be much."

Well, that's good at least. Knowing Emilio isn't part of this sends relief through me. But then again, Damien is unpredictable and there's no telling what he might do.

"Thanks, Emilio," I grind out between my teeth. It bites my balls to be grateful to the man, but he's actually made this situation a tiny bit better by answering my questions. Emilio is a hard-ass and rules his streets with an iron fist, but I've never had any personal beef with him. It still doesn't make me like him any more, though. I've heard some shit about him that's made me cringe. If I never hear from or see him again, it'll be too soon.

"Don't sound so enthusiastic in your gratefulness," he chuckles, but then sobers. "I've never had any problems with you, Jase. You always stayed out of my business. That's the only reason I've left you alone. A bit of advice: watch your back. You know how crazy Damien is when it comes to his family. He's out for blood and it won't be pretty."

His words ring true. Damien is extremely protective of his family, willing to do anything to protect them, even taking things overboard. There was a time his little sister, Marie, was having problems with a boy in school. They were in tenth grade. He'd pick on her, nothing extreme, just name calling and other stupid shit kids do at school. Damien found out and beat the shit out of the kid. He ended up with a broken jaw and arm. I didn't find out about it until weeks later, when his punk little brother was bragging to some guys at a party.

We hang up a few minutes later, after Emilio tells me to contact him if I'm ever in town. Yeah, like that shit will ever happen.

I get up and pocket my phone, only then bringing my eyes to Mac and Jase.

"He says he has no idea where Damien is. Damien came to him asking for some men, but he refused," I tell them.

"Thank fuck for that," Andrew mutters.

"Do you believe him?" asks Mac.

"Normally I wouldn't trust Emilio, but this time I think he's telling the truth. He's got nothing to gain by putting himself and his men in the middle of this. Emilio only does shit if he gets something out of it. There's nothing Damien can offer him that he wants or doesn't already have. So, yes, I believe him."

"Well, at least we have a better picture of what we're dealing with," Mac says, and stands. "I need to get home. There's not much more we can do until Damien shows us his next move."

I understand his words, but they still piss me off. With us not having a clue where Damien is or what he's planning next, we have no idea what to plan for. It just feels wrong sitting around doing nothing. Damien could show his face at any moment and this time he could actually hurt Chris, not just scare her. My body vibrates with anger at the thought.

"We'll be home day after tomorrow," Andrew tells Mac, then looks at me. "I just want one more day here while Ally has the transplant done."

I nod, letting him know I understand the importance of him being here. His kid was on the verge of dying, no way would I let him leave before he deems it safe enough. This is where he needs to be at the moment, and I need to be with him. I honestly believe Chris is safe where she is. I may not know Jaxon well, but he's a brick house, and I know he knows how to keep her safe. If I thought for one second Jaxon wasn't capable of watching out for Chris, I'd be back in Jaded Hollow in a heartbeat.

Even so, I still turn to Mac. "You keep my sister safe." It comes out more as a demand than a request, but I know Mac will do what I said. He's another person I trust with Chris's life.

"Alright, you two stay safe. And you take care of that little girl of yours, Andrew." With a nod, he leaves me and Andrew standing in the hotel room.

"If you need to head back now, I'll understand," Andrew says, coming toward me.

I watch as he crosses the room, his strong legs eating up the space between us. He's wearing a pair of gray sweats, recommended by the doctor because they're soft and won't press against the site where the bone marrow was drawn, and a black shirt with the sleeves pushed up to his elbows. His dark hair is a mess and the scruff on his jaw brings my body to life. This man gets my blood pumping like no other.

When he's standing in front of me, he lays one arm on my shoulder, and I feel him fiddle with my hair. He's watching me, waiting for my answer.

"No, I'm staying. I know Jaxon and Mac will keep Chris safe until I get back. You need me here."

I know it's not the others' responsibility to watch after Chris and make sure nothing happens to her, but I also know Jaxon and Mac are friends and they understand the need for me to be here. It doesn't mean I care for Chris less than Andrew, it just means Chris doesn't need me as much as Andrew does because she has people there for her who can protect her.

As selfless as Andrew's offer was, I still see relief flicker in his eyes. He's torn between the shit that's going down with Damien and being here for Ally. I know Andrew loves Chris, but his love for Ally is stronger. She's a child and she needs all the support and love she can get right now.

"You sure?" At my nod, he grips my hair and pulls my head back for a bruising kiss. I noticed he likes doing that; controlling me for his kiss by my hair. I have no problem with it; it's hot as fuck.

Our tongues plunder each other's mouths. The grip he has on my hair tightens when I nip his bottom lip, which only spurs me on more. I like rough sex and Andrew gives just the amount of roughness I need.

He pulls my head back and attacks my neck. I feel him sucking, and I know there will be a mark left behind.

Grabbing the hip that didn't have a needle poked in it, I grind my rock-hard dick into his. He growls against my throat and takes a bite, causing me to hiss in pleasure.

He releases my hair and takes a small step back. Planting his hand on my chest and looking at me with scorching heat in his eyes, he shoves me backward, until my back hits the wall. He stalks forward, taking his shirt off as he goes, and doesn't stop until we're lined up, touching from head to toe. He grips the bottom of my shirt, yanks the material over my head, and slams his mouth back on mine.

I run my fingers through his hair and yank him closer. Our chests meet, and I feel the rapid beat of his heart, just like mine.

Andrew palms my ass through my jeans, making me wish the damn material wasn't there.

He must sense my need because he pulls back and growls, "Take those fucking things off."

Not needing to be told twice, I reach down, unsnap, unzip, and yank down my jeans, leaving me standing there with my hard dick swaying. I palm it and give it a few strokes. Andrew follows my movement as he tears off his own pants. When he's standing in front of me in all his glory, I want to drop to my knees and worship the ground he walks on, after I worship his body, of course. I've had plenty of lovers in my life, but none of them compare to Andrew.

"Turn around," Andrew says in a gravelly voice. I again do what he says, wanting and *needing* whatever Andrew is about to give me.

I feel his chest hit my back and the bristly hair has my hips grinding back against him. My ass meets his cock, and I groan deep in my throat. I want it in me now.

"No fucking around, Andrew. Fucking fuck me," I snarl over my shoulder at him.

Instead of answering me right away, he reaches around my chest, puts his hand on my throat, applying light pressure, and brings my head back. He assaults my neck, sending shivers down my spine.

Once he releases his lips and teeth from my neck, he whispers in my ear, "I'm in control here, Jase. You do what I say, and I'll give you what you need. You don't tell me to do jack shit, you hear me?"

I tip my head back and rest it against his shoulder. His words send sparks throughout my body. Controlling Andrew is what I crave right now.

"Yes," I groan. I'll tell him any damn thing he wants right now, as long as he continues touching me.

Satisfied with my answer, Andrew lets go of my throat and glides his hand down my chest, until he reaches a nipple and tweaks it. I lift my head from his shoulder and let my forehead fall against the wall. With his other hand, Andrew grabs hold of his cock, pushes it down, and fits it between my legs. I tighten my legs around him and feel the tip rub against my balls.

"Put your hands on the wall and leave them there. Then spread your legs," Andrew says, and pulls my hips back a little.

I bend and place my hands on the wall in front of me. Andrew still has his dick between my legs, and I feel him pump his hips a few times, before I spread my legs and release the hold I have on him. He runs his hands down my back until he reaches my ass. Once there, he spreads my cheeks and notches the length of himself against me. It feels so fucking amazing, and I can't help but push back against him.

He slaps my ass and snarls, "Don't fucking do that. Stay still."

I want to turn around and growl at him to stop fucking around, but I clench my jaw and hold myself still.

Andrew wiggles his hips a couple times, causing my dick to jump in response.

A minute later, Andrew runs his finger along my lips. "Suck."

I open my lips and draw his finger in my mouth, sucking hard on the digit.

Once his finger is well lubricated, he pulls it free and places it at my asshole. He takes the tip and rubs it along the bundle of nerves, before slowly pushing it in. He slips it in and out a few times before pushing all the way through to his knuckle.

"Oh yeah," I groan and drop my head forward.

I barely hold on to my control, needing him to give me more. I need his dick in me. His finger is not nearly enough. He slides it in and out a few times, and I feel myself clenching around him.

Andrew withdraws his finger, and I feel the tip of his dick at my entrance. I hear a click and a second later feel liquid dribbling down my ass crack. Andrew uses his dick to smear the liquid around, making sure I'm wet for his invasion.

I ball my hands into fists with the first inch he slides in. My muscles spasm around him. Andrew grips my hips and pushes in another couple of inches. Our heavy breathing and moans are the only sounds in the room.

Working his hips back and forth, he slides the rest of the way in. The fullness is mind-blowing and so fucking intense. I know damn good and well I won't last long.

"Shit, baby, you feel so goddamn good. You're gripping me so fucking tight," Andrew groans from behind me and holds his hips still.

"Please, Andrew, just move." I'm not above begging if I have to. I'll damn near do anything at this moment.

Before the words even leave my mouth, Andrew withdraws and slams back, over and over again.

"Ah, fuck, yeah!" I shout.

"You like that, Jase? You like my cock buried deep inside you? You like me fucking you hard and dirty, baby?"

This is what I need, right here. I need him to fuck me hard and fast, like it's the last time he'll do it and he wants to imprint me so fucking deep that I'll never forget the feeling of him inside me.

Barely able to form a coherent thought, much less a word, I grunt out, "Harder."

"You got it," he rasps, before grabbing a handful of my hair in each hand and using it as leverage as he continues to fuck the living daylights out of me. His hips piston back and forth and his balls slap against mine. My muscles tighten up as I get closer and closer to release.

ALEX GRAYSON

Letting go of my hair, he circles his arms around my chest and stomach, bringing my sweat-slick body tight against his. With the close proximity, his thrusts become shallow, but no less intense. He hits just the right spot and my body tenses, ready to let loose.

"Don't come yet. I want it in my mouth," Andrew says at my ear.

I have not a fucking clue how I'm going to pull off not coming, especially with him whispering shit like that in my ear. My body is in control here, but I push the need to release away.

Just as I'm about to say fuck it and let go, I hear Andrew grunt in my ear and grind his dick in my ass as far as it will go. He jerks and spasms and it nearly sends me over the edge. Only the promise of coming in Andrew's mouth, holds me back.

Andrew stills behind me and licks and kisses my neck, his hot breath fanning over me. Once his breathing has somewhat regulated, he slowly pulls himself from me and turns me around.

I watch with anticipation as he immediately drops to his knees in front of me. One of my hands grabs my dick to aim it at his mouth, while the other grips his hair. Andrew opens wide, and I stick my dick inside.

Fuck!

The warm wetness of his mouth is almost too much. I have to force myself not to unload. I don't want it to end just yet.

Andrew uses his tongue on the slit at the tip of my dick, and it feels so good my dick jumps. He then takes the head into his mouth and swirls his tongue around it. After a few seconds of torture, he opens his mouth wider and takes half of me in.

I move my hand from my cock and use both hands to grip his hair. "Take all of it," I growl down at him.

He grabs my ass and in one smooth motion, engulfs my cock with his mouth, until I hit the back of my throat. I hold his head there for a few seconds before releasing.

The tightness of his throat and the slight hum of his moans send me soaring higher than I've ever been before. I slam my hips forward, and with my head thrown back, I shout out my release as jet after jet of cum shoots from my dick and into his mouth. Andrew greedily swallows every last drop.

After licking and sucking the very sensitive tip, Andrew stands and places a kiss against my lips. The taste of my cum on his lips is both thrilling and erotic. Our breathing has evened out slightly.

Ending the kiss, Andrew says "sleep" before grabbing my hand and walking to the bed, flicking the lights off as we go. The covers are thrown back and we slip underneath the sheet, the coolness of it feeling good against our heated skin. It's still early evening, but the events of the day and last night and the thorough fucking we just had, has worn us both out.

"Roll over," Andrew says quietly into the darkened room.

I comply and feel Andrew's heat against my back. He wraps his arm around my chest and his face in my hair. I'm normally not the type to snuggle with my lovers, but having Andrew wrapped around me feels different. Hell, everything about Andrew is different from any lovers I've had in the past. I can't quite explain it, but it's a feeling I don't want to ever let go of.

"Night, baby," Andrew murmurs, his voice deepened with sleep.

"Night, Andrew." I drift off to sleep a few minutes later.

Chapter Sixteen

Andrew

A WEEK LATER, I'M STANDING behind the bar at Jaxon's slicing lemon and lime wedges. Mia and I are singing along to Kansas's "Carry On Wayward Son." Mia is in an exceptionally silly mood tonight, something you don't see very often, but something I enjoy.

Jase and I have been back in Jaded Hollow for several days and tonight is my second night back at work. I've missed the place and the people here. This is my family. I feel lost without them.

Ally is doing much better. So far, her body has taken to the new marrow. If all continues to go well, she'll be released from the hospital tomorrow. This is the first day I haven't been to the hospital and I miss seeing her. A couple of days after Ally's released, Becky and Brent are throwing a small get-together for family and close friends, nothing too big so it doesn't overwhelm Ally. Just a small gathering to celebrate her leukemia going into remission and to show everyone she's doing much better. I'll see her then, if I can force myself to not go sooner. I talk to her every day, but it's not the same as seeing her beautiful face in person.

I look across the room and see Jase with Chris and Bailey, playing pool. They're all laughing and goofing around. My mom talked her way into watching Amari for the night for Jaxon and Bailey. I was grateful to them both. I think she misses Ally more than usual, and having another little girl in the house helps keep her mind off things.

Jase laughs at something his sister said and my body tingles with the sound. It doesn't matter what Jase is doing or what sound comes from him, my body reacts to everything.

Mia comes to stand beside me and bumps my hip with hers. She's so tiny it's actually more of her bumping her hip to my upper thigh.

"How are things going with Jase?" she asks, just loud enough for me to hear over the music, but low enough for others not to hear.

I look down at her and give her my trademark cocky grin. "It's going great. He loves me."

Her eyes twinkle when she laughs. "Did he tell you that?"

"No, not yet, but I know he does," I say and look back over to Jase, who's looking back at me with hooded eyes.

I'm not being cocky. I know Jase loves me. It's written all over his face when he watches me sometimes. The love and affection so plain to see. The way his body reacts so readily to mine. It's in the way his eyes always seek mine, like he doesn't like the thought of not having me in his sights. How he was by my side every second I spent in the hospital with Ally. I have no doubt about it.

"I think you're right," Mia murmurs beside me.

When I look at her, I see her watching Jase. She sees it, too. It excites me that I'm not the only one who's noticed. I want to shout it to the world, but I'll wait until Jase actually says the words.

"And you love him." She doesn't say it as a question, but a simple fact.

"Fuck yeah, I do." I couldn't help but love Jase even if I tried. The man is everything I've ever wanted in a partner and so much more than what I thought I'd get.

"I'm happy for you, Andy," she says with a smile. I grin down at her, the nickname not bothering me anymore. Before it was a reminder of the secret I kept hidden and the little girl I couldn't really have. But now, with my friends knowing about Ally, I have nothing to hide and can share her life with them.

"Hey there, sexy. Would you mind getting us a couple of beers?"

Mia rolls her eyes at the request. I give her a wink and turn toward the two girls standing at the bar. I've only seen them in here a couple of times. If I remember correctly, they're from the next town over. They've always been flirty.

Walking over, I bend and rest my arms on the bar, giving them a sexy grin. "What kind you want, sugar?"

The brunette on the right says in a breathy voice, "Anything."

"You got it."

I stand back up and get their beers. I set the mugs down in front of them and offer another smile. Before I get a chance to turn around and start back on my lemons and limes, the redhead on the left asks, "Hey, do you want to get a drink sometime?"

I saunter back to them and again lean on the bar. I crook my finger at the redhead. She leans over the bar, excitement and anticipation clearly written on her face. This doesn't surprise me. I'm not full of myself, but I know I look damn good. I'm used to girls coming on to me.

When she's a few inches away from my face, I look toward the pool tables. I point and say, "You see that man over there?" She and her friend both look to where I'm pointing. Turning back to me, she nods. "Well, see, he might have a bit of a problem with me having a drink with you, since he's my lover."

At first her eyes go wide as saucers, and I can't help but laugh. I feel bad for the poor girl.

Once she composes herself, she leans back and her lips form a pout. Looking at her friend, she says, "That's no fair. All the good ones are always taken. I say fuck it all to hell and just fuck each other. What do you say, Amanda?"

Amanda taps her chin with her forefinger, like she's contemplating her friend's suggestion. Coming to her decision, she says, with mischief in her eyes, "Okay."

I burst out laughing as the redhead's eyes bug out of her head. "Shit, girl, I was only joking."

"I know, Stacey," Amanda says, patting her friend on the leg. "So was I." She turns back to me and rolls her eyes.

"I'm sure you ladies will come across the right man someday. No need to switch fields just yet." They're funny and damn pretty. It'd be a shame for them to give up.

"Yeah, yeah," Amanda mutters. "I just wish someday were right now. A girl needs a good fucking just as much as a man does and it's been too long of a dry spell for me."

Stacey nods in agreement.

Just then, Jesse walks up to the two women and wraps his arms around both their shoulders.

"Hey, ladies. I can help you out with your little problem."

Chuckling, I walk away from the budding threesome. My eyes seek out Jase, and when they find him, I'm instantly hit with a powerful wave of jealousy and rage.

Still by the pool tables, Jase is standing with some guy I've fucked before. I'm not ashamed to admit I can't recall his name. He was an asshole and wasn't worth shit in the sack.

I watch with anger surging through my veins as the guy leans a little too close to Jase. He takes a step back from the guy, but the douche bag doesn't take the hint and inches forward again, reaching out to grab Jase's arm. I see anger form on Jase's face, and I'm about to storm over and smash the fucker's face in with my boot when he grabs the guy's arm and does something to it that has him falling to his knees.

Hell, yeah, my man is hot and *kicks ass!*

My dick hardens in my jeans as I watch Jase bend down and whisper something in the guy's ear, before yanking him to his feet and marching him to the door. He throws the door open and tosses the dickhead out.

"Jase!" I boom across the room, once Jase closes the door.

Jase glances over at me. I lift my chin in a gesture for him to come to me. I meet him at the bar partition, and before a word is even said, I take possession of his lips.

The vibration of Jase's moan causes my own moan to slip free. I grab his ponytail and twist his head to a better angle. Slipping my tongue inside his mouth, I taste Jase's unique flavor and the Jack Daniels he had earlier. It spikes my desire up several notches.

I force myself to pull back from Jase's delicious lips before I do something Jaxon will kick both our asses for.

"Watching you manhandle that fuckhead was hot as shit."

His pupils dilate and his nostrils flare with my words.

"You can show me just how hot it made you later, baby," Jase says, and reaches down and palms my cock before winking and turning to walk away.

Before he's out of reach, I slap his ass. "Damn straight I will. You better be ready for it too, 'cause it's going to be hard, fast, and rough."

"Wouldn't have it any other way," he says, laughing as he walks away.

Shaking my head at Jase's comment, I walk back behind the bar. That's just one of the many things I love about him: he likes fucking hard just as much as I do.

I finish the lemon and lime wedges and then move on to stocking the fridges with bottles of beer and bringing liquor we are low on up from the basement. A few customers come up, and I serve them their drinks. It's getting late, so most of the patrons are heading home, leaving only about a dozen people.

Jaxon came out from his office about an hour ago and he's been playing pool with Bailey, Chris, and Jase. From the looks of things, his teaching Bailey to play pool is biting him in the ass. She jumps up and down, with her pool stick above her head, while Chris cheers her on. Jaxon watches from the side, a slight smile on his face. Jase stands at the end of the table laughing.

I notice the door opening and glance over to see Nick walking in. It's been three weeks since he's shown his face around here. Jaxon went to his place the other day and found him passed out on his bedroom floor. He'd gotten drunk off his ass and never made it to bed. There's been several times Jaxon and Bailey have called him, but he either doesn't answer or he's too busy to talk. According to him, he's been out of town a lot lately, but I personally think he's hiding from the world.

With the way he's walking, I can tell he's already had one too many drinks. He staggers to the bar, his hair a mess, his face unshaven, and his clothes wrinkled. The damn man is declining fast and won't let anyone help him. I understand his grief, but it's been over two years and you'd think he would be getting better by now, not worse. Someone needs to give him a swift kick in the ass and send him back to reality. Right now he's living in what I'm sure is no less than hell.

Once he's seated at the bar, he mutters, "Jack, no ice."

I look down at him with pity and firmly say, "No."

He brings his bloodshot eyes to me, narrowing them slightly, before saying, "Why the fuck not?"

Instead of answering him, I ask a question of my own. "Did you drive here?"

He better fucking say he didn't, because so help me God, if he did I'll kick his ass myself. Grieve all you want, but you don't put others in danger through your grief.

"What's it matter to you if I did," he slurs at me across the bar.

"Because I'm your fucking friend. I don't want you to hurt someone and grieve over that shit as well. I don't want you thrown in jail because your dumb ass didn't think before you got behind the wheel."

"Fuck you, Andrew." He bares his teeth at me. "I fucking walked. Now get off my back and get me a damn drink."

Mia comes up beside me, and I see Jaxon walking over. Nick slumps down in his chair, looking down at the bar in front of him.

"What's going on here?" Jaxon asks, once he's standing beside Nick's chair. He looks from me to Nick.

"This asshole won't give me a damn drink," Nick says, and slowly lifts his bobbing head to Jaxon, damn near falling off his seat in the process.

Jaxon reaches out to steady him. "I can see why he won't. You're a fucking mess, Nick."

Nick snatches his arm back. "I'm fine. I don't need a damn babysitter."

"I'm thinking maybe you do," Mia says, and earns a "Fuck off" for her efforts.

Chris, who is beside Jaxon now, sees the state Nick is in and sucks in a sharp breath. "Oh, Nick," she whispers, tears gathering in her eyes. The sadness I hear in her voice is heartbreaking.

Nick hears Chris's whisper and shoots his eyes to her. They immediately turn to slits. He points at her and growls, "Not fucking her again! What the hell is that bitch doing here?"

The crowd around Nick tenses, me included. Being pissed at the world is one thing. Mouthing off at the guys because you're pissed? Whatever. But you don't get to be a complete ass to the women and think you can get away with it. Friend or not, that shit doesn't fly.

"Nick," Jaxon and I both warn him.

"Hey, asshole!" Mia yells, and tries pushing me aside so she can get to Nick over the counter. I pull her back with an arm around her waist.

Her attempt to rip him a new one is not needed. Jase steps in front of Chris and gets in Nick's face.

"Alright, you bastard, you got a problem with my sister, you take that shit up with me. You're done disrespecting her. I've held my tongue out of respect for these guys and because Chris asked me to. For some reason she thinks you're so goddamn special. No fucking more."

Nick's eyes are glazed over as he stares up at Jase unfazed. Jaxon sticks close to Jase's side, just in case he needs to break shit up. Mia is panting in my arms, her anger and adrenaline making her breathless. Bailey has a weeping Chris in her arms, her own eyes shiny with tears.

"What the fuck are you going to do? Beat my ass? Teach me a lesson? You go right ahead, *Jase*. I fucking dare you," Nick taunts.

From the look in Nick's eye, I can tell it's not just words. He's actually begging Jase to do it. He wants Jase to hurt him. Beneath the drunken stupor, the deep-rooted pain he's been dealing with is still very much alive. Realization dawns. If Jase hurts him with his fists, it may help ease the pain in his heart.

It's hard seeing Nick this broken. The fun-loving and sweet guy he was before is lost, and I don't know if he'll ever be found again.

Jase must realize this too, because he takes a step back and says, "You know what? You're not worth the trouble. I think the pain you're in right now is punishment enough."

"Whatever. You don't know jack shit. Pussy."

"Call Mac. Get his ass down here," Jaxon says, his voice hard. The look on his face says he's done.

"No!" Chris says, pulling herself from Bailey's arms and coming to stand beside Nick. Placing her hand on Jaxon's arm, she pleads, "Please, Jaxon, just let me take him upstairs. He can sleep it off. He'll be fine in the morning."

Nick pays her no mind and lays his forehead down on the bar. Jaxon watches him for a few seconds before looking back at Chris.

"Fine," he agrees, and then turns to Nick. He grabs the back of his shirt and pulls his head off the counter so he can look in his eyes. "You don't come here like this again. You come back sober and you're welcome, but not when you fuckin' drunk. You hear me? And be nice to Chris, fuckface, or you'll deal with me." He growls the last.

"Yeah, whatever," he mutters.

"You're not taking him up there alone, Chris," Jase says.

"Yes, Jase, I am," she tells him softly. "I'll be okay. He won't hurt me."

"Chris—"

"Please, Jase, just let me do this for him. I *need* to do this alone. I can handle him." Chris begs him with her eyes. "He won't hurt me," she says again. "I promise."

Jase looks around to the others, his eyes finally resting on mine. I know he's asking me if she'll be okay. Nick may be in a bad place right now and being a complete dick, but I know he would never hurt Chris, or any female for that matter.

I give him my honest answer. "She'll be okay. The last thing Nick will do is hurt Chris. It may not look like it now, but Nick is a good guy and would rather cut off his own dick before hurting a woman."

Nick wouldn't ever physically hurt a woman. But what I don't tell Jase is that I'm afraid that he'll hurt her emotionally before it's all said and done. Looking at the way Chris cares for Nick and the way Nick is so against it, makes me think she may be the only one who can pull him from this hole he's fallen into. He needs someone who won't give up on him, and as much shit as he's put Chris through, she's stuck by him. I worry that Nick hasn't hit rock bottom yet and hope he doesn't do irreparable damage to Chris on his way down. Chris is strong though, and I believe she can handle it.

After a few more seconds of indecision, Jase finally relents. "You don't stay there tonight. You go home with Jaxon and Bailey." At her nod, he turns to Nick and pins him with a glare. "You hurt my sister and I'll fucking end you."

Nick doesn't respond verbally, just shoots his middle finger up at him. Jase grits his teeth, but lets it go.

Chris steps up to Nick and wraps her arm around his waist. He seems to be mostly out of it, because he allows it and even puts his arm around her shoulders. When she rests her hands on his stomach, he tenses, but doesn't say anything. Slowly, they make their way down the hallway to the back entrance, where a door leads outside. From there, another door leads to the apartment upstairs.

"I don't care what anyone says, I'm checking on her before we leave," Jase says, as he watches them until they disappear.

"I'll go with you," I tell him.

"Me and Bailey are staying until the place closes down. I'll grab her when we leave, if she's not down before then."

Jase grunts his acceptance.

"Something's got to give with him," Mia says to no one in particular. "He can't go on like this. He's destroying himself."

We all nod, knowing Mia's right, but having no clue how to help him. Nick has to want help first, before he can start to mend.

"What can we do?" Bailey asks everyone.

Jaxon drags her closer and kisses her forehead, before voicing my thoughts, "The only thing we can: be there when he needs us. There's not much more we can do unless he asks."

We all stand there quietly, mourning the loss of Nick. He may still be with us physically, but emotionally and mentally he's in a dark hole somewhere.

Just as we break apart to get back to the rest of our night, a loud pop comes from the back of the bar. Jaxon, Jase, and I all look to each other before we become a flurry of movement.

Jase takes off down the hallway. Jaxon yells at Bailey and Mia, "Stay here," over his shoulder, before he takes off after Jase. I jump over the counter and follow them both.

The back door is wide open by the time I get there. Running outside and then back in the door that leads upstairs, I come to a halt when I see Chris hunched over a groaning Nick.

Jaxon and Jase move to them and squat down. Nick has blood dripping from his head, but it doesn't seem bad, just a scratch.

"What the fuck happened?" Jaxon growls.

Chris stares up at him with wide tear-filled eyes. The hand she has on Nick's shoulder is shaking.

"I—I don't know." Her voice is wobbly. "We w-were walking upstairs when the d-door suddenly slung open. A guy tried grabbing me, but Nick s-stopped him." She stops and takes a shuddering breath, before continuing. "He pulled out a gun, but N-Nick knocked it away. It went off when it tumbled down the stairs. The guy was trying to get away and Nick was trying to grab him, and he lost his balance and fell."

By the time she gets done talking, tears are falling freely down her face. Jase grabs her by the shoulders and hauls her to him. He looks at me over her shoulder, and I see the torment written in his eyes. We both know who the guy was and what could have happen if Nick hadn't intervened.

I take off out the door, not surprised when I don't see anyone out back. I'm sure the coward wasn't going to stick around to be caught.

Bastard.

I notice a hole in the wall at the bottom of the stairwell when I step back inside. It's about five feet from where Nick is currently moaning. Chris pulls away from Jase when she hears him. Jaxon, who is still squatting beside Nick, pushes his hair back to get a closer look at the cut on his forehead.

"It's not bad. Just a scratch. You want to go to the hospital?" Jaxon asks Nick.

Nick scowls up at Jaxon and grunts, "No."

"Fine, but your ass is coming home with us tonight. Someone needs to keep an eye on you."

Jaxon stands and helps Nick to his feet. He seems to be steadier than he was a bit ago. I guess the adrenaline of almost getting attacked and rescuing Chris has sobered him up some.

"Will someone tell me what the fuck is going on? Who in the hell was that guy?" Nick asks, the scowl on his face meant to intimidate, but failing when it switches to a wince.

"Tomorrow. When you're sober and can comprehend and remember what I'm going to tell you," Jaxon replies, and Nick bares his teeth at him.

I hear a sharply indrawn breath behind me and we all look to the doorway. Both Bailey and Mia are standing there with shocked faces.

"I told y'all to stay inside," Jaxon barks.

Bailey rushes to Chris while Mia walks up to Nick, both ignoring him.

"What in the hell happened?" That question is being asked a lot tonight.

While Jaxon recounts the events and Bailey has her arms around Chris, Jase walks over to me.

"I'm gonna fucking kill him," he seethes. His body is shaking in rage.

I understand his anger. His sister was nearly taken or hurt and Nick was hurt in the process of protecting her. I want the fucker just as bad as him, but he can't go out there half-cocked. We have no idea where this guy is and no way of finding out the information. Unfortunately, we're in the same position as before.

I grab Jase's shoulder. "We're going to get him, you hear me? That fucker's going down, but we have to be smart about it."

I can tell he doesn't like my words. Hell, I don't like them either, but we've got no choice but to wait. We can't magically snap our fingers and poof the guy to us.

"We need to call Mac," Jase says.

Jaxon already has his phone to his ear, talking to, I assume, Mac. I look over at Nick, who is slumped against the wall. Mia is beside him, looking at the scratch on his forehead. His eyes are on Chris. They don't hold the normal malice he normally reserves for her. Instead they look confused and worried.

I grab Jase's hand and walk over to Chris and Bailey. They are both a blubbering mess. Jase once again engulfs her in his arms. I grab Bailey's hand. She looks at me and tries to smile, but it comes out twisted. She releases my hand and slowly walks over to Jaxon, Mia, and Nick.

What a fucked-up bunch we are. Can we never have a time where bad shit isn't happening? This shit is getting old really fast.

I lean over and kiss the top of Chris's head and then Jase's lips.

Tonight was a close call. Too close. One slip or clumsy move and Chris could have been in Damien's hands right now, or worse, dead.

Something has to be done or the next time the outcome could be deadly.

Chapter Seventeen

Andrew

A COUPLE OF DAYS AFTER THE incident with Damien, we're at Becky and Brent's. Luckily, Ally did well enough to come home. Her doctors still want to keep a close eye on her, but so far there haven't been any set-backs. I haven't been able to see her the last couple of days because of everything that's been going on. As soon as I stepped foot into the house, she rushed to me as fast as her weak body would allow. Ally and I have always had a close relationship, and I thank God every day that he allows us to continue it.

The day after Damien showed his face to Nick and Chris (and we confirmed it was indeed Damien through a picture Mac showed her), a sober but cranky Nick called Jase to get the story. To say Nick was pissed was an understatement. I could hear him yelling from my seat across the room.

At first Nick was pissed at Jase because he thought Jase was careless when he came to town, not caring he was bringing trouble with him. I was on the verge of snatching the phone from Jase and giving him what for when Jase gave me a firm head shake and explained his reasons for coming here. After a few minutes of listening to Jase, Nick calmed down, and I sat back down.

Since then, no one's heard from Nick. He's back to not answering his phone. As far as we can tell, he hasn't been home either. He's probably out on some job site.

Damien hasn't shown himself since that night, but we all know it's only a matter of time before he does. The question is whether or not he'll do real damage next time. Chris, of course, is never let out of any of the guys' sights. We're even taking precautions with Bailey, Amari, Mia, and Trent. Crazy people do crazy shit. I'm sure Damien's been watching us and knows how close we all are. Jase is now part of our group, has been since he walked into town. If one gets hurt, it affects us all, including Jase.

We all just got done eating outside at the picnic tables. I decided to take Ally inside for a bit because she was looking a little tired. Everyone in our group is here. There's also Brent's family and a few close friends of Becky and Brent's. Becky's family was invited, but weren't able to make it because her dad couldn't take off work. They'll be coming in a couple of weeks.

I'm sitting on the couch with my arm thrown over the back. Ally is snuggled up beside me with Amari in her lap. I'm on Ally and Amari duty while Bailey and Becky clean up in the kitchen. I have no complaints though. These two are my favorite girls to be around.

Ally giggles as Amari kicks her legs and squeals. Watching the two of them play and interact is something

I'll never forget. For a while there I secretly feared Ally wouldn't make it. There's still a chance she could relapse, but for right now she's doing much better. I'll take anything I can get. She has a mask over her nose and mouth to keep exposure to germs and viruses to a minimum. Her body is still weak and needs to be given the opportunity to build her immunities back up. This doesn't stop her though. Her body may be weak, but her spirit isn't. The old Ally is returning, and I'm eating up every second of it.

"Watch this, Uncle Andy!" Ally says, her voice muffled by the mask.

I watch as Ally runs her small finger along Amari's foot. Amari smiles big, her beautiful two-toned eyes lighting up. Ally looks at me with her own smile. She fell in love with Amari the first time she saw her. I think she'd spend all her time with the baby if given the chance.

Trent, Mac's son, plops down on the chair next to the couch, handheld game in hand.

"Hey, Trent, how's it going?" I ask him.

He's only ten and he's already five and a half feet tall. He looks just like Mac, which he doesn't get from Mac because he's not Trent's biological father, but his uncle. To make a long story short, Tessa, Trent's mom, was obsessed with Mac back in high school. She drugged Mac with rohypnol the night of Mia's eighteenth birthday and took advantage of him. Mac ended up marrying Tessa because she became pregnant. It wasn't until recently that Mac and Mia found out that Mac never had sex with Tessa. He also found out the son he thought he fathered was actually his brother, Shady's. A brother he didn't know he had and one he wished he didn't, because he was just as sick and twisted as Tessa. Both Shady and Tessa are in jail.

"Hey, Andrew," Trent acknowledges. "It's going good. Dad and Mia are taking me to Cedar Point in a couple of weeks."

"That's great, kid. You're going to love it."

"Yeah. I've never been to a theme park before. Hey, I have this new game. You wanna play?" he asks, head bobbing up and down from me to the game.

"Can't. I'm on kid duty," I tell him. "But hit me up later, and I'll play."

"What are you playing?" Ally pipes up.

As soon as the words leave her mouth, Trent looks up at Ally, his attention no longer on the game.

"Team Fortress," he says.

"Can you come sit beside me so I can watch?" Ally asks tentatively.

"Sure."

Trent's reaction is immediate as he stands and comes to sit beside Ally. She beams a big bright smile at him.

Trent is another person Ally took to quickly. You could see in her eyes that she was curious about him and wanted to get to know him. Ally has plenty of friends at school, but she's always eager to know more people. Not to mention she hasn't been able to go to school for a while because of the leukemia. With her being so sick lately, I'm sure Becky and Brent have limited, if not stopped, her play dates.

I watch as Trent patiently tells Ally the logistics of his game. She nods and asks questions and he answers them in a way she'll understand. To see the two interacting so well together brings a smile to my face.

I glance up when Jase walks into the living room. He takes the seat Trent vacated a few minutes ago. I pucker my lips up at him in a kiss, and he chuckles.

We both sit and listen to Ally and Trent talking for a while. Bailey comes and gets a sleeping Amari from

Ally's lap, kissing Ally on top of her head and thanking her for watching Amari.

When I look down at Ally a few minutes later, I see her head resting on Trent's shoulder. She's asleep. Trent doesn't seem to mind as he continues to play. The scene of her sleeping against Trent is sweet.

When Becky comes into the living room, she moves to pick Ally up, but I shoo her away. I slowly get up to grab Ally to put her in her bed.

Trent looks up when I slide my arm under her knees. "She's okay."

"I know, buddy, but she'll be more comfortable in her bed. Thank you for showing her your game."

He watches as I gently gather Ally in my arms. His face shows he's disappointed I'm moving her. I like that he feels that way. I hope they are given the opportunity to form a bond.

Becky trails behind me as I walk down the hallway toward her room. After laying her down and pulling the blanket across her, I bend and kiss her forehead. Becky does the same and follows me out.

"Trent seems to like Ally," Becky comments, after quietly closing the door.

"Yeah. I'm glad they're getting along. I wanted to thank you for having my friends over. I know they want to be a part of her life now that they know about her."

She smiles and grabs my hand. "They're welcome anytime, Andrew. Having all these people here gives Ally more family. They love her already."

I'm grateful for her words. I know Ally isn't mine to have, but it's nice knowing Becky welcomes my friends in her life. I want to share Ally with everyone. She's special and deserves for everyone to know her.

I throw my arm around her shoulder and turn us to walk back down the hallway.

"So, once Ally is better, you going to let me take her for a weekend so you and Brent can have some hot sex time? I know you both have been slacking in that department."

I laugh when she smacks my stomach. "Seriously, Andrew? How could you possibly know that?"

Giving her a devilish smile, I say, "Because of all the come-fuck-me glances Brent keeps sending your way. You should really put him out of his misery and fuck him good and hard tonight."

"Oh, God! You noticed?" she asks, a blush creeping up her cheeks.

"Oh, I noticed alright. I'm sure everyone noticed. My dick almost went hard, the looks were so scorching."

Instead of smacking me, she pinches my side. "Ouch! What was that for?" I ask, rubbing the tender spot.

"Because I'm the only one allowed to get turned on by my man. You've got your own man to keep you satisfied."

"That I do. And he satisfies me very well. Speaking of, I need to go find him and see if he can satisfy me now."

This time I'm ready for her and laugh as I dodge her hand.

"I swear, Andrew, you better not do anything dirty in my house," she warns with narrowed eyes.

"Hey, all I meant was I was going to ask him if he'd rub my shoulder. It's feeling a little tight from having my arm on the back of the couch for so long."

She glares at me for a moment before laughing and shaking her head. She knows I would never disrespect her or Brent like that.

She goes to hunt down Brent, while I go find Jase. I was serious when I said my shoulder was hurting, but it's worth it to just sit with Ally. Having that little girl close to me is something I'll always cherish.

LATER THAT NIGHT, JASE AND I are in the living room at home watching TV. Jase is sitting on the couch with his feet propped up on the coffee table, while I'm lying on my back with my head in his lap. I have my hands clasped together, resting on my stomach.

He laughs at something on the TV, and I feel the vibrations in his stomach. When I glance up at him, his eyes are straight ahead. He has a beer in the hand that's on the arm of the couch. His other arm is thrown over the back. My eyes eat up the hot man sitting above me. His hair is loose, but pushed behind his ears. His chin and cheeks are covered in a thin layer of hair. I like that he doesn't shave every day. The bristle feels damn good against my skin when he kisses me. I wonder if I can talk him into growing a beard. Nothings hotter than a sexy man with a beard. I almost shiver at the thought of him kissing down my chest while sporting a beard.

"I love you," I tell him out of the blue. I was going to wait until he told me first, but that just seems childish. I'm tired of holding it in. I know he feels the same way, so if I need to say it first, then so be it.

He looks down at me with surprise at my sudden confession. The look doesn't last long though. It's soon replaced with his trademark Jase smile. The one that shows his dimples.

"What are you smiling about?" I ask.

"Nothing," he says, smile still in place. "I just love hearing you say that."

"I love you," I say again, because he loves me saying it, and because I love saying it.

He laughs lightly before his features become serious.

"I love you, too," he says, his voice deep with emotion.

"I know," I say, and give him my own smile.

He lifts a brow. "You know?"

"Hell yeah, I know. Umm… hello? How could you not?" I ask playfully, and to add more humor, I run my hands down my chest and grip my dick.

He laughs again at my playfulness. "You're right. How could I not?"

"Tell me about you parents," I say, changing the subject. We haven't really talked about his life in Georgia because I know it's a touchy subject, but it's something I really need to know, especially since we've thrown out the love word.

He looks down at me and I see a frown line appear on his face.

"What do you want to know?" he asks.

"Whatever you want to tell me. From what Chris said, I know they haven't treated you fairly."

He barks out a humorless laugh. "You could say that. Chris didn't have it as bad as me, and I thank God for that. My dad and I have butted heads for years. My parent's religion forbids any body modifications." He throws his arms out wide, showing off his naked tattooed chest. "As you can see from my ink, I don't agree with it. My dad hates it."

"And what about your mom? How does she feel?"

"My mom's not as bad as my dad. Don't get me wrong, she looked down her nose at me the first few tattoos I got, but after a while, she realized no matter what she or my dad said, it wouldn't make me change."

Anger shoots through me. How in the fuck could any parent look down on their child? Kids are supposed to be able to express themselves in different ways. They need to be encouraged to be different. They need to stand out from each other.

"When I told my dad I was gay," he continues, staring off into space as he talks, "I had never seen him so disgusted. Their opinion didn't really matter anymore at that point, but I needed to tell them. I don't know, maybe I told them because I knew I'd get the reaction I did. Or maybe it was a test to see if they could finally overlook something I've done or become. Either way, once I told them and watched my dad recoil in revulsion, I knew I was done. I haven't seen or talked to them since."

"I'm sorry," I tell him. White-hot rage still simmers in my blood. His parents better hope to God I don't ever meet them, because it won't be my face his dad will be meeting first, but my fist to his jaw. The bastards can stay far away as far as I'm concerned.

Jase looks down at me, smiles, puts his hand under my shirt, and starts rubbing my upper chest. "Don't be. It used to hurt when they rejected me, but I got used to it quickly. I still had Chris and my friends so it wasn't so bad."

"It still must have been hard not having parents that supported you."

He shrugs. "Not really. I learned to accept their behavior. Besides, I became close with a couple of my friends' parents. When I needed advice and shit, I went to them."

Still not the same, but I'll give him that. At least he had some form of adult guidance and support.

"What about your dad? Tell me about him," Jase asks me, bringing me out of my dark thoughts.

I turn away from him and look up at the ceiling, a smile forming on my face.

"My dad was great. The best there was. He was always there when I needed him. We had a tradition. He'd come home, pin my mom to the kitchen counter, wall, whatever was closest, and greet her with a big sloppy kiss, something I gagged over many times." I stop and chuckle at the many memories. "Then we would go out back and play soccer, football, catch, whatever we were in the mood for. We did that every day for years. Even when he became so weak he couldn't stand on his own, we'd push his wheelchair out back and between him, my mom, and me, we'd still play."

"He sounds like a great person. You were lucky," Jase says, and I look back at him.

"He was. You would have liked him. And he would have loved you."

And I know my dad would have. My being gay wouldn't have mattered to him. He always told me to be happy. No matter what anyone thought, I needed to do what I had to to be happy and be me.

We lapse into silence, thinking about the difference between our childhoods and wondering what it would have been like to have the other's. I can't imagine not having the emotional and physical support that a parent is supposed to give to a child. It pisses me off that Jase didn't. It also makes me sad.

Jase's hand starts tweaking my nipple under my shirt and my dick reacts, giving a little jerk in my sweat pants. I turn my head and plant a wet kiss on his stomach right below his belly button. When I look up at him, he's gazing down at me with hooded eyes.

"What do you want, baby?" I ask huskily.

"Suck my cock," he replies.

My body trembles. Having my mouth filled with Jase is one of my favorite things to do.

Instead of getting straight to it, I grab his hand and shove it into my sweats. He knows exactly what I want and wraps his palm around my hard length. I close my eyes for a brief second and suck in a harsh breath, savoring the feeling of his hand on me.

"Oh shit, that feels good, Jase," I groan.

After he pumps my cock a few times, I turn my head and run my tongue along his stomach. I feel his stomach muscles tighten and the length of his cock grows hard under my head.

Impatient for a taste of him, I get up from my lying position, which dislodges his hand from my cock, almost causing me to stop, and get down on my knees on the floor between his legs.

Jase has his eyes on me once I'm kneeling before him. The pure desire I see flashing in them has my body tensing in anticipation. I grip the sides of his pants with greedy hands and yank them down. He lifts his ass off the couch to make it easier. When his cock slips free my mouth waters.

"Hold it for me," I growl at him.

Jase grabs himself and gives it a few strokes before aiming the tip at me. I waste no time licking and sucking my way down his entire dick, but instead wrap my lips around him and slide my mouth down until he reaches the back of my throat.

Jase doesn't expect that and throws back his head and shouts.

"Fucking hell, Andrew!"

I hum in the back of my throat, knowing the vibrations will feel divine for him. The taste of his precum nearly has me shooting my own load. I reach in my pants and palm myself, gathering my own precum and swiping it across the tip.

With his free hand, Jase grips a handful of my hair and starts moving my head up and down, setting the pace to his own liking.

"That's it, Andrew, suck my cock. Faster, baby," he says, his voice low.

Ready to please my man, and with the guidance of his hand, I pick up my pace. The hand wrapped around my cock speeds up to match. I release it for a moment and give my balls a tug. It shoots fireworks through me and I have to force myself not to come. I don't want to come by my hand. I want it either in his mouth, his ass, or by his hand.

Just as I feel him stiffen in my mouth, I pull back. Jase groans and grips my hair, trying to pull me back.

"You come in my ass tonight," I tell him, and watch his jaw clench and his eyes flare. "Bedroom, now."

I get up, grab his hand, and we walk to the bedroom, where we devour and drain each other's bodies until there's nothing left to give.

Chapter Eighteen

Andrew

"HEY, NITRA, CAN WE GET another pot of coffee over here please?" Mia calls.

"Sure thing!" she hollers back

Chris, Mia, Jase, and I are sitting in a booth at Maggie's eating lunch. Mac was supposed to join us, but he said something came up and was running late. It's just after the lunch crowd, so the place isn't too busy. Mia was just telling us that her mom wants to have a barbeque one last time before winter hits. She wants me to invite Ally, Becky, and Brent. She hasn't gotten to meet Ally yet and is dying to.

"You sure your mom's up for throwing a party? I can just bring them by," I tell Mia.

"I asked that and she insisted we all get together. You know she's stubborn. The doctors have given her the all clear."

Lilly just recently had surgery on one of her ovaries to remove a cyst. There was a scare for a while that it might be cancerous, but the doctors discovered it was benign. Unfortunately, the pain became so unbearable that she was left with no other option but surgery.

"How's Levi?" Jase asks. He and I went over to Lilly and Levi's the other day to check on things for Jaxon. Jaxon had something come up at work and he was worried about his mom. When we got there, Levi looked haggard and worn down. I know the feeling of having someone you love become ill. It's not good and it leaves you exhausted.

"He's better. Still not letting mom do anything. She has to threaten him with bodily harm to let her walk anywhere," she says, laughing.

Levi is our old science teacher. He and Lilly started dating a couple years ago, but no one knew about it until a few months ago. We were all surprised by the news. Jaxon was pissed, but he got over it quickly.

"Will Tricia, Hunter, and the kids be there?" Chris asks, taking a sip of her coffee.

"Yes. They're excited to meet Ally as well. When I told them about her, it took me thirty minutes to convince them I wasn't joking." She rolls her eyes.

Nitra walks up to our table and deposits a fresh pot of coffee.

"I just heard over the scanner Mrs. Cranny was found dead in her house," she says sadly.

"Oh my God!" Chris says, throwing her hand up to her mouth in shock. "Do they know what happened?"

"I don't know. All I heard was she was found in her bed not breathing."

Grief hits the table. Mrs. Cranny was a ninety-year-old lady who loved calling the sheriff's department to have a deputy come by the house. Most times her excuse was spiders, rats, or snakes in her house. Everyone knew she just liked looking at the deputies, especially Mac. We used to always pick on him about it. She was crafty and sneaky, but also a part of our community. Losing that hurts.

Unfortunately, her husband passed away years ago and her only son died while serving overseas. She has no other family left.

"We need to ask Mac what arrangements are being made," Mia says, mirroring my thoughts. "She has no family left. I want to help if I can."

"Me too," says Chris.

"Let Jase and me know if we can do anything." I look to Jase for confirmation and he nods.

After the news of Mrs. Cranny, the mood around the table is dampened, and we decide to call it and go our separate ways. I pay the bill while the others gather their things.

"I'll see you tonight at the bar," Jase says, once we're outside. He's headed back to Joe's, while I'm headed to Jaxon's to do inventory.

"Yep." I lean in for a kiss.

"See you ladies later." He waves at Chris and Mia.

Just as he turns away to walk to his Jeep, Jaxon and Bailey come up. Jaxon's holding a squirming Amari in his arms. Both of their faces are somber.

"You heard?" Jaxon asks.

"Yeah," Mia says.

"It's a shame. She was a pain in the ass sometimes, but she'll be missed."

We all nod in agreement.

"How did the appointment go?" Mia asks, a moment later. She grabs Amari from Jaxon's arms. He doesn't protest, which is strange for him. He's normally very possessive of Amari and likes to keep her to himself. It just shows how distracted we are by the sad news.

"It went fine," Bailey answers. "She has an ear infection. The doctor gave her some medicine and said she'd be fine in a couple of days."

Chris's phone starts to ring and she takes a few steps away from the group to answer it.

When Amari starts to whimper, Jase reaches over and lightly runs his fingers along her stomach, giving her a little tickle. She perks up a bit and gives him a smile.

"Mom said to call her after the appointment to let her know what's going on," Mia tells Jaxon, without looking away from Amari.

"Already did."

I feel a vibration in my pocket and pull out my phone. Mac's name is displayed. Swiping my finger on the screen to accept, I put it to my ear.

"Hey, Mac, we just heard about—"

"Where are Chris and Jase? I can't get in touch with them" he says, out of breath, interrupting me.

"At the diner. Why?"

"They need to get the station right now." The urgency in his voice is telling. Something's wrong.

I hear a shuffling on the other side of the line, almost like he's running. His breathing is hard over the line.

I look over at Jase and demand, "What happened?"

The others go quiet, eyes focused on me. Jase takes a step closer, pinning me with hard eyes.

"No time. Just get them—"

He's interrupted by a scream. We all whip around and see a dark-haired man of average height with his arm around Chris's neck. His other hand is pointing a gun at her head. His eyes are sunken and his skin pale. His clothes are unwashed and stained, and his hair looks like it hasn't been brushed in a week.

This must be the bastard Damien, and he's not looking very good. Which could be bad for us.

"He's here," I rumble into the phone, and pocket it, leaving the call connected for Mac to listen.

Jaxon steps in front of Bailey, who had just taken Amari back from Mia. Mia's at Jaxon's side. He tries to push her behind him as well, but she ends up staying beside him in front of Bailey and Amari.

Jase and I both take a step closer to Damien and Chris.

"Let her go, Damien," Jase growls. His hands are clench at his sides, and I can tell he's barely holding on to his anger.

"I think I'll keep her right here for now," Damien says. "It's good to see you again, Jase. Still looking good, I see."

"You want me? I'm right here. Let her go and you and I both will leave." Jase tries again, and takes another step closer.

I match his step. He better be bluffing because there's no fucking way I'm letting him leave with Damien. Chris isn't either. We'll find another way to get Chris away from him.

A malicious smile creeps across his face before he says, "How about I take you both?"

"That doesn't work for me, fuckface," I tell him, trying to draw his attention away from Jase.

Chris starts squirming, desperately clawing at Damien's arm. Her face is turning red from the pressure on her throat. Damien clocks her upside the head with the gun. "Stay still, bitch," he snarls at her.

Jase growls in the back of his throat, and I throw my arm out to catch him before he goes after Damien. "No," I tell him, my voice low. I turn back to Damien. "She can't fucking breathe, you jackass. Ease up."

I'm so pissed right now that my body is shaking. I want to wrap my hands around the fucker's throat and watch as I squeeze the life out of him. These are my people he's threatening to harm.

He turns his eyes in my direction and gives me a lecherous grin. "Ah, Andrew. So good to finally meet you. I've seen you with my boy Jase. He fucks good, doesn't he? Likes to get it hard, just as much as he likes giving it hard." He looks me up and down and licks his lips. "I'd let you fuck me."

"Not in this fucking lifetime," I tell him, my voice laced with revulsion.

He just smirks at me.

I see out the corner of my eye Jaxon trying to slowly walk Bailey, Amari, and Mia behind a car parked at the curb. Damien notices the movement, his eyes moving beyond me and Jase.

I'm about to divert his attention back to us, but Jase beats me to it.

"How's your mom?" Jase asks.

Damien swings his eyes back to Jase and they narrow. "She's fucking devastated," he growls, and spit flies from his mouth, hitting Chris on the cheek. "You fucking killed her youngest son. How in the hell would she be?" He's shaking by the time he gets done talking. A shaky hand is not a good hand to be holding a gun with.

"Let my sister go and you can do whatever you want with me. You know your mom wouldn't want you to do this."

He laughs harshly. "You don't know jack shit, Jase. Mom's all for hunting you down and killing you just like you did Drake. She begged me to do it, even though I had already planned on it. No, I think I should have a sibling for a sibling."

Out the corner of my eye, I see Mac slowly creeping closer to Damien from across the street. He has his gun drawn and two deputies with him. The streets, which only had a few people milling about, are now deserted, but I'm sure there are plenty of faces pressed to windows and glass doors.

From Mac's angle, he doesn't have a good shot at Damien without putting Chris in more danger. Something is getting ready to go down, and I pray no one is hurt in the process.

Jase notices Mac too and he shifts his body slightly. The move is almost unnoticeable. My body tenses, preparing to distract Damien when Mac gives the signal.

Jaxon has Bailey, Mia, and Amari behind a car. At least they're out of harm's way. Damien must have let up on the pressure on Chris's throat because there's a little color back in her cheeks. She has tears falling down her face, but I can see hatred in her eyes.

That-a girl. Be pissed. Don't let the fucker see your fear.

Just as Mac is raising his gun to take aim, there's a loud wailing behind us. Damien shifts his body to the side, which fucks up Mac's shot again.

"Shut that damn baby up," Damien growls at Jaxon, his eyes turning frantic.

Jaxon, still standing by the car the girls are hiding behind, says, "She's a baby. You can't just make them stop crying. She's scared." His voice is calm, but I can still feel the rage emitting from him. His family's in danger. Jaxon doesn't do well when his family is in danger.

Everything happens fast after that point, and I swear my heart rips from my chest and plummets to the depths of hell. Damien aims the gun at Jaxon. Bailey screams, I assume because she can see over the car. Chris digs her nails into Damien's arm, causing him to yell and release her. She falls to the ground. Jase, playing the fucking hero, shoots forward to tackle Damien, but before he reaches him, Damien adjusts his aim and fires at Jase at the same time Mac fires and hits Damien in the chest.

I watch in horror as a small red spot appears on Jase's chest. "Jase!" I yell. He crumples to the ground at the same time I reach him.

His eyes are closed and his breathing is labored. The breaths that do leave his lungs sound broken. The spot on his chest is getting bigger.

"Fuck, baby," I rasp. I get down on my ass and pick his head up and put it in my lap. "Someone call an ambulance!" I yell.

"Already on it," I vaguely hear Jaxon say.

His face is starting to pale and my heart squeezes in my chest. My vision blurs, but I force the tears back. I want him to open his eyes. There's no fucking way this is happening. He's got to be okay. I can't lose him. I refuse to even think that possibility.

Mac rushes to our side and gets down on his knees. "I've got to put pressure on the wound. The ambulance is on its way."

When Mac presses down on Jase's chest, he moans and his eyes snap open. A trickle of blood seeps out the side of his mouth.

"Jase, baby, look at me," I tell him hoarsely. He focuses on me. "You're gonna be okay. The ambulance is coming."

"Chris?" he wheezes.

"Fuck!" Mac says harshly. "The bullet hit his lung."

I faintly hear sirens in the background and they're music to my ears.

"Chris is fine. She wasn't hurt," I tell Jase, my throat tight with emotion.

His body relaxes and his eyes start to drift closed again. I gently grip his hair to get his attention. "No, Jase! You stay awake. Let me know you're okay. I need to see your eyes, baby. Please," I add, when he doesn't respond.

When he opens his eyes again, they are no longer the clear blue I love. Instead, they are pale gray and glazed over with pain. I want to grab the motherfucker who did this and rip him limb from limb. My own chest starts to hurt and my hands shake. I feel sick to my stomach knowing Jase is in pain. I want to take it away and make it my own.

There's movement behind me, and a second later an EMT squats down beside Mac.

"Sir, you need to move back," he says.

I scowl at him and am about to tell him I'm not leaving Jase's side, but Mac grabs my arm, stopping me.

"Let them do their work. You can ride in the back of the ambulance with him."

Knowing he's right, I gently place Jase's head back on the ground, kiss his forehead, and stand. Jase's eyes have already drifted closed again and fear races through me. I don't like when his eyes are closed. It makes him look too close to death.

My eyes stay on Jase, waiting for them to open back up, but they don't. The longer they stay closed, the deeper the fear becomes.

Please, God, let him be okay. I send up the silent prayer. There's no fucking way I can manage if he doesn't make it. Jase is so much a part of me that if dies, a vital part of me will too.

ALEX GRAYSON

"Tell me he's going to make it, Mac," I beg the man beside me. I need something to help me through this. I need him to tell me Jase is going to be okay. I know Jase is the one on the ground fighting for his life right now, but I feel like I'm right beside him, lying there bleeding out too.

"You know I can't do that, Andrew," he says sadly, and grips my shoulder.

I close my eyes at his answer, tears spill over my cheeks.

When I open them again, the EMTs are lifting the stretcher Jase is now on. They have a breathing mask on his face and are pumping the big bulb thingy. I quickly follow them as they rush the stretcher to the ambulance.

On my way, I briefly notice Jaxon has a crying Bailey and Amari in his arms. Mia is off to the side with Mac, watching me with scared eyes. There's another EMT working on Damien. Rage fills me at the thought of them trying to save him.

Let the bastard die. If he lives, I can't promise I won't go after him and finish the job myself.

When they lift the stretcher into the ambulance, I climb in and sit beside Jase. I grab his hand, lying limply by his side. His eyes are still closed. I squeeze his hand to try to get a reaction out of him.

"Jase," I whisper.

I don't know if it's my voice or if it's my hand squeezing his, but his eyes flutter open for a second before closing again. Just that little sign helps alleviate the pressure building in my chest.

I lift his hand to my lips and pray the entire way to the hospital.

Chapter Nineteen

Jase

I GROAN AS I SHIFT IN THE BED. A hiss leaves my lips as a sharp pain pierces my side.

What the fuck is that?

I try to open my eyes, but they feel too heavy. My mouth is dry and my head is starting to pound. A strong smell of antiseptic tickles my nose, and I wrinkle it. The bed I'm lying on is too firm and lumpy to be Andrew's.

Where in the hell am I?

"Jase, baby, can you hear me?" Andrew says from somewhere beside me. The warmth of his hand envelops mine and it's nice. I wiggle my fingers.

"Open your eyes, baby," he says.

Yeah, easier said than done.

I try opening my eyes again, and they do, just a sliver. I can see the bright light through the slits and it makes my head pound harder.

"Lights," I croak.

"Shit! Hold on."

Andrew releases my hand and moves away. A second later, the light dims, and I crack my eyes open a bit more. It's blurry at first, but then it clears. Andrew's face appears in front of me, and he looks worn-out. His hair is more of a mess than usual, his eyes are red rimmed, and his skin is pale. I don't like the look and want it gone.

I take stock of my body and see an IV in my hand. I touch my side on my lower ribs and feel a bandage wrapped around my chest. I look down and see a long tube about the size of a pencil sticking out of my side. It's painful to touch, so I move my hand away.

I'm obviously in the hospital, but my brain is fuzzy and the visions in my head are unclear.

"How are you feeling?" Andrew asks, after pushing a cup and bendy straw in my face.

I take a sip and moan as the cold liquid slides down my throat. Water has never tasted so damn good in my life.

I clear my throat a couple of times before my voice starts working properly. The pain in my side is getting worse.

"Hurts like a bitch. What happened?" I ask, my voice still sounding weak and scratchy.

"You don't remember?" he says, and places the cup back down on the table beside the bed. There are flowers in a vase on it, along with a "Get Well Soon" balloon.

"Bits and pieces. Damien showed up, didn't he?" A flash of Damien holding Chris at gunpoint pops in my head. Other images slowly start to swirl around as well. "Chris? Where is she? Is she okay?"

I try to sit up, needing to get to Chris, but fall back.

Fuck! That hurts!

"Stop, baby," Andrew says, and puts a hand on my chest, his face etched with pain. "Chris is fine. She's in the cafeteria with Jaxon and Bailey getting something to eat. You have a tube sticking out of your side. Your lung collapsed when the bullet grazed it."

"Shit," I mutter, and close my eyes. "Everyone else okay?"

"Yeah. Except for Damien. That fucker is dead." The vehemence in his voice brings my eyes open again. Andrew's jaw is clenched and he's scowling. The hand on the bed beside my hip is balled into a fist.

I can't help but feel satisfaction knowing Damien is gone for good.

"You scared the shit out of me," he whispers. The anger of before is now replaced with worry. "Don't fucking do that shit again," he growls. "Mac was there and would have taken him out without you getting hurt."

I try to draw in a deep breath, but the pain is too intense. "I couldn't take the chance, Andrew. I had to get him away from Chris. The gun could have gone off at any minute."

He closes his eyes and lays his head on my arm. After a moment, he lifts his head and the stark pain there has my gut twisting.

"I could have lost you. Do you have any fucking clue what that would have done to me? I love you, Jase. I'm not the self-harm type, but if I ever was, I'd do it then. Living without you is something that's not possible for me. I *need* you."

I reach up, grip his hair, and bring his mouth to mine. "You won't have to. I'm here. I'm okay," I murmur against his lips.

He rests his forehead against mine and nods.

224

The pain in my chest is growing and it's getting harder to breathe. Andrew must sense my pain, because he pulls away and pushes the call button at the side of my bed.

A couple minutes later, a nurse and doctor walk in. They check my vitals, see that everything is okay, explain my injuries, and shoot me up with pain medicine through my IV. Before the medicine takes effect, the doctor explains I'll be in the hospital for a least a week. I'll have to do breathing treatments so they can monitor my lung to ensure it inflates properly and stays that way. If all goes well, they'll pull the tube out in a week and see how I'm doing then. Unfortunately, when the bullet went in, it cracked a few ribs and nicked my lung. They had to do surgery to remove some bone fragments.

Andrew stands to the side the entire time, watching, his brows still pulled down with concern. I know I was lucky. Things could have been so much worse, for both me and Chris. Hell, for anyone there. I know if it were Andrew lying here in this bed, I'd be out of my fucking mind with worry. I hate he went through that. I hate that I can't get up right now and comfort him.

The doctor and nurse leave a few minutes later, leaving Andrew and me alone. He comes back and gently sits on the side of the bed.

"I don't know if I'm going to last a week here. I fucking hate hospitals," I joke, trying to lighten the mood.

His lips quirk up a bit, but I still see the frown lines. I grab his hand and bring it to my chest, over my heart.

"I'm okay, Andrew," I tell him.

He doesn't say anything, just nods.

There's nothing I can say to reassure him. I know he's got shit rolling through his head right now. Scenarios of what could have possibly happened. He's just going to have to realize on his own that I'm here and going to be okay. I hate seeing him upset, but there's nothing I can do at the moment.

My eyes start to become heavy and it's hard to keep them open. The medicine running through my veins is taking effect, ensuring I get the rest I need. Giving up the fight, my eyes drift closed, and the last thing I see is a single tear trickle down Andrew's cheek.

TWO WEEKS LATER, I'M FINALLY home. After having the tube in my chest for a couple of days, the doctors discovered that the top part of my lung wasn't inflating all the way. They had to take the smaller tube out and put in a bigger one. Putting in the bigger tube hurt like a son of a bitch. I'm still in pain, but it's mostly because of my ribs being cracked. The doctor said it'll be a few weeks before I'm properly healed. He also warned me that my lungs could possibly collapse again in the future due to the trauma to them.

Mac came by while I was in the hospital to get my statement. He also informed me that it was because of Damien that Mrs. Cranny died. Apparently, he had been holed up in her house, without her permission. He barreled his way in and held her hostage. Toxicology reports showed drugs in the old lady's system. He kept her drugged up so she couldn't escape or call someone for help. Her old body finally tired out, along with the help of the drugs, and she passed away, hopefully painlessly. She had been dead several days before someone reported they hadn't seen her for a while. Mac went to investigate and discovered her body. He saw the condition of the house and found a picture of Damien, his brother Drake, and his mom in a duffle bag. That's when he knew Damien had been staying there and called Andrew. He was on his way out the door of Mrs. Cranny's house with Andrew on the phone when Damien showed up.

I wasn't able to attend Mrs. Cranny's funeral, but Andrew told me the whole town showed up to pay their respects. He also said Mac is the one who took it the hardest. He complained of her shenanigans constantly, but he was still very fond of her.

I was surprised when Mac told me he found the girl who had been tied up in the shed. Her name is Bryanna Canton. She had just turned fourteen the week before she was taken. Drake had her in that shed for five days, doing numerous horrible things to her. Her parents were worried sick about her and had called the cops the first night she went missing. Her physical injuries were extensive, but nothing she wouldn't heal from. It's the emotional trauma she'll deal with for years to come. I ache for her and what she went through.

Her dad, who happened to be a government official, came to visit me at the hospital. With tears in his eyes, he thanked me for saving his daughter and told me he was pulling strings to ensure I wasn't charged for the murder of Drake. I told him I wasn't sorry for what I did, that I would do it again, and I was prepared to face the consequences. He was adamant I let him help. I'm not sure if or how he'll pull it off, but if he feels he needs to do, then I'll let him. I didn't need his gratitude or his help, but I understand *his* need to give it.

His wife and daughter want to meet me. I told him when the time is right and they're ready, I'd like to meet them too. Seeing the girl I pulled from the shed and seeing with my own eyes that she's okay will be the final closure I need.

Chris called our parents to tell them about the accident. I wasn't surprised when they refused to come visit. They've written me off just as completely as I have them. I'm just sorry Chris is stuck in the middle. I hope she's able to hold on to a relationship with them.

Andrew and I have both just sat down on the couch. When we got home, the house was full of guests welcoming me back. They left about an hour ago, and while it felt nice to know so many people cared, I'm grateful the house is now quiet.

"Do you need anything? Are you hungry? Thirsty?" Andrew asks, for what feels like the hundredth time.

"Andrew, baby, please stop, okay? I can get my own food and drink," I tell him. My head, resting on the back of the couch, turns his way.

He's been trying to baby me for the last two weeks and it's starting to grate on my nerves. I appreciate his help and his caring, but I'm not an invalid. I understand his concern, but he needs to chill. I still see the worry in his eyes sometimes, but it's not as pronounced as it was when I first woke up in the hospital.

"That's probably not gonna happen," he says honestly, which I figured. "I need to be able to do stuff or my mind starts to wander. My mind wandering right now isn't a good thing. I keep seeing you on the ground with blood all over your chest." He squeezes his eyes closed for a brief second and when he opens them again, the pain is back full force.

I scoot over and turn my body to face him, the pain in my ribs sending a jolt through me, but I ignore it.

"What's it going to take for you to believe I'm not going anywhere? That there's nothing that could take me away from you? Even a bullet."

"Time," he says. "I can't help what I feel in here." He puts his hand over his heart. "Or here." He taps the side of his head. "When you were laid out the ground, my whole world stopped, Jase. It felt like I was the one on the ground with a bullet in my chest. That bullet could have landed in your heart or your head. It could have been over so fast." He scoots closer to me, so my bent leg is hanging over his. "I'll eventually get to the point where the visions don't almost debilitate me, but I'm just not there yet."

I nod, understanding his meaning. A scare such as ours doesn't just go away quickly. Emotional pain can be just as painful as physical pain. It needs time to heal as well. I can put up with Andrew's hovering if it helps him deal with it.

"Now stop complaining, lie down and rest, and give me your feet."

I laugh. "You're going to rub my feet?"

"Yes, because what I want to rub, I can't." He wiggles his eyebrows at me. "So it's the feet instead."

Not about to give up a foot rub, I do what he says and lie down with my feet in his lap. I took a pain pill after everyone left, so it's not long before Andrew massaging my feet and the medicine have me falling asleep.

LATER THAT NIGHT, ANDREW and I are in bed. I'm lying on my back with my hands behind my head. Andrew is on his side facing me with his hand on my chest over my heart, asleep. I'm not sure what time it is, but I know it's late.

I look over at Andrew and see his features peaceful. It's the most relaxed I've seen him since before the shooting. His messy brown hair looks tousled in sleep. His jaw sports a two-day shadow. I know he's been stressed lately, and it shows. I also know the stress will slowly leave him.

I reach over and gently run my fingers through his hair. It's soft. He mumbles something in his sleep, but I can't tell what it is. I remove my hand, not wanting to wake him.

There's no way to explain the feelings I have for this man. They are far beyond anything I've ever felt before. He barreled his way into my life and gave me no choice but to let him. I love him with everything I have in me. I've always known everyone has one person in this life they're meant to be with, but I never realized how thoroughly deep and abiding these feelings could be.

The day I walked through the doors at Maggie's Diner was the day that changed my life forever. I came to town thinking my days were numbered. Damien and his revenge were to be my end. What I ended up getting after I got here was my sister, who I adore, a town full of people who care for each other, friends I now consider family, and a man I will spend the rest of my life loving.

I roll to my side and feel Andrew adjust behind me, putting his arm around my lower stomach. Even half-asleep, he's careful not to put pressure on my side.

"Love you," I murmur into the darkness, not expecting a response.

"Love you, too, baby," Andrew mumbles. I tip my lips up into a smile and drift off to sleep.

Epilogue

Andrew

Nine Years Later

I WATCH AS ALLY AND TRENT huddle their heads together, looking at something on Trent's phone. They're sitting on the picnic table in Lilly's back yard. My eyes narrow when Ally throws back her head to laugh at something Trent said, and leans over to kiss his cheek. She's fifteen. Too young for that shit.

I look around the yard through the throng of people milling about until I spy Mac just a few yards away.

"You tell your boy he better watch himself with Ally," I warn him.

He looks to the pair still watching whatever on Trent's phone before looking back at me. "What are they doing?" he asks, his eyes dancing in mirth.

I shoot daggers at him with my eyes. "He keeps making her laugh and she kisses his cheek. She's fifteen, he's nineteen."

"Ah, come on, Andy." Mia butts her nose in. "You know it's innocent. They're best friends."

"I still don't like it," I growl at them both.

I've seen the way Trent looks at her when he thinks no one is looking. On several occasions, I've had to force myself not to go over and smack the look off his face. However, Mia's right. Over the years, they've grown extremely close. Any time I have Ally over at my and Jase's house, he's always around. I can't fucking get rid of him.

At first I thought it was a great idea for them to bond. I liked that Ally found someone in my family to attach herself to. But now I'm thinking it was a mistake. Watching the two of them across the yard all huddled together like two peas in a pod has my fists clenching. It's not that I don't want them close together, but I know what goes through the head of a boy Trent's age. All they think about is sex or anything to do with the female body.

"You don't have anything to worry about, Andrew. You know that. They are both smart. Ally won't do anything until she's ready, and you know Trent wouldn't push her." Mia comes to my side and places her hand on my arm.

Again, she's right, but it's still hard to watch. I also know Ally has feelings for Trent. She has stars in her eyes any time she looks at him. It's there for everyone to see. If Trent ever hurts her, I'll make his life miserable. Ally's had enough pain in her life. She doesn't need any more.

Two years after Ally's leukemia was announced to be in remission, it came back. Luckily, the cancer wasn't as harsh the second time around, but it was still painful to watch her body go through the chemo treatments again.

She didn't wait for her hair to fall out in chunks. She bit the bullet and shaved it the first day of treatment. In an effort to support Ally, Trent shaved his head as well. She cried when he came to see her after she got back from her appointment. Her body became weak again, but she pushed through it.

Becky and Brent's families and my family were all there to support her and give her courage. I'm proud of her for staying strong. It's been a little over six years since she's been cancer-free. She has yearly check-ups, just in case it returns.

Jase walks up and hands me a beer. He pops the top of his own, takes a swig, and turns to face the direction of my gaze. Jase and Ally have also become close, something that makes me happy. It didn't take her long to start calling him Uncle Jase. Ally knows who I am to her, a decision that Becky and Brent made on their own and then came to talk to me about. I told them to be sure that was what they wanted and they assured me it was. Ally was okay with it. Becky and Brent are still her mom and dad and I'm still Uncle Andy. Nothing's changed. Everything stayed how it should.

"Knock it off, Andrew," Jase says beside me, laughter in his voice. "You're going to scare the boy."

I take a drink of my beer and turn to him. His beautiful eyes watch me take him in. His hair is still long, carelessly thrown in a ponytail. His face is covered in a trim beard, something he started growing years ago when I told him I wanted to feel it on my body. The sleeves of his black button-up shirt are rolled up to just below his elbows, showing tanned tattooed arms. His stomach is flat and his hips, encased in jeans, are trim.

I never get tired of looking at him and my body still reacts every time I do. I feel a twitch in my jeans, and I discreetly adjust myself.

"What's wrong, baby? Jeans getting too tight?" he asks, smirking.

I take a step toward him and grab his ponytail. "Fuck, yeah, they are. Care to take care of it for me?"

His eyes flare with heat, and a rush of air leaves his lips. Yep, I still affect him, too.

"Cut that shit out," Jaxon growls, walking up to us with Bailey.

After giving Jase a deep kiss, leaving us both moaning, I turn to face them. I'm disappointed I have to wait until later to have Jase, but it's a family barbeque, so we need to behave.

I see Amari taking off toward Ally and Trent, and I sigh in relief. There will be no more sexy glances and whispered words with little Amari around.

We all laugh as Amari situates herself between the two.

"You need to bring Amari around more often when those two are together," I tell Jaxon, and he chuckles.

"Mama," a little voice calls, and we all look down to Belle, Mac and Mia's four-year-old daughter. She has a hold of Mia's pants, tugging on them. "Nanna said I can have a popsicle, but I haveta ask you first."

Mia squats down to her level before asking, "Did you eat the hot dog I gave you earlier?"

"Uh huh," Belle says, nodding vigorously.

"Okay, sweetie, you can have one." The words have barely left Mia's mouth before Belle takes off running toward the house. "But only one," Mia calls after her daughter.

"Okay, Mama," Belle yells, without looking back.

We all laugh as she dashes into the house, no doubt in our minds that Belle will end up with however many popsicles she wants. Lilly spoils all her grandkids, including the ones she's adopted.

I take another drag of my beer as I turn back to face the yard. This has always been a gathering place for us. Every chance we get, we end up here.

I look over at Jase, who's talking to Jaxon and Mac. Bailey and Mia are whispering something to each other and giggling. Unfortunately, Chris and Nick couldn't be here today. Nick's out on a job site and Chris went with him.

Looking back at Ally, my heart swells. I hate that I kept her from my family for so long. There're so many things they missed. But having her here, surrounded by the people I love, is something I cherish every day of my life.

I turn back to Jase and watch him interacting with our friends. I remember the day Chris showed me his picture. I felt a punch in my gut and my heart began pounding rapidly in my chest as soon as I laid eyes on him. I knew with everything in me that my world would change once he walked into my life. And it did. It may sound clichéd and girly as shit, but having Jase has made my world so much brighter. I had a good life before he came into it, but the moment he strolled through the door of Maggie's Diner, it became perfect.

Turn the page for a sneak peek at Awaken Me (Book 4 in The Jaded Series), Nick and Chris's story.

CHAPTER
ONE

"NICK." I HEAR THE SOFT BROKEN whisper and whip my head around.

The once beautiful eyes are now dull and almost lifeless. The stark pain radiating from them sends a sharp pain to my chest.

"I'm here, baby," I whisper, my voice no longer sounding like my own.

A whimper leaves Anna's lips when she tries to move. I have to force my body to relax, when all it wants to do is lock up and seize. I look down at Anna's broken body, covered in a dirty piece of cloth I found on the floor of the house, and every part of me aches with her. Every mark on her body, I feel on mine.

"No, Anna, stay still," I tell her, and take a deep breath before continuing. "The ambulance is on their way, okay?"

She ignores my plea to stay still and lifts an arm covered in marks. A flash of rage runs through my blood at the sight, but I push it away. My focus needs to be on her right now, not the fuckers who did this to her.

My gut clenches and my stomach plummets when she winces in pain and drops her arm. I gently grab her wrist and bring her hand to my lips, kissing the back before placing her hand on my cheek. It's ice cold and fear almost cripples me.

She closes her eyes and takes a few shallow breaths before opening them again.

"I love you, Nick." Her voice is barely audible.

As much as I love hearing her say those words, they scare me. They're too final. I know the broken woman lying in front of me is dying. I know her condition is dire. But I refuse to think of any outcome other than her surviving. This is my Anna. She can't leave me.

I bend over and lay a soft kiss on her forehead. "I love you too, Anna Banana," I whisper.

My lips are still at her forehead when I hear her weak voice say, "Be happy for me."

I close my eyes and pull in air that no longer feels life sustaining. All it does now is remind me I'm whole and safe while the woman I love with my entire heart lies broken and bleeding in my arms.

Anger at the injustice of it all has me pulling back and growling, "Don't do this, Anna! Don't you dare die on me! You hang on, goddammit. You can't die on me!"

My voice cracks and rises with every word I say. By the time I'm done, I'm panting. This isn't the way it's supposed to be! She's not supposed to leave me! We're a fucking team!

"It's... too late... for me, Nick. I need... you to promise... you'll be... happy. Promise... me. Please."

My heart cracks wide open at her words. She doesn't realize it, but pieces of my heart lie right beside her, a ruined and bloody mess. She's asking the impossible. There's no way I could ever be happy if she's not with me. She can't expect that of me.

"No!" I tell her angrily, and bring her body closer to mine. "I can't promise that! I can't be happy without you. You're my happy. Please, Anna, just hang on a little bit longer."

"Promise me, Nick," Anna says, her voice weaker than it was before.

"Fuck!" I snarl to the sky.

How can she think I could ever be happy again? I've loved this woman from the time I was old enough to know what love was. We've made plans together. We were supposed to grow old together. Without her, there is no happy.

As I glance back down at Anna, I know I have to give her what she wants, at least in words. Her eyes are begging me. I've never been able to say no to her.

Gathering up every bit of courage I have, and praying to God that he and Anna forgive me, I utter the lie, "I promise."

The smile that graces her face almost has her looking like my Anna again. My heart pounds in my chest, and I freeze when she slumps in my arms, her eyes closing with the smile still on her lips.

Ah, fuck no!

"Anna?" No response. "No, no, no! Jesus Christ! Please, Anna, baby, answer me!"

She still doesn't respond. The breath I'm holding whooshes out, and my lungs won't allow me to bring in more air. A piercing pain shoots daggers in my chest where my heart use to beat. It feels like it's not there anymore.

I can't believe she left me. The reality of it hits me, but I still don't want to accept it.

I gather her in my arms and bring her body up mine. Her limbs hang like dead weights and her head rolls to the side. I bury my face in her hair and breathe in her unique scent. Even through the filthy smell of the bastard, I still smell my Anna.

I gently rock her back and forth, waiting and praying she comes back to me. I know in my head it's in vain, but the place where my heart is supposed to be won't believe it.

"Please come back to me," I murmur in her ear, my tears soaking her hair. "I can't do this without you, Anna. Please, baby," I continue begging her, but she stays quiet in my arms...

I jerk awake and snap up in bed. My chest heaves up and down from the hard work of trying to pull air into my lungs. My heart's pounding so hard I can hear the thump-thump in my ears. Breathing in through my mouth and out through my nose, I try to settle my churning stomach. I release the death grip on the sheets, lean back on my hands, and let my head fall back on my shoulders.

That damn dream is going to be the death of me. I squeeze my eyes closed, trying to push back the images. It doesn't work. They slip through the cracks and crevices I never manage to seal shut when I sleep.

"Fuck!" I snarl to the ceiling.

Frustrated, I yank the damp sheet off my lap, swing my legs over the side of the bed, and plant my feet on the floor. I lean forward and drop my head into my hands, squeezing my hair so tight I feel the strands biting into my knuckles and hear the pop of them coming loose of their follicles. My body is covered in sweat and the cool air in the room sends goose bumps across my skin.

No matter what I do, I can't escape the visions. I've relived Anna's death hundreds of times and each time it feels like the first. I wake up smelling her scent, and I swear I still feel her limp body in my arms. Memories of her still body play out in my head over and over again, bringing the crippling pain of losing her to the forefront.

I lift my head and look around the barren hotel room I'm in. Overall, it's a shitty room with its germ-infested linens, outdated TV, stained carpet, and a shower and toilet that barely function. I can afford better accommodations, but with what I plan to do in these rooms each time I rent one, this type seems to fit more.

I look to my right and see the single bullet and 9mm pistol I have lying on the nightstand. Picking up the gun first, I release the clip and let it slide into my hand. The metal is cool and smooth. I reach over without looking and pick up the gold-tipped silver bullet. I flip it around a few times, before I push the bullet into the clip. The clip slides smoothly into the gun next, with a click.

Memories of Anna sitting on the tire swing I have in my backyard flash through my mind. She always loved that tire swing. She used to say when we got married our kids would play on the same swing. At the time I could picture Anna pushing a little girl with sandy-blonde pigtails.

Another memory surfaces of Anna and me playing house in the fort we built in her backyard. I built the unsteady frame out of leftover two-by-fours from my house and sheets and she decorated the inside with unused items her mom let her have. We even had hand-drawn family pictures hanging from the walls. Most boys my age at the time were out playing sports and riding their bikes, and sometimes I was, but I always made time for my Anna.

From the time I reached twelve years old, I knew I was going to love Anna. She was my everything. She was the air I breathed, the reason my heart beat, and everything I saw. She was the first thing I thought of when I woke up and the last thing I saw before I fell asleep. She was my sunshine, my moonlight, and my stars. There was absolutely nothing I wouldn't do for her, and nothing I wouldn't give her. She had my heart so tightly wrapped around her, I'm surprised it didn't suffocate her. Anna was my reason for living, and with her gone, I no longer have anything to live for.

Looking down at the gun in my hand, regret and guilt churn in my stomach. I flat-out lied when I made that promise to Anna two years ago. I promised her I'd be happy, knowing I never would be again. But I had to give her what she needed. Knowing deep down she was saying good-bye and that was the last time I was going to see her beautiful face, I said the only thing that would give her peace.

It's been over two years since my heart turned cold and stopped working properly. Two years since I've seen Anna or held her in my arms. Two fucking years since I've looked into her bright blue eyes. Two years, and it still feels like yesterday. Some people say I should move on and let my grief go. But it's not just the grief I hold on to. It's the guilt of lying to Anna and not keeping my promise. The regret for not being there when she needed me. The rage for not killing the bastards that took her away from me.

Yes, I still grieve for her with my whole being and have not let go of her, but she hasn't let go of me either. It's like there's still a connection between us that can't be severed.

I grip the cool black metal in my hand tightly and bring it closer to my face. I flipped the safety switch so the little red dot is visible. Red means fire. With shaky hands, I bring the barrel of the gun up under my chin. My finger slides across the trigger and rests there.

Of their own accord, my eyes flicker over to the picture I have on the nightstand. It's of me and Anna. I have my arm wrapped around her neck. Her head is tilted up, while mine is bent toward her, our foreheads resting against each other's. I had just pulled away from kissing her.

I squeeze my eyes shut and try to block out the picture, but it's no use.

I take a deep breath and apply light pressure to the trigger. I know at this point asking for forgiveness is useless, but I still send up a silent prayer, asking Anna to forgive this one last sin.

Gathering my courage, I squeeze the trigger the rest of the way…

Click.

All I hear is a fucking click.

I pull the gun away from my chin and look down at it. I didn't chamber a damn bullet.

A big rush of air leaves my lungs, and I glare down at the gun. Knowing that I won't have the courage again tonight, I put the gun back down on the nightstand and pick up the bottle of Jack instead. Uncapping it, I take a big swallow and relish the burn it leaves in my throat.

Anger and disappointment rush through me. With a roar, I rear back and throw the half-empty bottle at the wall. It connects with a loud crash and the amber liquid goes everywhere.

I'm angry because I couldn't follow through. My beautiful Anna is dead, and I'm left here. I was the one who was supposed to protect her. I should be the one in a cold grave. Not her. I'm the one who failed her.

I get up from the bed, ignoring the mess across the room, and walk the short distance to the bathroom. Once I'm in front of the mirror, I grip the edge and look at my reflection. I look like shit. My eyes are bloodshot with shadows under them from drinking too much and lack of sleep. My face is pale and gaunt. My eyes travel to my naked chest and stomach, and I notice that I've lost weight. The muscles are still there, but not as bulky. My stomach is starting to sink in.

I release my grip and turn to the shower. Once the water finally turns hot, I pull the shower curtain back and step inside. The hot water does nothing to settle my nerves or help the never-ending sorrow.

Knowing I need to present myself halfway decently, I start the task of doing just that. The last thing I need is people knowing just how dark my world has become. I have to mentally prepare myself for what's to come and the pitying looks I know I'll receive.

Because tomorrow I go home.

ACKNOWLEDGEMENTS

First and foremost, I want to thank my husband, daughter, and son. They are the ones who suffer every time I sit in front of my computer to write. Every hour I spend writing is an hour taken away from them. Thank you so much for understanding my need to do this and having patience. I love you all!

Next, I want to thank my good friends Hope and Allison. I have no idea what I would do without you three. Each of you play such an important role in my life, and I'd be lost without y'all. You ladies are my saving grace and sanity in the oftentimes madness of being an author. Thank you and I love you!

I also want to send a special thank you to Daqri with Covers by Combs. Once again, you amaze me with your mad designing skills. I couldn't have asked for a more beautiful cover! Thank you!

Alex's Jaded Angel's, you ladies (and one gent ;)) rock my world. Thank you for being there and supporting me. There's no way I could thank you all enough for everything you do.

Kaila! My teaser girl! I have no idea how I got so lucky in finding you, but I'm not giving you back! You're amazing, and sweet, and so damn talented! Love you!

Becky and Olivia at Hot Tree Editing, I KNOW you both hate me at times and I wear your patience, because my writing skills DO NOT extend to editing and grammar. Lol. Thank you both for taking on my books and making them the best they can be. You both are such a pivotal part in this process and there's no way I could thank you for taking care of my babies! But I'll start with a simple thank you!

Beta readers, you help me so much. It's your advice and guidance that makes my books more readable and dependable. Thank you so much for everything! Love y'all.

Readers! Thank you so much for taking a chance on me and giving me the opportunity to entertain you with my imagination. You are the glue that keeps this industry together. There are no words to express my thanks to you all.

Bloggers, you're last, but certainly not least. Indie authors would be nothing without you. YOU are the ones who promote our books for others to see. YOU are the ones who take time out of your day to show readers they need to take a chance on our books. My gratitude for each of you is endless.

OTHER WORKS BY ALEX GRAYSON

The Jaded Series
Shatter Me
Reclaim Me
Unveil Me
Awaken Me
The Jaded Series: The Complete Collection

Stand Alone
Endless Obsession
Whispered Prayers of a Girl
Pitch Dark
The Sinister Silhouette

The Consumed Series
Always Wanting
Bare Yourself
Watching Mine

Hell Night Series
Trouble in Hell
Bitter Sweet Hell
Judge of Hell

ABOUT THE AUTHOR

Alex Grayson is the bestselling author of heart pounding, emotionally gripping contemporary romance including the Jaded Series, the Consumed Series, and two standalone novels. Her passion for books was reignited by a gift from her sister-in-law. After spending several years as a devoted reader and blogger, Alex decided to write and independently publish her first novel in 2014 (an endeavor that took a little longer than expected). The rest, as they say, is history.

Originally a southern girl, Alex now lives in Ohio with her husband, two children, two cats and dog. She loves the color blue, homemade lasagna, casually browsing real estate, and interacting with her readers. Visit her website, www.alexgraysonbooks.com, or find her on social media!

Connect With Alex:

www.alexgraysonbooks.com

For exclusive giveaways and sneak peeks of the series, sign up for Alex Grayson's newsletter:

http://eepurl.com/bAxPLf

Made in the USA
Middletown, DE
25 February 2021